I0564300

WDM PRESENTS: SHORT FICTION FROM 2021

DEB LOGAN
DEBBIE MUMFORD

WDM
Publishing

COPYRIGHT

CONTENTS

INTRODUCTION

Welcome to WDM's Short Fiction of 2021.

In this volume you'll find five short tales written by Deb Logan, and ten stories by Debbie Mumford.

Deb Logan typically writes contemporary and urban fantasy for kids and teens, and four of these five tales fit that description. The fifth is a cross between science fiction and mystery - a tale of a little girl growing up on a space station who dreams of becoming a detective... just like her dad!

Debbie Mumford enjoys writing lots of different genres, and the stories in this book illustrate this beautifully. They run the gamut from urban fantasy to historical to cozy mystery.

So sit back, relax, and enjoy the stories WDM published in 2021!

FIVE STORIES

BY DEB LOGAN

PART I

PALADIN SHIELD

DEB LOGAN
AUTHOR OF *FAERY UNEXPECTED*

Paladin Shield

SPUN YARNS
A *Seer Chronicles* Short Story

y name is Artemis Lucia Woodward-Kendrick. My husband, Jedidiah Amos Woodward-Kendrick, and I recently purchased our first home.

I stared at the words I'd just written in the journal that Jed and I had decided would hold the record of our lives together in this house, our first home.

Our home.

Not my parents' home, or my in-laws, or even Grannie O'Toole's quaint cottage in Dublin. No, this sweet little house on the outskirts of McIntosh, Colorado was *our* home. Jed's and mine. Since we were newly married and as yet unemployed, we'd been able to afford this investment in our future thanks to the generosity of our friend and benefactor, Laird Angus O'Connor.

Life had been a whirlwind since I'd rescued Jed from enthrallment to the fairy queen in Ireland last Halloween. But that horrendous ordeal was behind us now. We were safely married, had enjoyed a fabulous honeymoon in Hawaii— again, thanks to Laird Angus— and had celebrated Christmas with friends and family here in Colorado.

We'd been home from our honeymoon for a scant three months, but already the new year had brought even more change. My parents had decided to downsize, moving from the home I'd grown up in to an upscale condominium on the shore of Lake McIntosh. Of course Jed and I helped with packing and their move, but since we'd been staying with Mom and Dad, that event had also necessitated a search for a home of our own. Jed's parents had offered us a room in their home, but we'd decided it was time to find our own place in the world.

And now, thanks to Laird Angus, we're the proud owners of this lovely little cottage situated on the very edge of national forest land. The cottage sits on an acre and a half of land, shaded by old growth pines and firs. Though it was only mid-March, crocuses and daffodils were already shooting up in the front garden and buds were showing on the apple tree in the backyard.

Inside, the cottage was snug and cozy, reminding me of Jed's grandmother's home in Dublin. The main floor boasted a comfortable living room which Jed and I had furnished with second-hand items, including a few pieces my parents didn't have room for in their new condominium. Like the well-worn brown leather sofa that used to live in the great room of my childhood home and the antique mahogany secretary Jed and I discovered when we were cleaning out the attic.

I smiled, well pleased with the look of the room. From the hardwood floors with their braided rag rugs to the mismatched sofa and overstuffed chairs to the secretary, lovingly cleaned and polished, the room spoke of comfort and contentment. Which was exactly what I wanted.

Opening my *sight*, I studied the room again, this time nodding with satisfaction at the warding runes glimmering on the walls and surrounding the windows and doors. Jed and I would be safe within these walls. No wandering Fae would break through those wards.

Moving into the kitchen, I sighed with happiness. From the cheery yellow walls and white pine cabinets to the farmer's sink, brushed steel appliances, and terra cotta floor tiles, the room suited me perfectly. I glanced across the half-wall with its serving counter to the dining area. Jed and I had found a wonderful pine trestle table and six matching chairs at an estate sale. We intended to share many meals at that table, enjoying the view from the wide windows that overlooked the tame carpet of our back lawn as well as the wild beauty of the old growth forest beyond.

Finally, I turned my attention to the bedroom... and shivered as a tingle of delight ran down my spine. The room was dominated by a king-size rustic aspen log bed topped with an heirloom log cabin quilt done in blues and reds and golds. The quilt was a gift from Jed's parents, but the bed itself was our gift to each other. We'd seen an example of the craftsman's work on a trip to Estes Park and had known instantly we had to have one. The bed was our one splurge. Everything else in our new home might be second-hand, but our bed would be our own. We'd special ordered it that very day, and now here it stood, in our own bedroom, in our own home.

Anticipating the night to come, my heart raced. I was almost as excited as I'd been on our honeymoon! Forcing my thoughts back to the here and now, I continued my examination of the house, moving to the narrow staircase.

Much like Grannie O'Toole's home, our cottage also included a second story—two small bedrooms tucked beneath the eaves with a shared bath. At the moment they both served as storage for the crates and boxes we'd yet to unpack, but we intended to set at least one up as an office.

Of course, an office suggested we had a clue about our future careers. Which neither of us did... at least not yet.

Sighing, I returned to the kitchen. Opening the refrigerator, I removed a pitcher of orange juice, grabbed a tumbler from the cabinet beside the sink, and poured myself a glass. Carrying the orange juice to the trestle table, I sat and sipped the tart liquid while staring at the huge trees beyond the yard and pondering our future. Life had finally settled down. Mom and Dad were happy in their condominium. Jed and I had a place to call our own. It was time to establish a routine, and that meant finding a way to support ourselves. We were adults now. Time to make our own way in the world. No more dependence on either set of parents, or even Laird Angus, the head of Clan O'Connor, and my friend and mentor during those dark days in Ireland.

We needed jobs, but what kind?

Sure, we had skills. Unique skills that had been passed through our bloodlines for generations, but those skills weren't exactly marketable.

Jed and I were hereditary *Sidhe Seers*. We could see what other mortals could not. We saw the Fae— in all their beauty and horror. And more than that, now that we'd found the journal left by my *Seer* ancestress, we were learning that we had the ability to banish the Fae from the mortal world.

But since regular folks had no idea the Fae existed, except in children's tales, our skills weren't exactly a hot commodity. Sure, we'd gone to college. Jed had decent IT skills and I was an excellent researcher, but information technology and library science were unlikely to support us; not when we might have to drop everything on a moment's notice in order to fight an incursion of Fae!

I had no idea how we were going to solve this puzzle, but knew we'd figure it out. I shook my head, remembering what was important: Jed and I were together. When he'd been enthralled by the fairy queen in Ireland, I'd been terrified that he was lost to me forever, that I'd never find a way to rescue him. Yet here we were, married with our own home in Colorado.

Finding jobs would be a snap compared to breaking the fairy queen's hold on my best friend... and the love of my life!

Before I could do more than take another sip of orange juice, I heard the front door open and footsteps pound across the hardwood floor.

"Artie!" Jed's voice called. "Where are you? I've got news!"

2

"*I*'m in the kitchen," I called, placing my glass on the table and standing to meet the man I loved.

Jed burst into the room, strode to my side and swept me into his arms, hugging me tightly. "You'll never guess," he said, twirling in a circle before setting me on my feet and holding me at arms' length.

"What?" I cried, laughing and working to find my balance after his enthusiastic greeting. "What are you so excited about?"

"Angus!" he said, his grin so wide it was a wonder he could speak. "Laird Angus is coming. I just got off the phone with him. He's at the airport now."

"In Dublin? When will his flight land in Denver?"

"No," he said, his eyes alight with merriment. "He called from Denver! He's renting a car and will be here within the hour."

My happy surprise turned to horror. "Here? Now? Jed! We don't have a spare bedroom set up yet." Not that we'd really planned to have a guest bedroom. We intended for those small bedrooms upstairs to be storage and an office. At the moment, both were disaster areas! I glanced toward our bedroom with its

13

beautiful king-size bed and sighed. Our first night in our new bed would have to wait. The laird would have our room and we'd make do with sleeping bags among the boxes upstairs.

Jed laughed and pulled me into his arms. "Don't worry about it, sweetheart. Angus can afford a suite at the Hilton, though I expect he'll make do with a less fancy hotel here in McIntosh."

I sighed, more relieved than I wanted to admit, and nodded. "Okay. Did he say why he was here?" I asked, and then hurried to add, "Not that I'm not delighted, of course, but Colorado is a long way from Ireland."

Jed released me and moved to the cabinet beside the sink. Grabbing a tumbler, he poured himself a glass of orange juice and we settled at the table.

"Not really," he said after chugging half of his juice. "He just said he needed to talk to us and he'd be on his way as soon as he had keys to a car."

I nodded and sipped my juice. I wasn't worried about him getting lost on the way; he'd made the drive from Denver to McIntosh last fall when he'd accompanied Grannie O'Toole to our wedding. But why was he here at all? What could the clan chief of the O'Connors need to talk to us about? I suspected there was more to the man than most people knew— when I first met Laird Angus my *sight* had hinted he was far more powerful, and far older, than he seemed— but I'd kept my suspicions to myself.

Perhaps we were about to discover more about our benefactor.

A little over an hour later, Jed and I stood on our front porch as Laird Angus O'Connor parked a dark blue Subaru Outback in our driveway. I reached for Jed's hand as Angus stepped from the car and made his way to us.

"Mr. and Mrs. Woodward-Kendrick," he said with a gallant bow. "It's pleased I am to see ye in your new home."

"Welcome, Laird Angus," Jed said, letting go of my hand and stepping forward to shake the Laird's. "We're always glad to see you."

Laird Angus turned to me, mischief sparkling in his eyes. "And ye, Artie? Are ye glad to see me?" He cocked his head and raised an eyebrow.

I laughed and threw myself at him, startling him so that I nearly knocked him to the ground, but he caught me in his arms and we hugged each other tightly. "I owe you my life and my happiness, Angus," I whispered, tears gathering in my eyes. "You will *always* be welcome in my home."

Jed cleared his throat and I stepped away from the Laird, wiping my eyes and smiling. "Well, don't just stand there," Jed said. "Come in and see the place you helped us buy!"

Jed and I proudly escorted Laird Angus through our home, even leading him through the mess of the upstairs bedrooms and detailing our plans for them once we'd finished unpacking and could find the floor. We finished by standing on the back deck, pointing out where our land ended and the national forest land began.

"Ah, 'tis a bonny place ye've chosen," he said as Jed opened the patio door and led us into the dining area. "I'm sure ye will be verra happy here." He glanced above the door, his eyes losing their focus, and I knew he was examining our wards. When satisfied, he nodded and smiled at me. "Ye've done verra well. 'Tis proud I am to have ye in my clan."

I grinned. "About that…"

"Aye, yer Grannie Maeve told me. The mystery of yer lineage has been solved," he said, his eyes twinkling. "I'd like to have a peek at that wee journal while I'm here."

"Of course," said Jed, "but before we start talking business, why don't we sit down? Maybe have a cup of coffee or tea?" He cocked his head and continued, "Here or the living room? Your choice, Angus."

The Laird clapped, rubbed his hands together, and nodded. "A cuppa wouldna go amiss," he said with a smile. "Tea, if it's no trouble, and let's settle in that pretty living room."

"No trouble at all," I said, moving around the counter to put the kettle on. "Jed, why don't you show Angus the journal while I make the tea."

Jed nodded and the men left the kitchen.

A few minutes later I carried a tray into the living room to find Angus standing by the window studying the journal Jed and I had discovered in the antique secretary in the attic of the home where I'd grown up; the same secretary that now stood in the corner of this room in all its newly refurbished glory.

"Well," I said, setting the tray laden with mugs of tea and a plate of oatmeal cookies on the oak coffee table, "I'm glad to see you haven't been wasting time."

Angus looked up and grinned. Closing the book he strode across the room and settled in one of the overstuffed chairs. Jed joined me on the sofa and handed out napkins and cookies while I arranged the mugs of tea within everyone's easy reach.

I took a sip of my tea before gazing directly at Angus and asking, "So, Laird Angus, what brings you to Colorado?"

He held up the small book he'd been studying. "This journal for one thing," he said solemnly, and then gestured to me, "and to welcome a long-lost daughter into the clan."

I frowned. "That can't be all. Regardless of that journal, I became part of your clan when I married Jed."

"True enough," he agreed, "but this journal clears up your bloodline. 'Tis good to know which line of my descendants you belong to." He laid the journal on his knee and patted it. "I lost track of this lassie when she came to America. I'm glad to know her line continued and her blood ran true."

Whether he'd intended to or not, Angus had just confirmed my long-held belief that he was far older than he looked. I glanced at Jed and saw with amusement that he'd had no idea. His eyes were fairly popping out of his head and his jaw hung slack.

I took the mug from Jed's hand and placed it on the coffee table, nudging him with my elbow as I did so. "Close your mouth, my love," I said quietly. "You look like he hit you with a two-by-four."

Angus laughed as Jed composed himself. "You're not surprised, Artie?" Angus asked in an amused rumble.

"My insight suggested as much when I first met you in the O'Connor archives," I said.

"But you never said anything!" Jed protested.

I shrugged. "I didn't know for sure. Besides, it wasn't my secret to tell."

"Ye are wise beyond yer years, lass," the Laird said. Turning to Jed, he continued, "I am not only the laird of the O'Connor clan, Jedidiah Amos Kendrick. I am *THE* O'Connor. The first and original *Sidhe Seer*. My longevity is due to the fact that I am half *sidhe*. My father is a *sidhe* prince; my mother was a mortal woman." He shrugged and took a swallow of tea. "And I? I am as you see me... and have been so since before the Romans invaded the British Isles."

"B...but...but," Jed stammered. "But the *sidhe* are FAE!"

Angus nodded. "Indeed they are. *Sidhe* is the old name, the Gaelic name. They've been known as the *fair folk*, which devolved into *fairy*, for centuries now. I prefer to name them *Fae*, myself."

Jed shook his head. "But if you're part Fae, aren't you, aren't *we* hunting your own family?"

Angus nodded. "I despised the way the Fae treated mortals, my mother included, and vowed to protect humans from the *sidhe*." He cocked his head and gazed intently at Jed. "I heard about your interactions with the selkies and that part-siren girl in Hawaii. You didn't banish them. In fact, you helped them."

"They weren't hurting anyone," I said quickly, my cheeks heating and my pulse quickening at the implied criticism.

He held up his hand. "Peace, Artie. I wasn't questioning your decision, merely making a point. If the *sidhe*, the Fae, leave mortals in peace, I'm content to instruct my clan to leave them be. 'Tis only when the Fae prey on mortals that me and mine intervene."

We were all quiet for a few moments, each considering the ramifications of the Laird's remarks. I bit into an oatmeal cookie, savoring the rich flavors of creamed butter and sugar, oats and raisins as I considered the man's long life. Not to mention the fact that I wouldn't exist if he hadn't married in the far distant past and sired children. I wondered exactly how many people alive today could trace their lineage back to Angus O'Connor? Certainly both Jed and I could.

My eyes widened and I inhaled so sharply I almost choked on a bit of cookie. Didn't that mean that Jed and I were related? Should we have married? Would the Laird's revelations end my relationship to the man I loved more than life itself?

My thoughts must have shown on my face, for Angus reached across the coffee table and patted my knee. "Relax, Artie. I checked. Yer line and Jed's parted company before America was even discovered. Ye are nowhere near being closely related, despite the fact that ye both descend from me."

My cheeks heated and I lowered my head, allowing my hair to fall forward, shielding me from his gaze. Before more than a heartbeat or two had passed, Jed touched my arm.

"Don't, Artie," he said quietly. "You're safe with me, and Angus means us no harm. You don't need to hide."

I straightened, pushed my hair behind my ears, and leaned

into Jed's arm. "Thanks," I told him. Turning to Angus, I said, "Forgive me, laird. It's an old instinct."

Angus studied me. "Yer defense is formidable, Artie. I almost lost sight o' ye, and I'm fully aware ye are here." He cocked his head, his eyes narrowing. "I don't think I've ever seen that ability before, though yer grannie did mention she'd seen it once."

Knowing I'd be embarrassed, Jed rubbed his hands together and said, "All right!" before grabbing a cookie, stuffing the whole thing in his mouth and chewing rapidly. He washed it down with a swig of tea, and said, "So, the facts as we know them." He held up a finger. "One: Angus is ancient." A second finger joined the first. "We're all related." His ring finger rose. "If the Fae don't bother us, we don't bother them."

He glanced around. "Is that all there is? You came all the way from Ireland to tell us not to bother any Fae that doesn't threaten us or the community around us? When you already had proof we'd do that anyway?" He narrowed his eyes and pointed at Angus. "I don't think so. I also don't think you came to confess your age. I'm guessing most of the O'Connor clan has no idea you're the original O'Connor. So what really brought you to Colorado?"

Angus smiled and nodded. "Verra astute, Jedidiah. Ye're correct on all counts." He picked up a cookie, took a bite, and chewed. Slowly and deliberately. As if he had all the time in the world. Which, of course, he did. Quite literally.

Jed bounced up and paced around the room, coming to a stop behind the sofa. Resting his hands on the back, he leaned forward and glared at Angus. "Come on, man! Spit it out!"

Angus's eyebrows rose almost to his hairline and he glanced at the last bite of cookie in his hand.

Jed scowled. "Not the cookie," he almost shouted. "The reason for your visit."

Angus finished his cookie, took a swallow of tea, and said, "Oh. That." He glanced at me. "This is verra good tea, Artie."

I tried not to smile as I said, "Thank you, Laird, but I think you need to answer Jed's question before he explodes. He's not as patient as I am."

Jed threw up his hands, muttering in disgust, and strode around the sofa to plop down beside me again.

"Fine," Angus said cheerfully. "If ye must know, I came to offer ye jobs. Both of ye."

3

"What?" Jed and I exclaimed together, though to be fair, Jed almost roared ,while I definitely squeaked.

"Jobs," Angus repeated. "Employment. Ye know, a way to earn money to pay for yer home and food."

"I know what a job is," Jed growled. "I just don't know how you expect to employ us when you're in Ireland and we're in Colorado." His eyes narrowed and he leaned forward. "We're not moving to Ireland, if that's what you're thinking."

Angus leaned back, comfortable in the overstuffed chair. "And why would ye be thinking I want ye in Ireland when 'twas I who ensured ye had the wherewithal to buy this house? Don't be daft, boy. A man who's lived as long as I have has varied business holdings and more capital at his fingertips than ye can imagine." He stopped talking, seemingly engrossed in examining said fingers.

"And?" I prompted before my husband could growl again.

Angus glanced at me and smiled. "I'm opening a Denver branch of one of my IT companies, Paladin Shield. I want the two o' ye on my payroll as consultants."

Jed sat back, his expression neutral. "What kind of IT company and how would we consult?"

"'Tis designed for computer security. Keeping systems up to date and impervious to hacking. I know ye studied information technology at university, Jed, so no one will question yer credentials, but I'm no interested in yer computer skills. I have experts on staff for that. Purely mortal men and women who have no knowledge o' the Fae."

He paused and studied our faces. "Nay, I want the two of ye to be my paladins. My knights— though ye willna be wearing shining armor— to defend humanity from malicious Fae. Ye'll be on the payroll of Paladin Shield, but ye'll have no need to set foot in the building; ye'll report directly to me. The only folk in the Denver office who'll know aught about ye will be the head of HR, who will have employment files that I'll create, and the financial director, who will authorize yer pay."

I frowned. "Why paladins?"

Angus shrugged. "A nod to my longevity. I knew Charlemagne's paladins. Rode with them on a few quests. A more noble group of knights never existed. They were honorable men who fought to protect the people given into their care."

He stopped, his eyes glazed with memories of the distant past. After a moment, he shook himself and met our gazes. "So? What do ye say? Want to become modern day paladins, roaming the earth to protect mortals from dangers they canna even see?"

"Of course," we answered together, then grinned at each other.

"Seriously, Angus," Jed said. "That sounds perfect."

I nodded. "Exactly what I dreamed of, but couldn't figure out how to achieve."

Angus slapped his hands on his knees. "Excellent! Ye'll have access to a private jet hangered at the Denver airport. I'll give ye each a dedicated cell phone just for this purpose and will let ye know where ye need to be when trouble arises."

"Wow," Jed said. "A private jet? Dedicated phones? This is starting to sound like James Bond."

Angus laughed. "Not quite. Ye'll have no 'Q' building fancy weapons and gadgets, but the O'Connor clan does provide me with an enviable intelligence network. Not all of my descendants have the *sight*, but enough do to keep me informed about conditions around the world, and fewer still have the means to fight the Fae. Most can only observe, and that only with great discretion. The two o' ye are unique. Which is why I want ye to be the paladins of the O'Connor clan."

Jed and I nodded, too overwhelmed to speak.

"When you're not on quest," Angus continued, "ye'll live and train here in McIntosh. I'll arrange for a mixed martial arts master to work with ye when ye are in residence." He turned his gaze on Jed. "I'd also like for ye to appeal to yer guardian angel. See if he will join ye in the physical world and train both of ye to fight the supernatural more effectively."

"How did you..." Jed began, then closed his eyes and answered his own question. "Grannie O'Toole."

Angus nodded. "Maeve O'Toole is an invaluable part of my intelligence network. Will ye make the request?"

"I will, but Michael visits when he sees fit, and then only in my dreams."

"I understand," Laird Angus said, "but perhaps a prayer would not be amiss?"

Jed nodded. After all, his father was the pastor of one of the local evangelical churches. "I'll visit my dad's church and pray for intercession."

"Excellent," Angus exclaimed again. He rose and clapped his hands. "Now that our business is concluded, may I take my favorite paladins out for a steak dinner?"

Jed and I agreed readily, and I moved around the coffee table to hug our ancestor, benefactor, and... employer!

4

_S_pring blossomed into summer before Jed and I were called upon to act as Laird Angus's paladins.

The months between the Laird's visit and our first assignment were busy ones. Angus arranged for a small dojo to be built at the back of our land once Master Kenji approved its placement.

"The trees enfold this space like the arms of the dragon," our sensei told us when we met for our first lesson in our private training space. "You will learn safely here." The sensei worked us hard, meeting with us three days a week and insisting we practice _tai chi_ every morning before breakfast.

But mixed martial arts weren't the total extent of our training. We also trained with Michael three days a week. Not the same days, thankfully, but between the sensei and the archangel, Jed and I had only a single day without scheduled training sessions.

True to his word, Jed had gone to his father's church the day after Angus's visit and spent an hour in prayer, asking for Michael's help in defending the human race from malicious Fae. The archangel had replied swiftly. He visited Jed's dreams that very night and listened attentively to Jed's description of the Laird's plan.

"When your training space is complete," the warrior angel had said, "I will come. But you and Artemis will be the only witnesses. I will be invisible to anyone else who happens upon our training."

While Master Kenji taught us to fight, he also taught us to meditate. To clear our minds of all distractions and to act with focused deliberation. We learned calmness in the face of danger, and practiced until our bodies could react without conscious thought.

Archangel Michael also taught us to fight deliberately and without fear, but his teaching concentrated on more arcane methods. From Michael we learned the uses of holy water, of specific prayers for the sanctification of weapons, places, and people. He taught us how to call upon the forces of light and life to aid us in the protection of innocent lives. Michael taught us faith. Not in church or creed, but in the god who created us and the forces of good he had set in motion in our world. Michael agreed wholeheartedly with Laird Angus (and us) that as long as the Fae were not in opposition to that good, they were not to be harmed.

It was an intense three months, but when the call came from Angus in early July, we felt ready.

Jed answered our dedicated phone and engaged the speaker function so neither of us would miss a word.

"And how are ye progressing, my paladins?" Laird Angus asked.

"Michael and Master Kenji are satisfied with our progress," Jed said. "Of course we won't know for sure until we're tested, but I'm confident in our abilities."

"And ye, Artemis?" Angus asked. "Are ye confident as well?"

I nodded, though the Laird couldn't see me. "I am. Jed and I fought well together before our training. We have a lot more techniques to put into action now."

"Verra well," Angus said, and I could almost see him nodding. "'Tis time for my paladins to take the field. Ye are needed in Glasgow. A particularly mean-spirited clan o' Fae have moved into the city. They're terrorizing the citizenry, though the locals are attributing the violence to gang wars and the like."

Jed and I glanced at each other, our expressions grave.

"How do you want us to proceed?" Jed asked.

"Get ye to the airport. I've already alerted the pilot. He'll have the jet fueled up and the flight plan logged by the time ye arrive."

I grabbed a pad of paper and a pen and wrote down the details as Laird Angus fired them off: which hangar to approach; where to park; the pilot's name. All the information we'd need not only for this mission, but for future ones as well.

When all the details had been passed along, Laird Angus said, "One o' my O'Connor lads will meet ye when ye land in Glasgow. He'll take ye to the clan keep. The other *Sidhe Seers* there will fill you in on the specifics. They won't be able to help ye fight, but they'll support ye in any way they can, so don't be afraid to tell them what ye need."

Jed and I nodded. "We understand," I said.

"We'll keep you posted," Jed said.

"Dinna worry about that, lad," Angus said. "The Glasgow clan members will give me regular reports. Ye'll be there to protect the city, not to be doing paper work and chatting with me."

"We won't let you down, sir," Jed said. I nodded my agreement.

"I've every confidence in ye both," the Laird said. A moment later he added, "After all, I've seen young Artie at work first hand."

Jed turned to me and grinned; my cheeks heated with a flush. "She's pretty amazing," he said. "I'm a lucky man."

"That ye are, lad. That ye are."

5

*T*he flight to Glasgow was amazing. I'd never set foot on a private jet before and was overwhelmed by the luxury. Comfortable white leather seats seemed to mold to your body and swiveled for ease of conversation or reclined for relaxation. Deeply cushioned chocolate brown carpeting. Cherry wood tables and architectural accents were polished to a velvety glow. Curved white walls with strategically placed windows for viewing the world as we skimmed above it.

Having only flown commercial flights before, and those only rarely, I was overcome with nerves. I closed my eyes and concentrated on the meditation exercises Master Kenji had taught me. I couldn't afford to allow the butterflies fluttering in my belly to get the best of me. If I gave in to nerves now— over the transportation the Laird had provided!— how would I ever manage to control myself when it came time to battle the Fae?

Jed didn't seem nearly as nervous as I felt. No, my tall, handsome husband acted like a ten-year-old boy turned loose in a candy shop! He sat in every seat but the one I'd chosen, checked out all the cubbyholes, chatted with the pilot, and asked if he could join him in the cockpit and check out the controls. The pilot laughed good naturedly and said not today, but he'd check with the Laird about a future flight.

At last the pilot retreated to the cockpit and Jed settled in the seat across from me. Buckling our seatbelts, we prepared for take-off, which was so smooth as to be practically unnoticeable. The minute we levelled off and the *fasten seat belts* warning clicked off, Jed jumped up and said, "This is awesome! Want a snack?"

I laughed, my nerves dissolving immediately. My Jed was irrepressible!

"Sure. Why not?" I unbuckled my seatbelt and joined him in exploring the compact, but well-stocked galley. We opted for fresh-baked chocolate chip cookies and bottles of spring water. I'd eyed the selection of fresh fruit— apples, oranges, bananas, and a medley of berries— but decided I could be health conscious another day. This first flight was all about luxury!

A little over nine hours after leaving Denver, we landed in Glasgow. While it was only early evening for me and Jed, it was past midnight in Scotland. We disembarked from the jet and were met by a sleepy-eyed man with auburn hair and beard in a rumpled dark blue suit.

"Jed Kendrick and Artemis Woodward?" he asked, stifling a yawn.

We nodded and Jed held out his hand. "It's actually Wood-ward-Kendrick for both of us," he said, shaking the man's hand. "We decided to combine our surnames when we married."

"O' course," the man said, extending his hand to me. "I'm Gareth O'Connor. Laird Angus asked me ta help ye get settled and act as yer guide." He motioned toward a waiting car. "If ye'll come this way..."

We followed the man across the tarmac, but as he opened the door of the car, I placed a hand on his arm.

"I know it's late here," I said, urgency buzzing beneath my

words, "but I feel a need to confront the Fae now. Before they're alerted to our presence."

Jed nodded. "She's right. It's not even time for dinner yet as far as we're concerned. Take us straight to the area most effected by the Fae's malice."

Gareth studied our faces, his expression revealing his skepticism. Then he shrugged and his face cleared. "Fine. Th' Laird ga' me no specific instructions about yer mission, only that I should gi' ye what aid I could. I ken where th' Fae are most active and if ye wish to go straight there, I'll take ye."

When we were settled in the car and underway, he added, "Ye do understand that I'll no be going wi' ye? If th' Fae know I'm a *Seer*, my usefulness to th' clan will be at an end."

Jed, who sat beside Gareth on what would have been the driver's side if we were in the States, nodded. "We understand."

"We expect to fight alone." I reached forward from the back seat and laid a hand on Gareth's shoulder. "It's what we've been training to do."

"Where are we going?" Jed asked. "And what types of Fae have you seen there?"

We'd left the airport behind and now drove through quiet streets. In the distance, across what I knew must be the River Clyde, lights shone in what was undoubtedly the vibrant heart of the city. But Gareth guided the car away from those lights.

"I'm taking ye to Easterhouse." Gareth's knuckles whitened with the strength of his grip on the steering wheel. "The Fae ha' been riling up those who're disaffected anyway, and the pubs o' th' area ha' been dealin' wi' even more violence than usual lately." He glanced over his shoulder at me. "Two men ha' died in th' last week alone."

Jed and I digested that information as Gareth guided the car across a bridge over the River Clyde. After a few moments, he spoke again.

"As to the type o' Fae, I've seen goblins and redcaps, and…" — he grimaced and swallowed— "and sluagh."

Jed whistled softly, and I shivered.

Sluagh. The Host of the Unforgiven Dead.

Jed turned in his seat and met my gaze. I nodded, knowing he was thinking as I was that it was a good thing we'd been training with Michael.

"Right," Jed said, directing his words to Gareth. "You'll want to stop a few blocks from where you expect the trouble to be. Artie and I will need to gear up."

We'd entered a part of the city that seemed less well kept. The houses, apartment buildings, and even the businesses had a disillusioned, unkempt air about them. Almost as if the structures themselves despaired of hope and happiness. Gareth pulled the car to the curb and Jed and I stepped out.

My spirit sank as I set foot on the pavement. The very air seemed to urge me to return to the car and escape. I straightened my shoulders and joined Jed as he pawed through the cases we'd brought with us.

"Let's see," he mumbled, almost to himself. "We'll want holy water and the swords Michael blessed." He handed me items as he spoke.

As I buckled on my sword and stowed the holy water in pockets of my calf-length black leather duster, I rehearsed the prayers of sanctification and protection Michael had taught us.

Jed also donned a black leather duster, though he cut a much more impressive figure than my five-foot-two physique could command. Tall and lanky, my warrior husband towered over me. His normally gentle gray eyes flashed with deadly fire as we prepared to battle supernatural forces for the souls of the people of Glasgow.

We moved away from the car as Gareth pointed us in the direction we should go. "I'll shadow ye," he said. When Jed cocked his head and lifted a brow, Gareth shrugged. "I'm ta report on yer success ta th' Laird." He grinned. "And if ye are no successful, I'll be there ta drag yer carcasses out o' danger."

I smiled, but Jed laughed out loud. "Good to know you've got our backs."

Finding the trouble wasn't hard. We heard the ruckus before we turned the corner toward the pub. When we came within sight, we saw a large gang of men slugging it out. Glass from the pub's broken front window glittered in the light spilling from the open door. Men and women stood just inside the door and others leaned carefully over the frame of the shattered window. Those who weren't fighting yelled catcalls, egging their favorite fighters on.

But this wasn't a friendly scuffle between mates. The atmosphere felt dark and malicious. Many of the catcalls were vicious, as if the bystanders thirsted for spilled blood.

I engaged my *sight* and saw the supernatural elements that orchestrated the brawl. Redcaps ensured that falls resulted in cuts from broken glass. Goblins pushed and shoved, making sure no combatants retired from the fight, while the sluagh flitted among the mortals, filling their minds with battle rage and lust for others' pain.

Jed and I glanced at each other, pulled our swords, and strode into the fray reciting prayers for protection of the mortals as we met the supernatural enemy.

Gareth told us later that it looked like a dance—a deadly dance. We slashed and cut, twirled and leapt, separating the Fae from the mortals they sought to harm. The skirts of our dusters flared as we moved from goblin to sluagh to redcap.

Lunge. Thrust. Parry. Feint.

We moved as a unit, always aware of where the other fought as we dodged and blocked, and swept our enemy from the street.

The mortal men and women stepped back as our prayers

took effect. They shook their heads and stared at each other as if wondering why they were bloody and bruised.

But they all turned to watch us fight, and since none could see the enemy, they told themselves they were watching a display of antique skills, for no one fought with blades in this modern world.

When the last redcap fled, Jed and I sheathed our swords amid cheers from the watching crowd. Gareth appeared at our sides, and the barman called everyone inside for a round of drinks... on the house!

6

"They are a sight ta behold, Laird." Gareth spoke into his cell phone while Jed and I packed the last of our belongings. "Th' locals won't be forgettin' the late night *exhibitions* the master swordsmen ha' been puttin' on this seven-day." He paused, listening. "Aye, I'll be tellin' 'em."

Gareth ended the call and turned to us. "He's right pleased, is the Laird. Says ye are ta rest up and be ready for his next call."

Jed and I glanced at each other and grinned. Rest up indeed! Our battles in Glasgow had shown us where our weaknesses were. When we got back to Colorado, we intended to train even harder. We had specific scenarios to describe to both Michael and Master Kenji, and we expected our mentors to help us work out new, more effective strategies.

As he drove us back to the airport, Gareth provided a running commentary on the effects of our work. "Even the locals, those wi' not a whit o' the *sight,* can feel th' change in Easterhouse. Friendlier, they say. There's hope in th' air and folk are cleaning up th' neighborhoods. Men as were fightin' and growlin' at each other a week ago are workin' together ta rebuild and refurbish."

He shook his head. "If I hadna seen it with me own two eyes, I'd ne'er ha' believed it possible." He parked the car near the private jet and helped Jed and I with our luggage.

When we were ready to board, he shook hands with each of us. "'Tis proud I am ta know ye and claim clanship wi' ye. Go wi' grace and know ye'll always ha' friends in Glasgow."

"Thanks," I said, "and the same is true of you. If you ever come to Colorado, we'll be glad of your company."

We boarded the jet, sank gratefully into white leather comfort, and smiled. Happy, but exhausted. We'd survived our first mission. More than survived! We were now full-fledged paladins. Battle-tested and ready to go wherever the clan needed us. We would fight to shield mortals from the wrath and spite of the supernatural enemies they couldn't even see.

Laird Angus had named his IT company well. *Paladin Shield*. We, Jed and I, were the true paladin shield... and we were proud to carry that responsibility. Blessed to be able to protect those given into our care.

PART II

SIREN SURF

Deb Logan

Siren Surf
A *Siren Tales* Short Story

PROLOGUE

*W*hat a difference a year makes!

Last year I thought I was a perfectly normal teenage girl. I lived in Wichita, Kansas and had never even seen an ocean. I'd definitely never been near salt water.

Now I live in Hawaii with my dad and swim in the Pacific Ocean every single day. And... I know the truth.

I'm not a human girl.

I'm a siren. A creature of the sea.

Kind of like a mermaid, but without a tail or scales or gills. When I swim in salt water, my body transforms. My hands and feet elongate and my toes and fingers become webbed. And my lung capacity goes off the charts! I don't breathe water, I just hardly need to breathe.

Well, to be honest, I'm only half-siren.

My mom rescued my dad when his small sailing vessel went down in a storm far out to sea. She was a siren; he was a human. They fell in love, moved to Hawaii, and lived happily ever after.

Until I came along.

Mom didn't know whether I'd have enough siren blood to transform, but she was sure I'd be drawn to the sea, so she convinced Dad to move inland to protect me. At least until I was old enough to understand the dangers and let Mom test me, slowly and safely, to see if I could handle myself in salt water.

Unfortunately, Mom died in a car accident before she got around to testing my abilities — or telling me what I am.

Poor Dad didn't know what to do. He was grieving for his lost love, didn't have a clue how to explain everything, and had no way to test me. So he just kept doing what he'd always done: kept me in Wichita, as far from salt water as he could manage.

That kind of worked. Until I told a little fib.

Okay. It was a full-blown lie. I admit it. I deceived my father.

My best friend in the whole world, Emma Walker, was going to the Oregon coast on vacation, and her family invited me to join them. Since we were flying to Portland, Oregon, I kind of *forgot* to mention to Dad that Portland wasn't our final destination.

I mean, really!

I knew he wouldn't let me go if he knew we were headed to the coast, so I just let him assume....

It was wrong; I shouldn't have done it.

But because I did, I finally learned the truth.

Fortunately, I lived to tell the tale.

After Dad and I had it out over the phone, we started making plans to move to Maui.

So here I am, a siren's daughter living in paradise and exploring the Pacific Ocean on a daily basis with my friends: bottlenose dolphins, Hawaiian monk seals, sea turtles, and the occasional humpback whale calf.

Life is good.

1
_____

*E*ven in paradise, a teenage girl has to go to school.
Bummer.

Especially when said girl is new to Hawaii, has no friends, and isn't even fully human. I'd much rather spend my time in the water, or even helping Dad wrangle tourists on one of Captain Bill's snorkeling cruises. But Dad insists I need my education.

I repeat, bummer.

So on Monday of the second week of August, I dragged myself out of bed, pulled on my best khaki walking shorts, the only blue polo shirt I owned that wasn't emblazoned with Captain Bill's logo, and stuffed my bare feet into a respectable pair of leather sandals, as opposed to the ratty flip-flops I usually wore down to the beach. Shuffling dispiritedly into the kitchen, I poured myself a glass of POG— a juicy blend of passionfruit, orange, and guava that I'd decided was the next best thing to ambrosia— and popped a couple pieces of bread in the toaster.

"Got everything you need?" Dad asked as he emerged from his bedroom.

We'd been really lucky to score a two-bedroom condominium just a block from the beach. It wasn't as roomy as our house in Wichita, but our building had two elevators and a coin-op laundry, and the seven acre complex boasted a water feature with a koi pond, swing sets for the littlest residents, and swimming pool and half-size basketball court for everyone else.

Why anyone would want a swimming pool when the ocean was less than a block away was beyond me, but it was a feature the sales rep had stressed while trying to reel Dad into a contract. Not that the guy had needed to work too hard to land us. The condo had everything we needed: two bedrooms, a kitchen, a bath, and easy access to the ocean. Anything else was a bonus. Nice, but unnecessary.

I sipped my POG and shrugged. "Everything but my freedom."

Dad laughed and tousled my short red hair. My human genes came straight from him. I'd inherited his red hair, gray-green eyes, and pale, freckled complexion. I looked nothing like my mother, who had been an exotic, dark-haired beauty. But there was no doubt I was her daughter. Not once I stepped into salt water!

"Come on now," Dad said, a slight wheedle to his tone. "It's not that bad. You always liked school in Wichita."

My toast popped up at that moment, so I turned away from him and flipped the hot slices of perfectly browned bread onto a plate. "In Wichita I knew everyone," I said, glad he couldn't see my face. "Here my only friends are bottlenose dolphins and Hawaiian monk seals."

Dad stepped to my side and draped an arm across my shoulders while I buttered my toast. "You'll make friends, Maris. In a month you'll feel like you've lived here forever."

I slipped out of his embrace, moved to the refrigerator and grabbed a jar of orange marmalade. "I guess," I said, slathering my buttered toast with the rich orange jam, "but that doesn't make today any easier."

Dad poured a cup of coffee from the pot that had just finished perking and followed me to the little glass-topped table on our lanai. We set our food on the table, plopped into its matching stackable metal chairs, and drank in the ocean view from our little second floor balcony. I inhaled the warm, balmy air, heavy with the delicious tang of salt water, and closed my eyes.

It was worth it.

Every uncomfortable moment in the day to come was worth it to live here instead of Wichita.

I turned to Dad and smiled. "I'll be fine, Dad," I admitted. "I'm just nervous. Sure, I have friends in Wichita, but here…" I paused and waved toward the ocean. "Here I know who and what I am and I can indulge my love of salt water every single day."

Dad nodded, but his expression was solemn, almost mournful. "Your mother would be so proud." He glanced out to sea. "I wish she were here. I wish she could teach you all the things you need to know."

I dropped the last bite of toast on my plate, pushed back my chair, and moved around the little table to hug Dad. "So do I," I said quietly, emotion thickening my voice, "but we're doing fine. You brought me here, Dad. You dropped everything and brought me to paradise. I'll figure out what I need to know. The dolphins and the seals have helped me a lot already."

Dad kissed the top of my head, and we separated. We both wiped our eyes, and then he smiled at me. "We're doing fine," he agreed, "but now you need to get moving. You don't want to be late for your first day at Kahalawai High."

I laughed. "You're right. The new girl should definitely not get off on the wrong foot on her very first day."

2

My first day at Kahalawai High turned out to be a no-brainer. Dad dropped me off at the administration office, where I met my counselor, got checked in, and received my class schedule. I was also given a map which, considering this school has twelve permanent buildings and a whole bunch of temporary ones, was actually a necessity.

Who ever heard of a high school with a 75 acre campus?

Anyway I managed to find all of my classes, following the map from building to building until the final bell rang at just after 2:00 p.m.

That's when my day *really* started.

I'd heard some kids in class talking about meeting after school at Kanaha Beach. I'd been here long enough to know that the beach wasn't far from either Kahalawai High or my apartment, but I hadn't brought a swimsuit to school, so I needed to go home first. I didn't know anyone well enough to ask for a ride, so I walked the mile and a half home as fast as my sandal-clad feet would carry me.

Once back in my apartment, I dropped my backpack, left Dad a note— just in case— and quickly changed into my favorite blue floral swimsuit and ratty flip-flops. Now, I could've walked to the beach, it was only a couple of miles, but I swim a lot faster than I walk so it only made sense that I should take the water route over to Kanaha Beach. I raced across Kahalui Beach Road to my own personal water access. Not that my ocean access was anything special— just a rocky strip between the street and the ocean— but that was all I needed. Leaving my flip-flops beside a convenient rock, I stepped into the water, waded out a few feet, then slipped beneath the surface.

The Salt Water Effect, my own personal name for the phenomenon, began as soon as I stepped into the ocean. My feet became long and slender, the toes splaying widely and webbing stretching between them. When I dove beneath the surface, my hands underwent a similar change, but that wasn't the really cool part. That belonged to my lungs. I didn't grow gills; I'm not a fish, but like the seals and dolphins who had befriended me, my lung capacity expanded off the charts. I hadn't really pushed myself yet, but I'd found that I could stay underwater as along as thirty minutes without a problem. And I had no idea how deep I could dive. Hadn't tested that either, and wouldn't until I had human back-up.

Or better yet, found another siren.

Seals and dolphins are great swimming partners, and I knew my friends wouldn't let me drown, but neither would they be able to provide CPR if I needed it. Nope, testing my limits wasn't on my list of 'must-do' accomplishments.

But I could swim near the surface for hours, and that was all I had in mind for today.

I swam out past the breakers and made my way east along the shore until I saw a bunch of folks snorkeling and body surfing just beyond a wide strip of white sand beach backed by the green canopy of heliotrope and milo trees. Kanaha Beach park was a picture perfect spot for a late summer afternoon gathering of teenage water lovers.

I made my way past snorkelers too intent on the fishy inhabitants of the Pacific to notice a girl whose flippers weren't plastic, and stepped out of the water in an area too rocky to be appealing to the masses. Choosing a convenient rock, I sat and waited for my body to return to its non-Salt-Water-Effect status.

The change didn't take long. In less time than most people spend washing them, my hands had returned to what I still thought of as normal. Taking a deep breath and hoping the drum roll of my pulse couldn't be heard on the outside, I walked over to join a group of ten or twelve kids I'd seen at Kahalawai High earlier that day.

Talk about sticking out like a sore thumb! Most of the kids had gorgeous, sun-kissed brown skin and straight black hair. The guys and gals in the group of European ancestry were also evenly suntanned from living under the tropical Hawaiian sun.

Me? Even after two months of cavorting in the Pacific and helping out on Captain Bill's island cruises, my skin was still fishy-belly pale, though I was sporting more and larger freckles than I'd had in Kansas.

And my hair? Far from the shiny, lustrous, straight black of the native Hawaiians, mine was red and naturally curly to the point of frizziness. At least at the moment it was slicked back from my face due to my underwater swim, though short tendrils at my temples were beginning to spring back into curls.

Whatever.

I am who I am... and I'm a lot more than what the kids on the beach could see.

As I approached the group, one dark-haired, perfectly tanned girl looked up, smiled and waved. I angled my steps to join her.

"Hi," I said, trying to infuse my voice with confidence. "I'm Maris. Maris Grainger."

"Anita Mukai," she said, holding out her hand. "I saw you in chemistry this morning. You're new to Kahului, aren't you?"

I nodded, shaking her hand firmly. "My dad and I moved here from the mainland a couple of months ago."

She smiled and turned to the others. "Hey, everyone, say hello to Maris. She's new to the islands."

Suddenly I was the center of attention. Everyone wanted to know who I was, where I'd come from, whether or not I liked Maui, and most importantly, could I surf?

I answered questions, shook hands, smiled, and tried desperately to remember names. The kids were all so friendly! Everyone was anxious to help the haole— someone like me who hadn't been born in the islands— find her way around.

When they learned I'd been on the swim team in Kansas, but had no idea how to surf, Daniel Garcia grabbed a board with one arm and my hand with the other and would've pulled me straight into the water if it hadn't been for Anita.

"Slow down, Daniel," Anita said with a laugh. "Maris hasn't said she wants to learn to surf." Turning to me, she cocked her head and raised an eyebrow. "Do you?"

My face flamed, a less than desirable trait I'd lived with my whole life. When I'm embarrassed or unsure, my face informs the world. Professional poker player is definitely NOT a career option.

I stammered a bit and finally managed to say, "No... at least... not right now."

Truth was, I'd love to learn to surf, I just wasn't sure how that would be possible. I mean, the Salt Water Effect would announce my difference to anyone who spent time with me in the Pacific. I was already the new girl; I wasn't anxious to become known as the not-quite-human girl, too.

Daniel's shoulders drooped, he dropped my hand and glanced at his bare feet, which he shuffled in the warm white sand. "Sorry, Maris," he mumbled.

I smiled and punched him lightly on the shoulder. "No problem. Maybe another time."

He looked up at that and flashed a brilliant smile. "Any time!"

With that, the group broke up. Daniel and Jason Okamoto ran into the surf with their boards, then paddled out to catch a breaker. The waves weren't high today, but they didn't care. Surfing was surfing, even if some of it was just body surfing.

Several of the others grabbed masks and fins and swam out beyond the breakers to snorkel, but Anita and a few other girls remained on the sand.

"You look like you could stand to catch a few rays," Anita said, gesturing to my pale skin. "Do you have a good lotion? One that will let you tan while protecting you from sunburn?"

I shrugged. "I'm lucky, I guess. Even here in the tropics, I don't burn, but I don't tan either. I just get more freckles."

Amy Lindsey, another girl of European descent, nodded. "One of my cousins has that problem. I always tease her that maybe someday her freckles will all run together... then she'll have a nice even tan."

Everyone laughed. "I can always hope," I said when I'd stifled my giggles. I didn't have a towel to spread out on the sand, but Jenny Yamamoto had an extra. She seemed a little surprised at my lack of beach necessities, but handed it over with a smile.

We spent a relaxing afternoon sunning, swimming, surfing, and snorkeling. And if any of my new friends noticed that I never so much as put a toe in the water, they chose not to comment. When it was time to leave, I walked the others to their cars, but declined to accept a ride home.

"No worries," I said. "I live nearby. I'll walk."

With calls of "see you tomorrow," we parted company, and as soon as my new friends were out of sight, I returned to the Pacific to let the Salt Water Effect take hold and swim home.

Tomorrow would be a better day. I had friends now.

----

3

*B*y the time October rolled around, I was well established at Kahalawai High. Anita and Amy had become my best friends, and Jenny accepted me easily into her circle as well. I still missed Emma, but she and i talked on the phone often and occasionally managed a video chat. Plus I had the wonders of the Pacific to keep me occupied.

The pod of bottlenose dolphin I often swam with introduced me to humpback whales, sea lions, and the awesome sea turtles who inhabited the waters and reefs near my home. But best of all was my discovery of a colony of selkies who lived on the Forbidden Island of Ni'ihau.

I knew intellectually that such creatures must exist— I mean, I'm half siren after all!— but I'm not sure I ever expected to meet one. Having a friend like Serena who could swim with me as a seal and then remove her sealskin and lounge on a beach with me as a teenage girl... well, let's just say it was very liberating!

And then there were the boys.

We left Wichita before I really had a chance to date. I mean, sure, a whole group of us would go out for pizza and a movie, but I was only fifteen when I discovered exactly who and what I am. After that, I was too focused on the move Dad and I were about to make to seriously consider any of the guys I knew as dating material.

But now I'm sixteen.

And living in paradise.

And I know who I am.

And... well... BOYS!

I know, I know. The Salt Water Effect complicates things, but as long as I stay out of the Pacific I can dream of dating. And I know some seriously hunky, athletically built guys! I mean, just about everybody surfs here, and surfing is an extreme sport. It takes muscles and coordination and good lungs and... let's just say the surfer guys are built!

Three guys in particular had caught my eye and any one of them could cause me to go all tongue tied if I wasn't prepared to chat. Kyle Lee, Jason Okamoto, and... Daniel Garcia.

Yep. The guy who'd nearly dragged me into the ocean when we first met had turned into a major heart throb for me. Danny was in several of my classes, and once we got past the embarrassed stage, I discovered he was smart, fun to hang with, and had a great sense of humor. Plus, it was a major rush to watch him surf. Danny didn't just have fun with a surf board, he was good.

So when the gang invited me to tag along to Ho'okipa Beach to watch the surfers do their thing, I was thrilled.

Dad, of course, gave me the third degree.

"How many kids are going?" he asked, frowning as he buttered a slice of toast Wednesday morning before our planned outing on Saturday.

I did a quick head count in my mind before I answered. "Ten. Anita, Jenny, Amy, me, and Fiona," I said, ticking each name off on a finger, "plus Danny, Kyle, Jason, Billy, and Adam."

"How will you get there?"

I bit into my own toast, chewed quickly and swallowed. "Honestly, Dad, it's only about twenty miles up the coast. I could swim it easily."

He glared at me and didn't say a word.

"Fine. We're taking three vehicles to accommodate everyone and all of the boards. I'll probably ride with Anita."

Dad considered. "From what I hear, there are some dangerous waves in that area. You won't try to surf, will you?"

I really wanted to roll my eyes, but controlled myself. "You know perfectly well I won't get in the water. The Salt Water Effect, remember?"

He shrugged, but nodded. "Don't your friends think it's odd that you don't swim or anything?"

My turn to shrug, and chug a mouthful of POG. "Probably, but they don't bug me about it."

"Okay," Dad said after taking a swig of coffee. "I know you're in no danger in the water, no matter what the waves are like. Just make sure whoever is driving is good behind the wheel. If you're not comfortable, if they've been drinking or anything, swim home. Or call me and I'll come get you."

This time I did roll my eyes. "Dad, my friends don't drink or do drugs. They get their kicks from catching waves."

He nodded. "Good enough. I'll be working a snorkeling cruise to Molokini on Saturday, but call me if you need me."

I grabbed my backpack, hugged him, and headed to school. "Don't worry, Dad. Everything will be fine."

Famous last words.

4

—————

Saturday dawned clear and gorgeous. Let's be honest. *Every* day dawns clear and gorgeous here.

I jumped out of bed, raced to dress in my new favorite swimsuit, a deep purple tankini with an awesome color shift design, shorts, T-shirt, and flip-flops, and packed my swim bag with the essentials, towels, sun lotion, bottled water, sunglasses, and a floppy hat. When everything was ready, I carried it all out to the kitchen, toasted a bagel and smeared it with cream cheese.

Dad was just finishing his coffee, and told me to have fun as he grabbed his car keys and headed to Maalaea Harbor and his job with Captain Bill's Island Cruises.

I'd just finished chugging my POG and rinsing off my dishes when a car horn honked. Opening the door, I stepped out, waved at Anita before grabbing my things and heading out for the day.

Anita's car was loaded with three surf boards, me, and Amy. Billy was also driving. He had Jenny, Fiona, and Kyle. Danny and Jason were bringing the other six boards. Nine boards and ten people. Everyone would be surfing but me.

Ho'okipa Beach boasts some of the best surfing on Maui.

Depending on where you paddle out, you can catch nice normal waves all the way to monsters. Most of the gang was planning to stay in the main flow, with a few of the more adventurous guys thinking about surfing the Point or even the Pavilions.

I didn't expect anyone to risk the Jaws. That's where the legendary swells can occur, and even the pros have to be towed in rather than paddling out to catch a wave. We didn't expect any tremendously huge waves today, but it was moving on toward winter, so anything was possible.

Once everyone was in the water, paddling out to ride their waves, I moved down to a deserted patch and slipped into the water. I wanted to be part of the action, I just didn't want anyone to catch me at it.

Diving down into deep water, I swam with my undulating stroke out well past the breakers where I could keep an eye on my friends, but not be seen. They'd be watching the waves, not staring out to sea for a single red-haired female.

It was a glorious day to be alive. Clear blue skies, hot yellow sun, just enough wind to provide decent waves, and a sea turtle circling my webbed feet. Every now and then, when it looked like some of my group would be taking a break, I'd head in, give the Salt Water Effect time to dissipate, and then race back to our beach towels. No one wondered at my wet hair, they just assumed I'd taken a dip in one of the safe-for-swimming areas.

We enjoyed a picnic lunch of turkey and cheese sandwiches, grapes, and cold, bottled water while everyone replayed their morning rides.

"You really need to let me teach you, Maris," Danny said around a mouthful of grapes. "You're missing all the fun."

I shook my head. "Are you kidding? I'm having a blast watching you guys ride."

He shrugged. "Whatever. If you change your mind, you don't

have to start here. We could do your initial lessons back at Kanaha Beach."

Amy batted his shoulder. "Leave her alone, Daniel. Not everyone has to surf."

Danny ducked his head. "Okay. Okay." Then he grinned at me. "But I'm available. Just sayin'."

My heart skipped a beat and my face flamed, so I grabbed a bottle of water and chugged it, using the motion to turn away. He hadn't meant it the way I wanted to take it. Not like he was available to date. Just that he was willing to teach me to surf. That was all.

Wasn't it?

After lunch, we all took a nap in the sun. There's nothing like reclining on a beach towel under a hot Hawaiian sun with a floppy hat over your face to make you feel like all is right with the world. Except maybe when the guy you have a crush on flops down beside you and offers to rub lotion on your shoulders!

I peeked out from under my hat to find Danny sitting in the sand beside my towel.

"Need anything?" he asked. "I'd be happy to add some more lotion... to your back... I mean..." He stopped, his cheeks flaming, and dropped his gaze. "I mean, if you're interested, I'd..."

"I'm interested," I said, sitting up and meeting his gaze, "but not in suntan lotion... or surfing."

His Adam's apple bobbed, and he stared at me with those gorgeous brown eyes in his awesomely handsome brown face. Slowly he nodded. "What about a movie and a pizza tomorrow night?"

I blushed, but grinned. "That sounds perfect."

He jumped to his feet and yelled, his arms spread wide. "I asked... and she agreed!"

Our friends sat up, laughing at him.

"Of course she did," Anita said as she turned over and laid back down.

"About time," said Jason, and threw an empty water bottle at Danny.

Danny hopped around, grinning like a maniac, and I grinned too. Suddenly, he grabbed his board and raced for the water. "Later!" he called and used his excess energy to paddle out to sea.

Everyone else returned to dozing in the sun.

But not me. I watched Danny's progress, frowning. I didn't like the angle he was taking. If he kept that up, he'd be swept out toward the killer waves at the Jaws.

He was too excited about asking me out. He wasn't paying attention to the currents.

Ignoring who might be watching, I ran for the water and dove as soon as the land dropped away. Danny was an excellent surfer, but I wasn't taking any chances. Not now that he'd asked me out!

Of course, I'd never risk losing any of my friends just to protect my secret, but Danny...

Danny was special.

As I'd feared, the currents were sweeping Danny and his board into dangerous waters. I dove deep beneath the waves and fought the current as only a creature of the sea can. I kept pace with him, and when a monstrous wave flipped him from his board into the swirling rage of the undersea chop, I was there to pull him to the surface, far beyond the wild breakers.

He gasped deeply, pulling as much air as he could into oxygen starved lungs, pushed the hair from his eyes and stared at me.

"How... what? Did you just pull me up from the wash? How did you do that? What are you even doing out here?"

"I thought you were in trouble," said, not meeting his eyes. "I'm a really strong swimmer."

He shook his head, his eyes narrowed against the sun. "No way. If I couldn't handle that wave with a board, there's no way you swam through it."

We were both bobbing and sculling to stay in place in the relative calm of the water beyond the breakers. I pushed my hair out of my eyes, and Danny grabbed my hand, staring at the webbing between my fingers with disbelief.

I cursed myself.

Why had I done that? Why had I raised my hand out of the sheltering water? Had I been trying to sabotage myself?

Whatever. The damage was done now.

I wrenched my hand away from him and said quietly and in a menacing tone, "Tell anyone, and I'll just say you hit your head on your board. You're hallucinating. No one will believe you."

His eyes widened and his face paled, but he didn't say anything.

Something nipped at my webbed feet, and I sank beneath the surface. A sea turtle nudged my shin and a bottlenose dolphin drew up beside me in concern. Using the telepathy I'd established with my fellow creatures of the sea, they asked if I required assistance. I held out my hands and stroked the dolphin's sleek side and the turtle's wrinkled neck, assuring them that I was fine. The dolphin nodded upward at Danny, was I sure?

Danny, though still on the surface, had dipped his face beneath the water and was watching us.

I'm fine, I said into our link. *He's a friend. You can go if you wish.*

At least, I hoped Danny was still my friend.

The dolphin and the turtle swam away, and I returned to the surface.

Danny stared at me, solemnly, but without fear. "Let's head

to shore," he said. "We need to talk."

I nodded my agreement, and towed him perpendicular to the shore until we arrived at a place where the waves were manageable. Then, after giving him fair warning, I pulled him into the depths and towed him through the breakers' chop until we surfaced in a calm swimming area.

Walking out of the water, I saw our friends down the beach, dragging Danny's board out of the water and searching the waves for some sign of him.

I nodded toward them. "Not now," I said. "We need to let everyone know you survived." I gave him a meaningful glance. "Think of a story while we walk. I just went for a quick dip. What's your excuse?"

Everyone was astounded by Danny's survival. Amazed that he'd gotten away from an undertow that had ripped his board away from his leash. When all were convinced that he'd suffered no ill effects, the group decided it was time to pack up and head home.

While we were loading the cars, Danny caught my arm and gazed at my hand. Shaking his head, he said, "I saw what I saw."

I wrenched my hand away, but refused to look at him. "My apartment as soon as you and Jason finish unloading." I gave him my address and stalked away to help Anita and Amy.

5

There's nothing worse than waiting for a friend to disown you.

Dad was still at work when I got home, so I put my things away, washed the salt water from my face and hands, and set out a plate of oatmeal cookies and a pitcher of lemonade on the table on the lanai. I didn't really expect Danny's visit to make it to refreshments, but I needed to do something besides sit and wait for the axe to fall.

When the knock finally sounded on the front door, I squared my shoulders, pushed my hair away from my face, and opened the door to the guy who had *almost* been my boyfriend. To my surprise, he held out a bouquet of pink plumerias, white tuberoses and red carnations.

"I never thanked you for saving my life," he said, pushing the flowers into my hands. "Thank you."

Tears welled in my eyes, threatening to overflow and stream down my face. I blinked as rapidly as I could, and taking the bouquet, stepped away from the door.

"Thanks," I said. "Let's sit on the lanai." I gestured to the little patio and turned to find a vase for the flowers. When I carried the bouquet to the table, I found Danny munching a cookie and staring out at the Pacific Ocean across the street.

"So what happened out there today?" he asked, gesturing toward the water with the half-eaten oatmeal cookie.

And just like that, the moment of truth had arrived.

"I'm, uh, not entirely human," I said as quickly as I could force the words out.

He nodded. "I kinda figured that. So what are you?"

I stared at him. This wasn't at all what I'd expected. He was so calm. I'd expected him to rant, to yell. I'd even wondered if I'd be safe trying to talk to him without my dad present. And here he was, calmly eating a cookie and asking for information.

Weird.

"I'm a siren," I said.

He cocked his head and raised an eyebrow. "A siren? Really? Aren't you kind of red-haired and freckly to be one of the legendary sea creature who lures sailors to their deaths?"

I glared at him for a second, and then relaxed and smiled. "Maybe, but I'm still a siren. Or at least, I'm half a siren."

He'd started to pour a glass of lemonade, but stopped when I said that. "Half a siren? And you're from Kansas?" He finished filling the glass, handed it to me, and poured another for himself.

And just like that I poured out my whole story to him, including the fact that everything I knew about being a siren had come from dolphins and seals.

"Wow," he said, when I finished. "If I hadn't seen your hands and watched you talking to a dolphin and a sea turtle, I'd never believe it. You look perfectly normal now."

I nodded. "It's the Salt Water Effect."

"The what?"

"The Salt Water Effect. If I'd never stepped into salt water, I'd never have known what I was. That's why we lived in Kansas. To protect me, in case being half a siren wasn't enough to let me survive in salt water. Can't get much further from the ocean than Wichita, Kansas."

His gaze softened. "I'm sorry about your mom."

I nodded. "Me too. I have a million questions, and no one to answer them."

"I bet."

I squirmed in my chair, and finally met his gaze. "Are you going to tell?"

His eyes widened and his eyebrows rose. "What? Of course not!" He picked up his glass and sipped his lemonade. "I mean, first off, who'd believe me? But more importantly, you're my friend, and you saved my life. I owe you."

I lowered my gaze and fiddled with my glass. "I don't want you to *owe* me. I want you to keep my secret because you like me and wouldn't want to hurt me."

"Look at me, please," he said, and I raised my gaze to meet his.

"I do owe you, but I also like you and I definitely wouldn't want to hurt you. I'll keep your secret," he said, and held out his hand. "Friends?"

I accepted his hand and we shook. "Friends."

"So," he said, his cheeks going a bit red, "are we still on for pizza and a movie tomorrow?"

I grinned. "You bet!"

EPILOGUE

So here I am, a red-haired, freckle-faced teenage siren living in paradise. I swim in the Pacific Ocean almost every day with bottlenose dolphins, Hawaiian monk seals, sea turtles, and the occasional selkie. But I also go to Kahalawai High School where I have good friends and a certain very special guy who not only knows my secret, but still wants to date me.

Danny and I have progressed from pizza and movies to surfing lessons. Since I no longer have to hide the Salt Water Effect from him, I'm fulfilling my dream of learning to surf... and Danny Garcia is an excellent teacher.

Dad was amazed and alarmed to learn that someone else knew about my heritage, but he's gotten to know Danny and agrees that he's trustworthy. Mind you, he did threaten Danny's life if anything bad should happen to me. A conversation that left Danny a bit unnerved.

But since our greatest danger exists when we're surfing, I'm not too worried. Danny's an excellent surfer... and I'm an even better siren.

Life is good.

PART III

THE CASE OF THE VANISHING PUPPY

The Case of the Vanishing Puppy
The Cinnamon Files
Case Four
DEB LOGAN

I sat at the table in our dining alcove across from Dad, my precious tablet clutched tightly to my chest. My heart beat rapidly, but I maintained a carefully neutral expression. Dad leaned forward, his hands resting on the permaplastic surface of the table. Mom stood off to one side, feet slightly spread in her ready-for-anything stance, hands clasped behind her back.

"Detective-in-training Chou," Mom said, "in accordance with our agreement you will unlock your tablet and surrender it for inspection."

"Sir, yes sir!" I responded. Pressing my thumb to the activation screen, I licked my lips and handed my tablet to Dad. "As you can see, sir, my case files are correctly labeled and saved appropriately."

Dad swiped the screen, smiled, and glanced at me, one eyebrow raised. "*The Case Files of Cinnamon Chou, Space Station Detective*. Really? That's a very ambitious title, Sugar Cookie."

My face heated, but I held my gaze steady and managed not to roll my eyes. Parents. They're incorrigible. No matter how many times I asked Dad not to call me *Sugar Cookie*, he persisted. His excuse? Force of habit.

"You've always taught me that I can do anything," I said. I wanted to shrug my shoulders, but controlled the impulse. "I intend to be a detective. Just like you, Dad."

Mom moved to stand behind Dad and studied the tablet over his shoulder.

"Very nicely arranged, Cinnamon," she said. "Your reports appear concise and to the point."

Dad nodded, swiped back to my home screen, and handed the tablet back to me. "I agree. You're doing a great job recording your case files." He paused for a moment, watching me thumb my tablet into dormancy. "Would you like to have a report template? One that my detectives use?"

My eyes widened. A real, live case report template? Just like the detectives on Dad's security team used? Wow! Like I was going to pass up that opportunity!

"That would be awesome, Dad," I said, barely managing not to squeal. When I couldn't contain my excitement, I bounced up from my chair, hugging my tablet to my chest and danced a little jig. "I'm going to be so far ahead of my class at the academy," I said, grinning happily. "I can hardly wait!"

Mom laughed. "Well, I can," she said. "You have years here on Space Station Zeta before you can apply for the USL Academy. Don't go wishing your childhood away."

"I know," I said, twirling around the dining alcove, "but I'm going to make the best use of my time." I stopped twirling before I got too dizzy to stand and raced to hug Dad. "Besides, detecting is in my blood. *Cinnamon Chou, Space Station Detective*. It's who I am!"

The USL Academy. That's where I was headed and everyone knew it. Mom and Dad were both Universal Star League officers. Mom commanded Space Station Zeta, Dad was the ranking security officer, and I was their only offspring. The academy was my destiny.

Dad stood, hugged me back, and ruffled my sleek black hair. "I'll see that you get that template right away, Sugar Cookie."

There it was again, the nickname that refused to die. Now, I don't really mind Dad referring to me as an overly sweet pastry, but I draw the line at casual acquaintances using the name, and when Dad called me that in public, other station inhabitants, both human and alien, seemed to think they could refer to me that way too.

Honestly! I appreciate the fact that Dad has called me his sugar cookie since he first set eyes on me mere moments after my birth, but I'm not a baby anymore. I'm twelve Earth-standard years old, and just because my skin tone, the perfect combination of Mom's ebony complexion and Dad's gold-toned coloration (a throwback to his heritage from the ancient Earth region known as China), reminded him of an old-fashioned cinnamon sugar cookie is no reason to call me that in public.

But, what can a detective-in-training do? Put up with it, that's what. Because Dad is the best dad in the universe and I couldn't imagine loving anyone more. Except of course Mom. I loved her equally as well as Dad.

Let's face it, nicknames aside, I was one lucky girl. Great parents. An awesome pet— how many kids do you know who can claim a Fornaxian dragon as their own?— and an ever expanding universe of friends.

My wrist link pinged and announced, "Samantha Lindstrom." I grimaced. Sammy really needed to change her link settings. She hated being called Samantha almost as much as I disliked anyone but Dad calling me Sugar Cookie.

I waved to Mom and Dad and rushed down the hall to my room. The door irised open with a nearly inaudible *whoosh*, and

I answered my link as I stepped inside, the door irising closed behind me.

"Hey, Sammy. What's up?"

A tiny 3-D model of my friend appeared above the link on my wrist, her eyes wide and swimming with tears.

"Emergency, Cinnamon," she wailed. "Fred has disappeared! We were playing in the recreation area, and... and..." She paused, swiped tears from her face with a hand, and took a deep gulp of air. "He vanished, Cinnamon. Fred just vanished!"

2

$\mathcal{N}$ow Sammy may not be a detective-in-training like me, but she is the daughter of a USL officer. Sammy doesn't lie and she doesn't distort the facts. If she said her puppy had vanished, then Fred had vanished. At least, he'd wriggled completely out of her sight. But before I could make an informed decision, I needed cold, hard facts. And to get those, I needed two things: a calm best friend and the opportunity to study the scene of the crime... er, incident... er, disappearance.

"Calm down, Sammy, and tell me what happened."

"Calm down?" she said, her voice rising into the squeaking range as she scowled at my image. "How can you expect me to calm down? Fred just vanished! My puppy is missing!" She paused again, took another gulp of air, and said in a more normal tone, "Besides, I already told you what happened. We were playing in the recreation area and... and... he disappeared."

Fine. Every good detective knows that witness statements can be unreliable. I needed to move on to option #2: investigate the scene of the... disappearance.

"Don't worry, Sammy. Rafe and I are on the case. Stay where you are and we'll be right there. Where are you, exactly?"

"The picnic table next to the jumpball court," she said quickly. "Hurry, Cinnamon. He could be hurt and I'm sure he's scared."

"We're on the way," I assured her and closed the link.

I grabbed the special sheath glove and the padded vest Dad had designed for me, pulled them on, and opened the door to Rafe's habitat. My Fornaxian dragon cocked his head and stared at me with beady amber eyes. He gave a little chirp, as if asking what we were doing.

"Fred's in trouble," I told him, gesturing for him to come to my gloved forearm. "We're going to meet Sammy in the recreation area."

He bobbed his head, ruffled his wings and glided from his permaplastic perch to land lightly on my glove. Well, *lightly* might be stretching the truth. Rafe (Raphael if you want to get formal) was about the size of a small earth dog with ruby red scales, a barbed tail that was nearly as long as his body, and seriously wicked claws. The sheath glove and padded vest with reinforced shoulders protected me from his claws, but I'd really had to work to build up my muscles so that I could hold my arm steady when he landed on the glove.

Transferring him to my shoulder, I waited for him to get settled before leaving my room and hurrying to the door to the corridor.

Mom glanced up from the table where she and Dad were going over some paperwork. "Where are you and Rafe off to, Cinnamon?"

I didn't even pause, just called over my shoulder, "We're meeting Sammy and Fred at the recreation area." At least, I sure hoped we'd be seeing Fred too!

Mom nodded. "Have fun, but be home in plenty of time for dinner."

"Will do," I said and slid through the opening iris into the corridor.

Some people think that space station corridors are confusing, but not me. I grew up on Space Station Zeta and I could navigate its corridors with my eyes closed. Yes, the corridors were color coded: blue for administration; red for engineering; green for hydroponics; white for medical; and purple for the market district; but each section also had its own, unique odors. I could follow my nose to any place I needed to go. But today wasn't even a challenge. Rafe and I wouldn't even need to leave the last and arguably most important sector: yellow— the central core that housed the space station's living quarters, educational units, and recreational areas.

I slowed from a jog to a brisk walk as we entered the large park at the center of yellow sector. The ground underfoot changed from permaplastic flooring to artificial turf, a springy green surface that supposedly mimicked the grass of old Earth. Glancing from the forest of Andolian fern trees that ringed the park to the game fields for soccer and baseball, my gaze came to rest on one of the picnic tables beside the galactic jumpball court. A small figure huddled on the bench, looking miserable and lonely.

Sammy.

Without Fred.

3

I hurried over to join Sammy at the picnic table. My friend looked up when I sat down beside her and tried to smile, but her lips trembled. Her blue eyes were swollen from crying, and her light brown hair was escaping from its usual neat braids.

"Don't worry," I said, giving her arm a squeeze. "We'll find him."

Rafe hopped from my shoulder to the picnic table and nuzzled Sammy's cheek, crooning softly.

"See? Rafe agrees. Everything will be fine."

This time Sammy's smile succeeded. She reached up and stroked Rafe's muzzle, then nodded at me.

"Okay," I said. "Walk us through it. What happened? Tell us everything you can remember."

Sammy nodded, took a deep breath, and stood up. "Right. We were over here," she said, walking to an open area a few feet away. "I was throwing his favorite yellow ball and he was chasing it and bringing it back to me."

I nodded and squinted me eyes. I could almost see the scene. Sammy tossing the bouncy yellow ball and Fred running to catch it and bring it back. Fred was an absolutely adorable little furball. Black and tan and wriggly, the Earth-normal puppy adored belly rubs and playing fetch. I liked the little ball of fluff, but even Sammy would agree that he wasn't exactly what you'd call smart. Not like Rafe, who understood Standard almost as well as I did.

But Sammy hadn't been looking for intelligence in her pet, she'd wanted cuddly, and Fred excelled at cuddles. Rafe? Not so much. When he'd first come to me, Rafe had been... well, *haughty* and *aloof* are probably the best words, but we'd grown on each other and now we were excellent friends. But no one would ever accuse my dragon of being cuddly.

"Where's the ball now?" I asked.

"That's the thing," Sammy said, "I don't know. The last time I threw it, it hit that big rock over there and bounced into the trees. Fred followed it. I heard him yelp, ran to check on him, and couldn't find him." Her eyes widened and her voice got kind of screechy. "He disappeared, Cinnamon. Vanished! Without a trace!"

I grabbed my friend and hugged her. "It's okay, Sammy. We're going to find him."

"But Cinnamon," she cried, her tears transferring from her cheek to mine, "you don't understand. He yelped! He's hurt and scared and I can't find him!"

"Hush now, Sammy. We're going to find him." I patted her back for a minute, then stepped out of our hug. "Why don't you go over there and lie down in the grass. The sunshine will warm you up. Rafe and I will look for Fred."

Now, Sammy and I both know that there isn't any grass or sunshine in the recreational area, any more than there are rocks, but she nodded and flopped into the pretend grass anyway. In reality, the recreation area consists of artificial turf, great lighting programs, and permaplastic boulders for the littlest kids to climb around on. The only living things in the recreational area, besides people and pets, were the Andolian fern trees, and those were grown in hydroponic solutions, their roots traveling deep beneath the permaplastic deck plating into reservoirs maintained by engineering and a special hydroponics team.

Once Sammy was settled, I motioned for Rafe to follow me into the forest. First we stopped by the boulder Sammy had indicated, made a guess as to where the ball had bounced and stepped into the shadows under the fern trees. I glanced up at Rafe— he'd landed on a branch just above my head— and said, "Fly around. See if you can spot Fred or his yellow ball. If you find anything, come get me."

Rafe bobbed his head once and launched into flight.

Great. Air support was on the job. Now for a close inspection of the ground. Noting the trees around me, I imagined a grid overlaying the artificial turf and began a careful inspection of the tree trunks and the turf. It was boring work. The blades of turf didn't bend or break the way living plants might. It just sprang back into shape after being stepped on. I had no way of knowing if Fred had raced over a particular spot as he chased his ball. And even though the fern trees were alive, they'd all been planted at the same time, had received the same nutrients and light, and had grown in very similar patterns.

The Andolian fern tree forest wasn't giving me the clues I needed.

I stopped, hands on hips, then turned and marched back to where Sammy rested in the grass.

When I stood over her, I said, "We need more people."

She shaded her eyes and stared up at me. "Why?"

"We need a line of people to walk from the edge of the open space through the forest watching for clues."

"What kind of clues?"

I threw my hands in the air. "I don't know, but by myself I

can't tell where I've been and what I've already looked at." I pointed at the trees. "Everything in there looks the same."

She sat up. "Okay. I see what you're saying. That's why I couldn't find him. I couldn't tell where he'd gone."

I nodded. "But we know about where he went in, and we know he wasn't out of sight long before he yelped, so we shouldn't need too many people."

"Let's call Rabbie and Ginger. I'm sure they'll help."

"Right, and Liu and Aaron and Jase will come... as long as their parents don't have plans for them."

4

_S_ammy and I got busy with our links and a few minutes later our friends rushed into the park to help us search for Fred.

Rafe perched on my shoulder as I outlined the plan. He hadn't found any sign of the missing puppy either.

"So," I said as I wrapped up the briefing, "Rafe will fly low, using his keen sense of smell as well as his eyes, so don't be surprised if he goes past you. Trust me, he won't do more than brush you with a wingtip."

All seven of us lined up near the rock that had deflected Sammy's ball toss. With our arms outstretched, we positioned ourselves so that our fingertips just barely touched. At my command, we dropped our arms and stepped forward into the trees.

"Remember," I called, "if you see anything suspicious, shout and everyone will stop until I examine the clue."

"Got it." "Right." Will do," called my friends.

I'd only gone about ten paces when Rabbie yelled. "I think Rafe's found something!"

"Everyone stop and hold you places," I said as I raced to find

Rabbie and Rafe. I found Rabbie first. He pointed to the base of a fern tree where Rafe sat staring at the ground, his tail barb beating the artificial turf in agitation.

I crept up to my dragon and stroked his shoulder. "What is it, Rafe? What did you find?"

He cocked his head and then bobbed his muzzled toward the spot he'd been observing. I leaned around the base of the fern tree and gasped. Rafe had found a hole in the artificial turf and deck plating. A hole big enough to swallow a puppy whole!

I edged closer to the hole and gazed into its depths. There, about five feet below me was the vat of hydroponic solution that fed the fern tree, and swimming around in the liquid was one very unhappy, very tired puppy!

"Rabbie," I called. "Get Sammy. Bring everyone else. We've found Fred!"

Reaching for my dragon, I stroked his shoulder again. "Well done, Rafe. You solved the mystery. Let's call Dad."

Dad answered my link immediately. "What is it, Sugar Cookie?"

I suppressed a grimace and said, "I need help, Dad. I'm in the recreational area with my friends and we've found a dangerous hole. Sammy's puppy fell through and is in one of the hydroponic tanks. He's swimming, but he's getting tired and we can't reach him."

"Stay where you are, Detective-in-Training Chou. Help is on the way." Dad closed the link and I breathed a sigh of relief.

"Don't worry, Fred," I called to the waterlogged pup. "Dad will rescue you."

Footsteps rushed to my side and soon I was surrounded by friends. Sammy was so relieved to see Fred, she cried and laughed at the same time. I frowned and stared at the edge of the hole. What had caused the opening? Was the edge stable? Possibly not.

"Listen everyone," I said loudly to get their attention. "I think we need to move away from the hole. The edge could give way."

"Right," agreed Rabbie. "I didn't think there could be a hole like that in the deck plating. Let's all move back." He turned to me. "You called security, didn't you?"

I nodded. "Dad said help is on the way, but until they get here, we need to be careful."

Everyone moved away from the hole and back toward the permaplastic boulder. Everyone except Sammy.

"No," she said, her eyes blazing. "I'm not leaving him. He's tired and wet and unhappy. He'll think I'm deserting him."

I nodded. "I understand, but don't kneel like that. At least lay flat so your weight is spread out more evenly."

"Okay. Maybe you'd better call Rafe away."

Rafe cocked his head, glanced from Sammy to me, then spread his wings and flew to a branch a few trees away, but still within sight of Sammy and the hole.

"Good enough," I said and gave him a nod.

The rest of us milled around the boulder while keeping an anxious eye on Sammy.

After a few nervous minutes, Sammy scrambled away from the hole and ran to join us, grinning broadly.

"A hydroponics worker showed up, scooped Fred out of the solution, and waved at me," she said happily. "He said he'd wash Fred off, blow his fur dry, and then bring him up to me."

She grabbed me and hugged me, bouncing up and down the whole time. "Thank you, Cinnamon! ThankyouThankyou-Thankyou!"

When I managed to disentangle myself, I grinned and said, "You're welcome, but it was a team effort," and gestured to all five of our other friends. "Rabbie and Ginger and Liu and Aaron and Jase came as soon as we asked." I beamed at each of them. "We couldn't have done it without you."

EPILOGUE

The next day, Sammy and I met our five friends at the recreational area for a picnic lunch. Rafe and Fred played chase in the open area, with Fred running and barking while Rafe flew back and forth, zipping down to brush Fred's fur with his tail barb or a wingtip. I'd given Rafe strict instructions to stay away from the trees, and to make sure Fred did the same.

The other kids and I scarfed down synth-chicken sandwiches, hydroponic apples, and soy-based cookies while we watched the engineers and construction team moving back and forth from the place where we knew the hole was to their equipment in a cordoned off section of the open space.

"What do you think made that hole?" Rabbie asked between mouthfuls of sandwich. "I mean, if the permaplastic plating can give way, we could all end up in space."

I shivered at the thought, but repeated what Dad had told me that morning. "Don't worry, Rabbie. Space Station Zeta has the best engineering team in the galaxy. Whatever the problem is, we've discovered it early, thanks to Fred. Engineering will figure it out, and if they can't, the best USL minds in the universe are just an ansible call away. No one is getting spaced."

Ginger nodded. "My mom is an engineer. She said the same thing. Space Station Zeta is safe."

Liu poked Sammy. "Who knows, maybe Commander Chou will give Fred a medal for alerting us to danger."

Sammy grinned. "That would be awesome, but I'm just glad to have my puppy back." She paused and made eye contact with each of us in turn. "And to have the best friends in the whole wide universe!"

We all gave a cheer and thumped our fists on the picnic table. I cleared my throat to get their attention and said, "Thanks, everyone, for helping me solve *The Case of the Vanishing Puppy*."

They all groaned, but Sammy laughed, shook her head, and said, "Trust Cinnamon to turn Fred's adventure into one of her case files!"

PART IV

THE TWELVE DAYS OF TRICKSTERS

The Twelve Days of Tricksters
A Prentiss Twins Story

Deb Logan
Author of *Thunderbird*

1

_____

*J*ake Prentiss woke with a start, sitting up in bed straight-backed and bleary-eyed. Blinking sleep from his eyes, he glanced around his bedroom wondering what could have roused him from a deep, sound sleep so suddenly? Nothing looked out of place. Early morning light was just filtering around the window blinds painting the room with dim, not yet distinct colors. The air was cool—he always turned the heat down overnight—but not cold. Especially not as cold as might be expected for Bozeman, Montana in mid-December.

Well, he was awake. He might as well get up and check the rest of the house, though he couldn't imagine anything or anyone entering his home unnoticed; not with the twins' bond animals on duty. Throwing back the covers, he swung his legs off the bed, stuffed his feet into sheepskin lined slippers, and pulled on the warm flannel robe Emilia had given him more than a decade ago. He fingered the well-worn shawl collar, remembering. The twins had just turned three that Christmas. They'd been a happy, busy, young family. A complete family. By the next

Christmas, the twins had been motherless and he'd been a widower.

Sighing, he knotted the belt around his waist and moved to his bedroom door. This robe was getting old. He really needed to buy a new one. After all, the twins were thirteen now. Teenagers. Emilia's babies were teenagers now. He sure wished she could see them. She'd be so proud. Of course, he also wished she were here to help him navigate the suddenly turbulent waters of parenting. There was just so much he didn't understand. He really wished his wife were alive to help him with all the decisions, choices that could affect the rest of the twins' lives.

His reverie was broken by a high-pitched shriek. Not his daughter's—thank all that was holy—but not something that belonged in his home either. He yanked the bedroom door open and raced down the hall to the family room. Where he skidded to a halt.

Why was there a cherry tree growing from the middle of the family room floor? And was that a parakeet hopping between the branches and shrieking?

"On the first day of Christmas," laughing voices sang, "my tricksters gave to me a parakeet in a cherry tree!"

Jake stumbled to his favorite overstuffed chair and dropped into it. Except for the tree growing out of the plush beige carpeting, the room looked completely normal for this time of year. The Christmas tree sparkled in the corner, its many strings of multi-colored lights giving it a merry glow. A fire crackled in the hearth, lighting the five festive stockings hung from the mantle. Dawn light crept across the floor from the patio door at the far end of the room, where the family room opened into the kitchen, its sliding glass providing a view of the snow-covered deck.

Well, not completely snow-covered. The wide oblong where

his daughter's thunderbird habitually rested (invisible to normal human eyes) was suspiciously snow-free. He frowned. If Winona was on the deck, then Janine must be... he scanned the room and found his daughter curled on the sofa, clearly enjoying his confusion.

But Janine wasn't a trickster. No, the voices that had sung had been her twin brother Justin and his spirit animal, Coyote... a trickster if ever there was one. A small, wry smile tugged at Jake's lips as he closed his eyes and massaged his temples.

Emilia would never believe what her babies had grown into. Especially since last summer.

"Really, Justin?" he asked. "A cherry tree in the family room? Besides, isn't it supposed to be a pear tree? With a partridge?"

Justin popped out from behind the couch where Janine sat curled, Coyote padding beside him. "I like cherries better than pears," he said with a mischievous grin, "and parakeets are more fun than partridges." He glanced at the small green and yellow bird. "Did you know parakeets can talk? Even without any magical prodding?"

Jake nodded, his eyes still closed. "I've never had one, but a friend did when I was a boy. It only had a few words, but it definitely talked."

Opening his eyes he studied his son. Justin and Janine were very alike in looks, except for the gender difference which was growing more pronounced every year. Both had straight black hair, copper skin, long straight noses, and high cheek bones. Both were athletic, a good thing considering the many adventures they'd had since Janine had discovered the egg that had hatched a thunderbird. His daughter hadn't wanted to go to field camp in the Absaroka Mountains last summer, but Jake had insisted. And look where *that* decision had led!

Jake drew a deep breath and exhaled slowly. Looked at in a particular light, everything that had happened to his kids was his fault. If he wasn't a paleontologist... if he didn't lead digs at field camps every summer... if he didn't insist that his children accompany him on those digs... but he was and he did and Janine had found what looked like a rock, but was really a living egg.

He shook himself. What was done was done and couldn't be changed. And truthfully, he wasn't sure he'd want it to—and he knew without a doubt that neither of his children would wish for the events of last summer to change.

He pushed his concerns away and resumed his study of Justin. The similarity between the twins ended with their looks. Much like her thunderbird, Janine was quiet and contemplative. But Justin? His son was anything but quiet. Justin was the proverbial man of action. Always in motion; had been since birth. Why even when Emilia had held him in her arms to nurse him, Justin's tiny feet had drummed against the arm of her chair.

And smart? Both the twins were too smart for their own good, but Justin.... Well, Jake had always known that scheming was Justin's super power. At least, he'd thought so until he'd discovered that his thirteen-year-old son was a shaman bonded to a trickster demi-god ... and a powerful magic user to boot! For on his thirteenth birthday, Justin had discovered that he was a *skin walker*, able to shift from an adolescent boy to a coyote in the blink of an eye.

And Jake had thought being a single parent of twins was tough!

"Seriously though, Justin," Jake said with a sigh. "What's with the tree? Christmas isn't for another two weeks." I glanced at Janine. "Are you in on this too?"

His daughter raised her hands and shook her head, aiming a long-suffering glance at her twin brother. "Nope. This is all Justin, though I'm sure Coyote was lots of help."

Coyote didn't respond. He simply sat on his haunches with

his bushy tail wrapped around his paws and stared at the cherry tree, pride and admiration shining in his canine eyes.

Justin cleared his throat. "Coyote and I know exactly what day it is, Dad. It's Friday, December 13th."

Jake suppressed a shiver. Friday the thirteenth... and he was sitting in a room with a couple of dedicated tricksters. He could hardly wait.

"We've decided to treat you to a *traditional* Christmas this year," Justin continued, gesturing to the cherry tree, "and this is our opening gift."

"Uhm, Justin," Janine said, her eyes sparkling with mirth, "don't you have your dates wrong? The twelve days of Christmas usually don't start until Christmas Day."

"Whatever," her twin brother replied, waving away her objection. "We're not *that* traditional. Coyote and I have everything worked out to perfection."

"Right," Janine said. "You two do know that starting on the thirteenth means your twelfth day will be on Christmas Eve, not Christmas Day, don't you?"

Justin glared at her. "Of course we know." His face relaxed into a mischievous grin. "Trust me, Janny. We have everything under control."

Janine rolled her eyes, and Jake dropped his head into his hands.

2

---

he next few days were a nightmare as far as Jake Prentiss was concerned. He went to bed each night dreading the next morning and the revelation of Justin and Coyote's next *gift*, not to mention their goofy rendition of the traditional Christmas carol. The song got longer and sillier with each passing day.

On the second day of Christmas... Jake woke to a pair of crows flying around his bedroom and cawing loudly.

On Sunday, the third day, three fat mallard ducks waddled past his desk as he worked on his computer in his home office, quickly followed by his son and Coyote popping in—literally! one minute they weren't anywhere around, the next they stood beside the mallards—to sing for him.

Day four brought four western meadowlarks swooping through his office at The Museum of the Rockies, their song echoing off the ceiling.

Tuesday, the fifth day, was actually a relief. No birds to shoo out of house or office. Instead, Justin presented him with a protective amulet woven from hairs from the five members of his family: Justin, Coyote, Janine, Thunderbird, and Jake's father, a shaman known to the spirit animals as *Steadfast Guide*. Hmmm. Maybe all of this wasn't Jake's fault after all. Maybe his dad's beliefs had set everything in motion.

The gifts went downhill from there.

On Wednesday, six dozen duck eggs were delivered to his home before breakfast.

Thursday night he found seven tiny swans swimming in his bathtub.

Eight milkweed plants were discovered in the museum's exhibit of fossilized dinosaur eggs on Friday.

A bouquet of nine pink and yellow ladyslipper flowers rested beside his plate of bacon and eggs on Saturday morning.

On Sunday, Jake's boss, Dr. Abernathy, called him in for a special meeting. Jake arrived only to find ten flyfishing lures decorating his desk... just as his boss stepped inside. That had been a true nightmare. Papers skewered by hooks in lures from black ghosts to woolly buggers, and Jake trying to explain to Dr. Abernathy that despite appearances Jake hadn't been spending his days tying lures instead of working on the important exhibit they were there to discuss. Fortunately, Justin and Coyote had waited until Jake returned home before serenading him with that blasted ever-lengthening song.

Yesterday had set Jake's last nerve on edge. Justin and Coyote had not only popped into his office themselves... they'd brought an eleven member pipe and drum corps with them. And every single member had been decked out in full regalia, including kilts! Jake still wasn't sure how his coworkers had missed that show since the corps had marched through the museum, bagpipes screeching.

Probably magic.

What was he thinking? Undoubtedly magic!

Today was the twelfth day. The tricksters' grand finale. Jake had been bracing himself all day, but his work day was at an end and nothing had happened. Yet.

As Jake trudged through the deepening snow to his car, he ticked off items on his to-do list. Today was Christmas Eve. The museum would be closed until next Monday, so he had a few days of peace. As if anything about life with his magical children could be called peaceful! But tomorrow was Christmas, and Jake had been so preoccupied with the aftermath of Justin's nonsense that he hadn't found time to wrap gifts and place them beneath the tree. Fortunately, he'd done his shopping early, so wrapping was all that he'd left to the last minute. That and filling the stockings, of course. He smiled thinking of the five stockings hanging on his mantle. This time last year he'd never have guessed that he'd need stockings for Thunderbird and Coyote! What a difference a year had made.

He drove home in a swirl of snow. Having a white Christmas was never a concern in Bozeman, but this year it looked like they might be in for an actual blizzard. Fortunately, once he got home, Jake and the twins would have no need to leave the house again for several days. They had plenty of food, a good supply of firewood should they lose power, and even several gallons of bottled water.

Not to mention magic.

He didn't know why he worried about things like food and shelter when Coyote and Thunderbird, not to mention his own children, could obtain anything they needed with magic. At least, he thought they could. But what did he know? He was just an ordinary guy with an extraordinary family.

Jake pulled the family Range Rover into the garage, parked, and headed for the door into the kitchen. Pausing, he braced himself. There was still the twelfth gift to endure, and it was bound to be a doozy. After all, the traditional song called for twelve drummers drumming. He winced. He'd already survived a pipe and drum corps, how many more drums could he take?

Taking a deep breath, he pasted a smile on his face and opened the door.

3

_J_ustin fairly danced with excitement. He could hardly wait for Dad to get home. This was day twelve of Dad's Christmas gift, and he and Coyote had worked really hard to make sure this was a twelfth night Dad would never forget.

"Are you sure everything is ready?" he asked Coyote.

Coyote rolled over on the plush beige carpeting of the family room and wriggled, scratching his back. "Of course," he yipped. "Just like it was the last twenty or thirty times you asked."

Justin stuck his tongue out at his bond animal before turning to his twin sister. "You and Thunderbird are ready too. Right?"

Janine rolled her eyes. "Yes, Justin. Relax. Winona and I are ready to follow wherever you and Coyote go. The only one you should be worried about is Dad. Have you given him any warning? His last trip through the Spirit World wasn't all that great, you know."

Justin grimaced. "I remember." He'd been incredibly proud of how his dad and his grandpa both had handled the battle with Unktehi, the demi-god of Chaos. "But this isn't the same thing at all. We won't be staying in the Spirit World, just passing through."

Janine cocked her head and narrowed her eyes. "Passing through to where?"

Justin grinned. He loved knowing something Janny didn't. "You'll find out soon enough. Now, we just need Dad."

Coyote rolled over and sat up, ears pricked forward. "Is that the Range Rover I hear?"

Justin concentrated, but didn't hear anything beyond the howl of the wind. He considered changing skins, becoming a coyote, but rejected the idea. He didn't need his other form's enhanced hearing, Coyote would listen for him. Besides, he needed to be a human boy when Dad walked through that door. If he were wearing his coyote skin, Dad would freak. He'd seen Justin transform before, of course, but Dad was much more comfortable with his son as a boy, and Coyote and Justin were about to make Dad uncomfortable enough without starting him out freaked.

A few minutes later, everyone clearly heard the Range Rover pull into the garage and park. It was almost time...and Justin danced from one foot to the other in excitement. This was going to be so cool. Beyond cool. Absolutely frigid!

Dad stepped into the kitchen, shrugging out of his down coat, and Justin and Coyote burst into song.

"On the first day of Christmas," they sang, "my tricksters gave to me a parakeet in a cherry tree!" On and on they sang until they came to *twelve tricksters tricking*, at which point Coyote opened a portal to the Spirit World and Justin grabbed his dad's arm and yanked him through.

4

*J*ake struggled to regain his balance as his son pulled him through what he recognized as a portal to the Spirit World. *Twelve tricksters tricking*? What in the world did that mean? Why the portal? Where was Justin taking him? Jake's mind reeled with questions, none of which had answers. He gulped, pushed the questions aside, and concentrated on steadying himself. He trusted Justin. Whatever this was, it was the culmination of a gift. Justin wouldn't design a gift that would harm his dad. At least, not on purpose.

Pushing his worries aside, Jake looked around. He stood in a wide meadow under a clear blue sky, with what could only be a banyan tree in front of him. A massive banyan tree.

"About time," Justin called, causing Jake to turn around in time to see Janine and her thunderbird step through the portal.

"We are here as requested," Thunderbird said. "Greetings, Dr. Prentiss."

Jake nodded his acknowledgement. Normally he couldn't even see Thunderbird, let alone hear her speak. At home, she communicated telepathically with Janine, who then told everyone else what her bond animal had said. Jake had seen her before of course, but her appearance always surprised him. She looked like one of the pterosaurs he studied as a paleontologist. The size of a small elephant, her wings were formed by a membrane of skin and muscle that stretched from her ankles to a dramatically lengthened fourth finger. When she walked, she folded her wings upward and carried her weight on her knuckles. Her nut brown hide was covered in short, cinnamon colored fur, and her long neck supported a slender crested head with brilliant green eyes and a long narrow beak.

"All righty," barked Coyote. "Let's get this party started."

"Uhm, party?" Jaked asked. "Your song said *twelve tricksters tricking*. Nothing about a party," he paused and glanced around, "and there are only two of you. Tricksters, I mean."

"Astute as always, Dr. Prentiss," Coyote barked. "I just meant, let's keep moving."

"Right," Justin said, a huge grin spreading across his face. "We're not there yet."

"And where exactly is *there*?" Jake asked, planting his feet and distributing his weight to keep Justin from yanking him off balance again.

Justin huffed and fisted his hands on his hips. He glared at Dad before glancing at Coyote. Coyote cocked his head and flicked his tail, his version of a shrug. Justin deflated a bit and threw out his hands.

"Fine," he said. "I wanted it to be a surprise, but we're going to Monkey King's banyan tree on Victoria Peak."

"You're taking me to Hong Kong?" Jake asked, his eyes wide.

Justin grinned. "Yep. Surprised?"

Jake nodded, swallowed, and said, "And tricked."

Coyote chased his tail in a circle, then stopped and said, "Can we go now? The Trickster Tribe is waiting!"

Jake closed his eyes and massaged his temples. "The whole tribe?" he asked, his voice barely louder than a whisper.

Justin danced from one foot to the other. Excitement shown in his eyes. "As many as can manage to get there. Come on, Dad! They're waiting, and I can hardly wait for you to meet everyone!"

Jake nodded, and Coyote opened a portal in the base of the banyan tree. All five of them stepped through into a jungle teeming with creatures of legend. The first to catch and hold Jake's eye was a monkey dressed in red and gold silk. At least, Jake thought it was a monkey. The creature was as tall as Jake and could have been the missing link between tree-dwelling monkeys and human beings. He wore soft, baggy pants gathered at waist and ankle, and a short vest. A gold band circled his furry head, and a single ruby dangled between his eyebrows.

Justin grabbed Jake's arm and dragged him closer to the creature, who sat on a living throne woven of banyan roots and runners. Giving a slight bow, Justin said, "Monkey King, this is my father, Dr. Jake Prentiss." Turning to Jake, he continued, "Dad, this is Monkey King, trickster god of China and chief of the Trickster Tribe."

Monkey King inclined his head. "Welcome, Dr. Prentiss. The Trickster Tribe is very pleased to claim your son as one of our number." The creature leaned forward and said quietly, "He's worked very hard on this gift. You have raised a fine son."

Jake nodded. "Thank you, Monkey King. I'm honored to meet you. Justin is very proud of you and your friendship."

Monkey King clapped and leapt from his throne. "Come, let me introduce you to our twelve tricksters. Coyote and Justin you already know, so besides me, there are nine others for you to meet."

Jake's head reeled as he met each trickster god. So many legends all in one place. And all real. As a scientist, a paleontologist, Jake had always relegated the tales his shaman father told to the realm of fantasy, just as he had all the other myths of the world. Until his twin children brought him face to face with two creatures of legend: Thunderbird and Coyote. Now he met ten more and he fought to expand his understanding of his world.

Monkey King was as real as Thunderbird and Coyote. So were the other nine.

Puck, also known as Robin Goodfellow, was a trickster out of the lore of the British Isles.

Kitsune, a small red fox with several tails, told him of her fame in Japanese mythology.

Anansi was polite enough, but the giant spider well known to the Ashanti people of Ghana in West Africa made him nervous. Spiders, even normal sized ones, weren't his favorite creatures.

Jake was more at ease with Azeban, the trickster raccoon associated with the Abenaki and Penobscot people of New England.

Kutkh, a raven from Eastern Russia, reminded him of the crows who were the namesake of his own tribe of birth.

Loki, Hermes, and Maui all wore human form, which made them much easier for Jake to relate to though they represented far flung cultures. Loki was Norse, Hermes, Greek, and Maui, Polynesian.

Last came Kokopelli of the Native American tribes of the desert southwest. Jake liked the hump-backed flute player, but couldn't decide if the trickster reminded him more of a man or an insect.

When the introductions were complete, Monkey King clapped his hands and announced, "Now that everyone knows each other, let the celebration begin."

Immediately tables appeared laden with every kind of food imaginable. Trickster Tribe roared their approval and fell upon the feast. Each was quick to point out their favorite delicacies to Jake. Janine and Thunderbird seemed as at ease with the food as they were with the tricksters. Jake marveled as much at his daughter's calm acceptance as at his son's friends. His children truly were extraordinary.

And speaking of extraordinary, the food piled on the tables was unexpected and delicious. Jake sampled sushi rolls from Japan, sticky rice, fish, and crisp vegetables rolled in seaweed wrappers. From Africa, Anansi's home, came a delectable mixture of rice and beans he called *Waakye*. Maui insisted Jake try a drink called *Nectar of the Islands*. Whatever was in it, the drink refreshed Jake and calmed his nerves, helping him feel more at home among this amazing group.

At last Jake settled himself on a banyan root beside his son. Justin was happily devouring a bacon cheeseburger along with a side of fries smothered in chili-cheese sauce.

"Think that'll hold you until we get home?" Jake asked, nudging Justin's shoulder and grinning.

Justin wiped his mouth on his sleeve and laughed. "Probably. How about you? Did you find enough to eat?"

"Definitely," Jake said, patting his belly. "If I ate like this all the time I'd be as round as Santa Claus." He stopped and stared at Justin, eyes wide. "You don't suppose..."

Justin grinned and nodded. "Yep. He's real too. Janny and I haven't met him yet, but the stories Monkey King and Kutkh tell... well, let's just say they're very exciting!"

They sat in comfortable silence for a few minutes while Justin finished his meal. Finally, Jake turned to his son, a solemn expression on his face.

"Thank you, Justin. This twelve days gift has been, well, unique and memorable." He cleared his throat as his emotions tried to clog it. "I'll admit, some of it annoyed me, but this," he gestured around the clearing beneath the banyan tree, "this has been amazing. I'm honored that you would think to introduce me to these tricksters, and that they would take the time to meet me." He stopped, swallowed, and took a deep breath. "You're growing into a fine man, Justin, Your mother would be proud of you. I know I certainly am, and I'm even more proud to be your father."

Justin ducked his head, a blush staining his cheeks. "Thanks, Dad. I'm glad you're okay with all of this," he gestured to the members of Trickster Tribe, "and with what Janine and I... well, what we are." He looked up and met his father's gaze. "I know you could've been disappointed or angry or tried to force us to be normal. I'm glad you didn't."

Jake shook his head. "I couldn't have changed what you are, either of you, and I wouldn't have tried. You're growing into your destinies, and even if those destinies scare me half to death, I know you must be who you are intended to be."

Justin nodded and lowered his gaze.

Jake slapped his hands on his knees and said, "Now, hadn't we better be getting home? We wouldn't want Santa to think we weren't excited about his visit."

Justin grinned, but before he could say anything, Monkey King joined them.

"I overheard your last comment, Dr. Prentiss," the trickster chief said. "I was just thinking the same thing."

"Please, call me Jake, sir."

Monkey King grinned. "Jake it is. You are welcome at any time, Jake, but for now, take your family home for Christmas." With that, he clapped his hands and the clearing under the banyan tree disappeared and Jake found himself in his own family room surrounded by Janine and Justin and Coyote. He glanced at Janine with a raised eyebrow and she nodded. Thunderbird had returned safely as well.

Hugging his twins, they dropped onto the couch, happily exhausted after an awesome day.

5

————

 ake groaned and dragged himself from bed. Dawn
had barely broken, but he could hear Justin and
Janine giggling in the family room along with
Coyote's excited yips and even an occasional screeching laugh
from Thunderbird. Jake hadn't had enough sleep. He'd been up
way too late wrapping gifts and filling stockings. He was
tempted to roll back over and catch a few more winks. The twins
knew the routine. They were allowed to enjoy all the treats in
their stockings, but wrapped gifts had to wait until after breakfast. They'd be fine if he slept in a bit.

He pulled the pillow over his head, but it was too late. His
brain was awake and working, remembering all the effort Justin
and Coyote had gone to over the last twelve days to make Jake's
Christmas memorable. He needed to get up and enjoy his kids
while he could. They were growing up even faster than he'd
imagined was possible.

Stuffing his feet into his slippers, he reached for his flannel
robe. Instead of shrugging into it, he held it to his face and
breathed a little prayer to Emilia. *They're not who we expected,*

sweetheart, but our twins are wonderful, thoughtful, and downright magical.

As he pulled the robe on and knotted the belt around his waist, he thought he heard an echo of her sigh, *I know, and I'm so proud. Of all of you.*

PART V

RUSH!

Deb Logan

Author of Faery Unexpected

Rush!

A Very Short Story

I'd spent my life testing boundaries. My parents, well, adoptive parents — I had no idea who had given me life — worried about me constantly, too aware that I'd do anything for an adrenaline rush.

That particular concern had just ceased to exist.

Now I knew I had limits, but the lesson came too late.

When Andy shoved me against the railing of Amber's high-rise apartment patio, he didn't mean to kill me. He was just expressing the general view of Skyline High's ultra elite in-crowd: *You can come to our parties, but hands off our girls.*

Unfortunately, my rail-thin, freakishly tall body's center of gravity was higher than the norm. Instead of hitting the railing and crumpling, I tipped over the edge, my hip acting as the fulcrum of my doom.

My arms flailed wildly, hoping to catch hold of something. Anything. Adrenaline fired my veins and my heart banged like a bass drum on steroids. Out of the corner of one eye I saw Jason lunge forward. I jerked to a stop as he caught my foot, and relief washed across my soul. I wouldn't die today after all.

Thank God for Jason.

People screamed and fingers snatched at the leg of my jeans. Too bad I'd worn the skin-tight pair; they were having trouble finding purchase. Beneath the chaos, my heart-rate slowed and peace settled comfortably across my mind.

Until my shoe came off.

2

---

*G*ravity jerked me downward; a happy dog proud of the bone it had wrested from its opponent.

Too bad *I* was the bone.

Peace lasted for the space of several floors before reality smacked me. This was it. Unless Superman flew past and scooped me into his arms, I was about to be sauce on the sidewalk.

Realization triggered *The Voice*.

From the dark recesses of my mind the gong-like tones of a masculine voice commanded, *Forget what you know. Do what you must.*

Forgetting wasn't an issue; my brain was about to splatter across the pavement, but what was I supposed to *do*?

Again *The Voice* ordered, *Do it now!*

My body responded without my direction. Arms snapped together above my head like they were preparing to execute a perfect dive. Legs straightened, toes pointed, and a sudden tension sang through my arrow-straight body. I closed my eyes, not to block out the sight of the rapidly approaching sidewalk, but to visualize the star-studded velvet of the sky above me. My back arched and my trajectory altered. I executed a perfect U-turn in space and raced upward, an arrow shot from an invisible bow.

When I reached Amber's balcony, I landed lightly, pulled my shoe from Jason's limp fingers and gave him an appreciative nod. Without bothering to put it on, I limped over to Andy and stuck out my hand. "No hard feelings, man," I said with wry smile. "I know that was an accident."

Andy swallowed, his expression stunned. He took my hand without a word.

I mean, really? What could he say?

TEN STORIES

BY DEBBIE MUMFORD

PART I

SEVENTH: FIRST FRUITS

DEBBIE MUMFORD

BESTSELLING AUTHOR OF *SORCHA'S HEART*

SEVENTH: FIRST FRUITS

SPUN YARNS

A *Gus & Ghost* Short Story

1

I'm a homicide detective. Portland, Oregon is my beat. It's also my hometown. Not a hotbed of crime, but not exactly peaceful either, and today was starting off with a bang. Barely zero-seven-thirty and we already had a murder to investigate.

My partner, Jack Barnes, parked our department issued dark blue sedan across the street from a marijuana dispensary on Northeast Sandy Boulevard. The uniforms had already cordoned off the area with yellow crime scene tape, but even this early in the morning civilians were piling up on the sidewalk to either side, trying to get a look. I'd been a murder cop long enough to know that regular, law-abiding citizens got a thrill out of being near the scene of a crime... as long as the police were already present and said citizens knew everything was safe.

Jack figured it was a result of too many cop shows on television. I thought their fascination with death was part of human nature and had existed long before TV crime shows found their way into our shared world view.

Whatever.

The civilians were there, and we ignored them as we exited our car and ducked under the crime scene tape. Occasionally the perpetrator would join that crowd, curious about how his work was perceived, but not often. A quick glance confirmed that one of the uniforms was scanning the civilians with a cell phone camera. Good. All the bases were covered.

Jack took the lead as we flashed our badges to the uniform in charge.

"I'm Detective Jack Barnes and this is my partner, Detective Gus Collier," Jack said, pulling a small spiral-bound notebook from his pocket and clicking his pen open. Glancing at the man's name badge, he continued, "What can you tell us, Officer Reynolds?"

The uniform nodded. He stood at ease, relaxed but ready, feet solidly planted, thumbs hooked in his belt. "I was walking my beat this morning and noticed the lights on inside. That's unusual at zero-seven hundred when they don't open until ten hundred hours. So I looked in, saw the body, and forced the door." He glanced at the building and shook his head. "Guy was already dead. I called it in and secured the scene."

"The door was locked?" I asked.

Reynolds nodded. "The back too. I checked when I cleared the building. No sign of a break-in. Everything seemed secure, except for the body... and it looked like he had help getting dead."

Jack grunted his thanks and strode into the building accompanied by Officer Reynolds. I hung back, surveying the scene. A normal, well-kept Portland sidewalk beside a busy four-lane street. The marijuana dispensary was a single story, stand-alone building— flat roofed, its exterior walls painted dark green with deep gold trim. The display windows were clean, the shop well-lit. In short, it appeared to be a solid small business operation.

Time to get moving and see what Jack had found inside.

Wait, Gus. Don't go in yet. Sarah appeared beside me, floating a few inches above the sidewalk and shimmering in the morning sunlight. My ghostly partner had been with me for close to six weeks now— ever since I'd investigated her murder at the summer solstice— but her unexpected appearance still caused an adrenaline rush that made my heart hammer.

I glanced around. The uniforms were all occupied and no one was close enough to notice, so I answered her. "Why not?"

Look at the threshold.

I knelt down and examined the space between the sidewalk and the doorframe. A fine line of some type of powdered crystal ran from one side of the opening to the other.

"What is it?" I murmured.

Part of a ward, Sarah answered. *Use your* sight. *Examine the doorframe.*

Six weeks wasn't really long enough to change the habits of a lifetime. I'd always considered myself a regular guy. Sure, I'd been teased my whole life about being the seventh son of a seventh son, but I never put any stock in the legends. After all, I'd never had any special abilities. At least, not until six weeks ago; not until Sarah's ghost turned my understanding of reality upside down.

My twenty-eighth birthday just happened to fall on the summer solstice this year, giving me a double whammy of weirdness. Twenty-eight is seven quadrupled, which makes it a very auspicious time for a seventh-seventh to come into his power. Plus, the summer solstice is one of the *Old Ones'* eight holy days.

The universe chose to celebrate my awakening by allowing a corpse— Sarah's as it turned out— to speak to me at the murder scene I'd been called to investigate. And while I've grown fond of Sarah, I've got to tell you, I've had better birthday presents.

I discovered that Sarah Allen was another seventh-seventh, and that she'd been murdered in a blood magic ritual in order to steal her nascent powers. My partner Jack Barnes and I solved the case... with Sarah's supernatural help. But by the time it was all over, Sarah and I had bonded. She chose to stay in this realm instead of moving on, and I was happy to have her help.

But she still freaked me out when she just appeared out of thin air.

Now, I know what you're thinking: "This seventh-seventh nonsense is just that... nonsense. Supernatural hooey dreamed up by superstitious people with too much time on their hands and overactive imaginations."

Trust me. I wish you were right, but you're not. Sarah is a real ghost, and I'm not delusional.

And yes, she's female, so how can she be a seventh-seventh? Well, it turns out that even though I fit the traditional profile— the seventh son of a seventh son— gender isn't really an issue. Birth order is the determining factor. Sarah is the seventh child of a seventh child. If she'd made it to her twenty-eighth birthday, she would've come into her power. Unfortunately Jason Morgan murdered her on the cusp of the summer solstice in order to co-opt her abilities before they had a chance to blossom.

Abilities I now possessed, but still needed to be reminded to use.

I sighed, ran a hand across my eyes, and allowed my *second sight* to slip into place. When I looked at the doorframe again I saw that the deep gold trim paint was covered in glowing glyphs and runes. The lowest ones actually touched the powdered crystal. The entire opening shimmered with power.

"But people have been moving in and out through that door all morning," I whispered. "Hell's bells! Jack went in just a couple of minutes ago."

It's not a ward against normal humans, Sarah said. *I'm not exactly sure what it protects against, but I'm betting I won't be able to cross it. I can feel the power from here.*

"What about me?"

She shrugged. *No clue. Try it and see.*

I scowled at her. "Thanks for your concern." I said, trying to keep my sarcasm in check.

Really. I tried. Scout's honor.

Sarah grinned, and I stuck a finger into the open doorway. A buzz of power stung me and I jerked my hand back. If a finger caused that much of a jolt, I didn't want to consider crossing that void with my whole body.

Jack appeared on the other side, a frown creasing his forehead. "What?" he asked. "You waiting for an engraved invitation or something?"

Jack's not the best looking guy in the world— his hair is thinning and going gray, his cheeks are constantly stubbled, and he's got a definite spare tire around his middle— but he's a solid detective and a good friend. He used to give me a lot of grief about the seventh-seventh thing, but after discovering it was the motive for Sarah's murder, he'd stopped teasing me. He decided if some loony took it seriously enough to kill for, it wasn't a laughing matter.

He doesn't know that I came into my power during that investigation, or anything about Sarah other than as a murder victim, but his decision has made my life easier, so I'm grateful.

"Look at this," I said and knelt down to examine the powder again. Jack mimicked me from the other side. "What do you make of it?"

"No clue," he said. "Might be important; might not. Better grab a sample just in case." He pulled an evidence bag out of his pocket and scooped a bit of the powder into it, breaking the seal.

The wards winked out of existence, allowing Sarah and me to follow Jack into the shop's interior. The corpse, a young man, sprawled face down in front of a softly illuminated, and very bloody, glass-front display counter. Blood pooled on the floor around his upper body.

"Someone slit his throat?" I asked Jack, glancing at the pattern of arterial spray that coated the front of the glass display.

He nodded. "The medical examiner will say for sure, but it looks like he was kneeling in front of the counter when someone grabbed him from behind and...." He didn't finish the sentence, but pantomimed slicing a throat.

I swallowed and nodded toward the counter. "Yeah. If he'd been standing, the spray pattern would be higher. On the top of the counter and the wall behind, not just on the front." I paused before asking, "Identification?"

"David Howe, according to his driver's license." Jack nodded to a wallet encased in a plastic evidence bag and resting on top of the display case. "That was in his pocket. Cash and credit cards are still there."

"So, not a robbery," I said. "Or at least, not of him. Any idea if anything was taken from the store?"

"Place looks pretty neat," he said, and I had to agree. Except for the blood, the display case appeared untouched and the shelves behind the counter boasted neat rows of various types of cannabis products.

Officer Reynolds approached. "Excuse me, detective. I've got the information you asked for."

Jack turned to confer with him, while I stepped aside to examine the scene... and talk to Sarah.

"Where's the ghost?" I asked quietly.

He's already moved on, she said. *I saw the light while we were still outside.*

I nodded and breathed a sigh of relief. I didn't really want to have to deal with another ghost. I'd learned with Sarah that even though the victim might know who killed them, they were incapable of providing the information. A fact that was frustrating to both the living and the dead.

"Reynolds is contacting the owner," Jack said, turning to join me again. "Nothing looks out of place, but there could've been a lot of cash on hand."

I nodded. Marijuana dispensaries were in limbo as far as finances went. They were legal in many states, including Oregon, but credit card companies wouldn't deal with them since they weren't recognized nationally. Most banks refused to do business with them as well. This meant that dispensaries tended to deal in cash, and often had to store that cash on the premises. A risky enterprise in more ways than one.

Hell of a coincidence, Sarah said, gazing at the sign proclaiming the name of the business.

I quirked an eyebrow at her to encourage her to elaborate. Jack was too close to risk asking her directly.

This place is called "First Fruits", she said.

I shot her an annoyed glare. I could read after all.

She glared right back. *I thought you were reading up on the ancient holy days,* she said, shifting her position so her cute little fists rested on her nicely curved hips. She'd been a very attractive young woman, blonde and blue-eyed with a lithe, athletic body. Too bad she was forever doomed to wear the blue hospital scrubs she'd been murdered in. Sarah had been a doctor, a resident in her last year of training at Sisters of Mercy Hospital.

Today is Lammas or Lughnasadh, she explained. *It's also known as the Celebration of First Fruits.*

My eyes widened and my jaw dropped. She was absolutely right. Today was August 1st, the traditional day to celebrate the early harvest. I was standing in a marijuana dispensary named *First Fruits* on an *Old Ones'* holiday of the same name... and I had needed Jack's help to pass through a powerfully warded door.

A shiver ran down my spine. I was very much afraid this investigation was going to involve the supernatural.

Good thing I had a ghost on my team.

*B*ack at the precinct, Jack set up our murder board— a whiteboard mounted on the wall directly across from our desks— while I pulled David Howe's information up on the computer. Nada. Howe seemed to be a solid citizen. No rap sheet. No arrests, no charges (false or otherwise), not even a list of shady associates. Just a single white male residing at the address we'd already determined from his driver's license. The one thing the background search did reveal was his employment record.

Since he'd been found in *First Fruits*, I'd assumed he was an employee. Not true. Howe was a certified public accountant and owned his own firm.

"Interesting," I said to Jack's back as he scrawled data on the murder board. "Our vic was a CPA. What do you suppose he was doing in the dispensary before opening?"

Jack's dry erase marker stopped moving, and he turned to face me. "A CPA?" he asked, a frown creasing his forehead. "What would an accountant be doing alone in a marijuana dispensary?"

I shrugged. "Well, not alone. He didn't slit his own throat. At least, it didn't look self-inflicted to me. The M.E. will say for sure."

"True, but Reynolds said the doors were still locked when he arrived on scene." He paused, capping the marker and flipping it in his hand while he thought. "If Howe was murdered, how did the perp leave?"

"Maybe he had a key," I suggested. "We don't have a time of death yet, so we don't know when this all went down. Do we have the owner's name and contact information? Maybe he can shed some light."

"Yeah. Reynolds pulled it from the dispensary license. Place is owned by a Gerald Adamson. I've got the address in here somewhere." He riffled through his notebook. "Got it." He turned, wrote a West Hills address on the board, and said, "Let's go see what Adamson has to say."

I pulled my dark tweed sport jacket from the back of my chair and shrugged into it as I strode to the elevator. I wasn't surprised to see Sarah appear in the elevator car when Jack and I stepped on.

I've been thinking, she said as I turned to face forward, appearing not to notice her. *The killer has to have been a normal human, otherwise he or she couldn't have crossed the wards.*

I cleared my throat, our signal that I'd heard and understood her comment.

But someone must've been worried about supernatural interference, or there wouldn't have been any wards.

I gave another little cough.

Jack glanced sideways at me. "You coming down with something?"

I grimaced and motioned to my throat. "Nah. Just a little tickle. I'm fine now."

Sarah snorted behind me.

Her comments were true, but there was another possibility,

which I couldn't share in our present circumstances. Whoever cast those wards could undoubtedly cross them. I'd have to watch Adamson very closely. I didn't have a clue what kind of an aura a witch would present, but that was the only mortal I could think of who would be able to cast the wards we'd seen. I might have paranormal abilities, but rune work and wards weren't among them.

If Adamson hadn't cast the wards, who had? And had that person done so at Adamson's request? And how was I supposed to ask those questions with Jack beside me?

Life had certainly gotten more complicated since my powers had manifested.

Jack guided our dark blue sedan out of downtown and up into the hills. Barely ten minutes later we were winding through Arlington Heights, a well-to-do neighborhood of classic homes owned by lawyers, doctors, and business owners. The inhabitants of this area appreciated being perched above the city, while staying only a few minutes from their downtown offices.

Adamson's home was a grand specimen of a Prairie style home, with clean horizontal lines that would've made Frank Lloyd Wright proud. I thought about voicing this opinion to Jack, but stifled the impulse. The style of the home wasn't germane to our investigation, and even though I'd taken a few architectural design classes in college and still found the subject interesting, Jack would think I was nuts to bring it up.

So I kept my thoughts to myself as we followed a walkway across an immaculately landscaped yard to the front door.

Jack readied his badge and rang the doorbell.

Sarah appeared beside me. *Nice place.* I gave her a tiny nod and readied my own badge.

The door opened and I had my first sight of Gerald Adamson. A tall, thin man in his late forties or early fifties, Adamson had silvery blond hair that allowed his pink scalp to show through. His eyebrows were similarly colored and his complexion such a pasty white that if his eyes, a light, watery blue, had appeared red or bloodshot I would have suspected albinism.

"Can I help you?" he asked, looking us over with suspicion.

Jack and I help up our badges. "Portland PD," Jack said. "I'm Detective Jack Barnes and this is my partner, Detective Gus Collier. We have a few questions regarding the murder in your marijuana dispensary this morning. May we come in?"

Adamson stepped back, opening the door wide and gesturing us inside. "Of course. I've been expecting someone to come by. Terrible business." He shuddered, shaking his head. "Poor David!"

We stepped into a spacious entry hall, well-lit with white paneling and polished oak floors. Adamson led us to the back of the house and into a lavishly decorated living room with floor-to-ceiling windows providing a panoramic view of the city below, as well as the mighty Columbia River.

Adamson gestured us to a silvery green couch while he seated himself in a pale brown leather armchair. "I was so distraught when the officer contacted me this morning," he said. "I wanted to rush right down to the shop, but the officer— Reynolds, I believe?— discouraged that, saying the building was an active crime scene and that someone would contact me."

He glanced back and forth between me and Jack. "I assume that's you. How can I be of help?"

Jack pulled out his notebook and flipped it open. I studied Adamson. That was our habit. Jack jotted down information; I kept my eyes open. We compared notes later.

"Do you have any idea what Mr. Howe was doing in your dispensary after hours?" Jack asked.

"I'm afraid I don't," Adamson answered. His eyes widened for a beat and then his brows drew together in a little frown of perplexity. "David was our accountant, of course, but I didn't have any meetings scheduled with him until the end of the quarter." He glanced from Jack to me before adding, "The end of September, when we'd finalize our quarterly report."

"Did any of your staff have dealings with him?" I asked.

"Well, I think everyone had met him, but no, I was the only one who met with him. For business at least."

Jack glanced up from his notebook, interested. "Did any of them have a personal relationship with him?" he asked.

Adamson lowered his gaze, leaned forward and adjusted a floral display on the white oak coffee table that separated us. "I don't like to say," he mumbled. "We're a small business, and I can't help but notice, but it's not my place..."

"Mr. Adamson," I said, "we're conducting a murder investigation, not writing a gossip column. Now what do you know... or suspect?"

He sighed, sat back, and met my gaze. "Of course. My apologies. As I said, I don't *know* anything, but I believe one of my clerks, Tammy Wilcox, was rather taken with David. As they're both unmarried and she doesn't deal with my bookkeeping, I noticed, but wasn't concerned. I've no idea whether or not either of them acted on the... attraction."

I nodded and exchanged a significant look with Jack before he scribbled down the name. "Thank you, Mr. Adamson. We'll look into it." I hesitated, glanced at Sarah who hovered near the picture window. "By the way," I said, trying for casual, "we noticed some kind of powdered crystal lining the threshold of your store's front entrance. Can you tell us anything about that?"

His brow furrowed and he glanced between us again. "Powdered crystal? At the threshold? I have no idea what you're talking about. Is it important?"

I've been a cop long enough to read most people, and he

came across as genuinely surprised and baffled. I shrugged. "Probably not. I just thought I'd ask since it seemed odd."

I paused a moment, and then said, "We'd appreciate it if you could meet one of our officers at *First Fruits* and go through the place. See if anything is missing. Do you know if there was much cash on hand last night?"

"Now that I can answer for certain," he said. "No. There was no significant cash on hand, only the petty cash in the register that would be necessary to open this morning. I took the deposit to our bank myself just after closing last night."

I frowned. "I thought banks were wary of dealing with marijuana dispensaries."

He smiled wryly. "They are, but they're happy to rent me a good-sized safe deposit box. I don't feel comfortable keeping too much cash on the premises, even in a safe, so I store it at the bank until it's needed."

"I see," I said, nodding. Watching his face for micro expressions that might call his words into question, I asked, "Do you know if Howe had any enemies? Anyone who disliked him enough to do him harm?"

Adamson shrugged and shook his head. "I'm afraid I can't help you there. He would've had no reason to mention anything like that to me. David and I had a business relationship; nothing more, nothing less."

Jack nodded, then flipped his notebook closed, pushed his pen into his breast pocket, and rose. "Thanks for your time, Mr. Adamson. That'll do it for now."

I stood and handed Adamson one of my cards. "If you think of anything that might be helpful, please call."

He accompanied us to the door and watched as we drove away.

"What did you think?" Jack asked. "Victimized business owner or murder suspect?"

I frowned and tapped my fingers against my leg. "His reactions seemed genuine," I said, "but it's too soon to take him off the list. What about you?"

"Same, though he did have his answers pretty handy," he said, keeping his eyes on the winding residential street. "Almost seemed rehearsed."

Agreed, Sarah added from her perch behind my left shoulder. *Something was off with him, but I'm not sure what.*

3

———

J opened the tablet computer mounted to the car dashboard and accessed Tammy Wilcox's information. Her driver's license was current and listed an address near Laurelhurst Park. A few minutes later Jack guided the car onto a narrow, tree-lined street of older homes.

"Nice neighborhood," he said, "but a real come-down from the boss's digs." He parked in front of the house, and we crossed the sidewalk and followed a neatly edged concrete path to the front door. The house was a blue two story bungalow with white shutters and several wind chimes dangling from the eaves. They jangled in the light summer breeze, serenading us while we waited.

A young woman opened the door and stared at us with open curiosity. From her license, I knew Tammy Wilcox was in her late twenties, but she looked like a high school girl. Her dark hair was pulled back in a high pony tail with stray bits curling around her face. She wore a sleeveless gold top and a billowy, ankle-length skirt; her feet were bare.

"Can I help you?"

We flashed our badges and repeated the standard police detective introduction.

"Oh," she said. "What's this about? I mean, I don't have any criminal tendencies." She smiled, displaying a cute little dimple. "Unless you count believing in the sanctity of Mother Earth."

Jack glanced at me, rolled his eyes, and then turned his attention back to Tammy. "I take it no one has contacted you regarding the incident at your place of employment?"

"*First Fruits*?" she asked, her eyes widening and her grip on the doorframe tightening to almost white-knuckle status. "No, I'm not scheduled to work today, so no one has contacted me. What happened?"

I answered before Jack could blurt out the news. "If we could step inside," I said, "we'll fill you in... and then we have a few questions." Her face paled and her breathing quickened. Time to calm the situation. "Nothing to worry about," I added. "Just routine police work."

She nodded, her lips pressed into a thin line, and opened the door wide. We followed her into a small living room with worn green shag carpeting and a drab brown couch whose cushions looked sprung. A black cat with white tips to its front paws watched us from a well-worn overstuffed armchair done up in a floral slipcover.

Tammy scooped the cat into her arms and dropped into the vacated chair. Jack and I perched on the couch. Sarah floated into the room and settled near a fireplace that looked like it hadn't been used in years.

A slight frown creased Tammy's brow as she followed Sarah's progress with her gaze.

This was going to be interesting.

"I'm sorry to have to deliver bad news, Ms. Wilcox," I said, reclaiming her attention, "but there was a murder at *First Fruits*."

She gasped, and squeezed the cat so hard it yowled and

wriggled out of her grasp. "Oh! I'm so sorry Prissy." She reached to pet the cat, but it hissed and ran from the room.

Closing her eyes, she inhaled deeply, exhaled fully, and then did so again twice more. When she was calm again, she opened her eyes, met my gaze, and asked. "Who died and when?"

I glanced at Jack, startled. The first question was expected, the second part, not so much.

"A man named David Howe," I said. "I understand that you knew him."

Her face paled and then flushed. "Yes," she said quietly, clasping her hands together and lowering her gaze to stare at them. "We'd been seeing each other for about a month. H-how did he die... and when?"

Jack took that one. "We aren't at liberty to discuss the manner of his death— it's an ongoing investigation— and we won't be sure of the timing until the autopsy is complete." He paused to let that sink in before continuing. "Is the time important?"

She sat back, closed her eyes again, and massaged her temples. When she opened them, she looked wan, but in control. "I doubt you'll believe me, but I'm a witch. I practice the old faith and observe the *Old Ones'* holy days."

"What's that got to do with the time of the murder?" Jack asked.

"Today is August 1st, the Feast of Lughnasadh or First Fruits. There should have been a celebration last night between sundown and midnight. A libation of oil and grain should have been offered. I told Mr. Adamson about it. I told him that especially in our business, the old rites should be observed."

"Why especially in your business?" I asked, ignoring Jack's squirms beside me.

She shook her head and sighed. "Our society has lost touch with the old ways. Our food comes from grocery stores, packaged and promoted. But *First Fruits*, the business, deals with products of nature. Marijuana is a plant with natural healing properties, and Lughnasadh recognizes the *Old Ones'* bounty." She stopped, gazed over our heads toward the window, then glanced at Sarah and quickly away again. "But what has been given can be taken away. A harvest can be lost."

"You warded the entrance to the store," I said quietly.

She glanced up startled, but Jack said, "What?" before she could respond.

I quelled Jack with a glance. "The powdered crystal," I said. "It was part of a ward against supernatural evil."

Tammy drew a sharp breath, glanced toward Sarah again, then met my gaze. "You know she's here?" she asked quietly.

I nodded.

"Know who's here?" Jack asked, irritation evident in his growling tone.

She shuddered, but didn't drop her gaze from mine. "Yes. I warded the entrance, both of them. The windows too."

"But Howe died anyway."

"If he died before midnight...." She swallowed, shuddered, and tried again. "If he died before midnight, he was a sacrificial offering."

"And if after?" I asked.

"It was the *Old Ones'* retribution."

4

On the way back to the precinct Jack grumbled about our interview with Tammy Wilcox.

"What was all that crap about wards and witches and what the hell are *Old Ones*?" he asked as he guided the sedan along the shortest route to the precinct. "You don't believe all that hooey, do you? And what was that about another female being in the room?" He glanced my direction with an expression of betrayal.

I shrugged. "I was just playing along with her fantasies. Seeing where the discussion led us."

"Right," he said, returning his gaze to the road. "And where, exactly, did it lead?"

"Well, we know that she thinks she's a witch and she was concerned enough about this supposed holy day to try to protect the windows and doors in a very non-standard manner." I stopped. I didn't like making light of Tammy's actions, because I knew her concerns were real... as were her powers as evidenced by the fact that she was aware of Sarah and that I'd been stopped by her wards. But Jack didn't, and I didn't have any way to explain what I knew. Not in a way he could accept.

I sighed and continued, "But I don't think she had anything to do with Howe's death. My take is that she was genuinely fond of him, and, given enough time, that fondness might have turned into love."

Jack grunted. "Yeah. She might be a sandwich or two short of a picnic, but I don't see her as a killer." He pulled the car into our assigned parking space, and we made our way back to our desks in silence, each thinking about what we'd learned and what was still a mystery.

I left Jack to notify Howe's next of kin by phone— his parents lived in Florida— while I wandered to the breakroom to think and hopefully confer with Sarah.

I poured myself a cup of coffee and settled at a table near the room's only window. I'd barely tasted the bitter, but hot brew when Sarah manifested and appeared to perch on the chair opposite me. Fortunately, we were alone.

"So," I said, setting the insulated paper cup on the table, "Howe's girlfriend is a witch."

Sarah nodded. *And she definitely has power, otherwise she wouldn't have been able to see me.*

"What do you think about her theory? Could Howe have been murdered in a ritual sacrifice?"

Possibly. If he really was kneeling, and if the killer stood behind him and used the knife as Jack suggested, it would fit.

"But if we're talking an offering of first fruits, why kill a man? Wouldn't the grain and oil Tammy mentioned make more sense?" I swirled the dark liquid in my cup while I thought. "A blood sacrifice seems like overkill."

Sarah grimaced. *Poor choice of words, but I agree.*

"And what about her other assertion? Do the *Old Ones* take retribution? In this day and age when practically no one has even heard of them, let alone believes in them?"

Sarah shrugged, floated to the window, and stared out. *I've never heard of them doing so, but I'm still very new to the supernatural world.* She turned to face me. *We need more information.*

"Agreed," I said, taking another swig of the swill the precinct called coffee. "Is there anyone you can ask about the *Old Ones*?"

A cute little frown creased her forehead as she thought. *Maybe. What are you going to do?*

"Time to check in with the medical examiner," I said, standing and pitching the remains of my so-called coffee in the trash. "If she's not finished with Howe, I'll see if I can hurry her along."

Great. You don't need me for that, she said with a delicate shudder, *and I don't want to ever visit that place again.*

If I could've, I would've given her a hug. Watching her own corpse being autopsied had been traumatic, even for a doctor who'd nearly completed her training. Instead, I gave her a sad smile and said, "Let's meet at my place after shift and compare notes."

Sarah faded out of sight just as two patrol officers entered the breakroom. Timing is everything, and except for her being dead when we met, ours has been pretty good.

Jack accompanied me to the morgue, having finished his notification of Howe's parents.

"They're pretty broken up," he said as we strode down the long, spotlessly white hallway that led to the M.E.'s office. "He was their only child, and they never expected to outlive him."

"Are they flying out?"

Jack nodded. "They want to arrange for burial here, where he had friends. He never lived in Florida. They retired there a few years ago, and he'd only visited over the holidays."

The M.E., Dr. Sandra Rayden, led us into the autopsy room

and gave us a full run-down on her findings. David Howe's corpse rested on a stainless steel table under bright white lights. A thin sheet covered his privates, but everything else was laid bare, including the neatly stitched Y-incision... evidence of Dr. Rayden's recent work.

Death doesn't leave a man much dignity.

"Your victim was a very healthy thirty-five year old male. His organs were in excellent condition and his muscle tone was exemplary. I found no evidence of drug use, legal or otherwise. His lungs were healthy and showed no indication of nicotine use; his liver showed him to be a non-drinker. In short, if he hadn't been murdered, he would've lived a long life."

Jack cleared his throat and swiped away a bead of sweat that was making a trail down the side of his face. My partner was an excellent detective, but visits to the morgue unnerved him. "So you're ruling this a homicide?" he asked. "He definitely didn't slice his own throat?"

Dr. Rayden glanced up, startled. "That's correct, Detective. This was no suicide. The angle and depth of the cut show that another hand, a very steady hand, inflicted the fatal wound."

She pointed to the angry red line across Howe's throat as she spoke. "The cut was made from left to right, beginning there, very close to his left ear, and ending here, just below the right jaw. In addition to the blood spatter evidence shown in the crime scene photos, subtle blood pooling around his knee joints indicate that he was kneeling at the time of his death. His head was jerked back with enough force that some of his hair was pulled out, his throat sliced, and his body allowed to fall forward into the position in which it was found."

"The cut was from the vic's left to his right, and the perp was behind him," I summarized. "So we're looking for a right-handed person?"

She nodded. "That's correct."

"Any indication as to whether the perp is male or female?"

"There's no way to assign gender based on the evidence I've seen. A woman would've been able to pull his head back and make that slice just as easily as a man, especially since there was no indication of a struggle."

Jack's eyebrows rose and he cocked his head. "So our vic just knelt down and allowed someone to slit his throat?"

Dr. Rayden shrugged. "That's what the evidence suggests."

"Was he drugged?" I asked, silently agreeing with Jack.

"Tox screen isn't back yet," she said. "I should be able to answer that question in the morning."

I nodded, waited a beat, then took a deep breath and, avoiding Jack's gaze, asked, "And the time of death?"

Dr. Rayden turned to a clipboard, flipped a page, and said, "Between 10:00 and 11:00 p.m."

"You're sure he died before midnight?" I asked, maybe a little too sharply since Jack scowled at me.

"Definitely," Dr. Rayden said. "His body temp and other factors are irrefutable." She turned to a tray, extracted a plastic evidence bag, and held it up. "Plus, his watch broke when he fell. It stopped at 10:38."

5
_____

*B*y the time I got to my apartment, all I wanted to do was grab a beer, put my feet up, and chow down on the pepperoni pizza I'd picked up on the way home. I was ready to put the murder on the back burner and unwind with a little mindless TV.

Unfortunately, Sarah had other ideas. She materialized in the kitchen before I even had a chance to put the pizza box on the counter.

So? she asked, perching on the counter right next to where I wanted to set the pizza down. *What did the medical examiner say? Did Howe die before or after midnight?*

"Hold your horses," I growled. "Let me get settled before you start the interrogation." Dropping the pizza box on the counter, I pulled off my jacket, tossed it on a chair, shrugged out of my shoulder holster and placed it and my service revolver carefully on the end of the kitchen counter. Yanking a plate from the cupboard, I slapped a couple slices of pizza on it, then turned to the refrigerator to grab a cold beer. Carrying my dinner to the living room, I toed off my shoes, sank onto the couch and put my feet up on the coffee table before biting into the warm, gooey bliss of a thick crust pepperoni pizza, heavy on the cheese.

Sarah floated over and hovered beside the coffee table, arms folded across her nicely padded chest. *Are we all comfy now? Ready to get down to business?*

I sighed and filled her in on Dr. Rayden's report between bites of warm pizza and swigs of cold beer. Sarah might not need to recharge, but I definitely did.

"So it looks like he was sacrificed," I finished, "by person or persons unknown."

Sarah, who had been pacing— if you can call it that since her feet had no need to touch the floor— while I talked and ate, stopped across from me and said, *Good.*

I frowned, a bite of crust suspended in midair. "Exactly what part of a guy having his throat sliced while he's kneeling in a marijuana dispensary do you consider *good*?" I asked, the day's stress revealing itself in my tone of voice, which was decidedly peevish.

Sarah waved away my comment. *He was murdered by another human. No ancient gods were involved.*

I nodded and popped the crust in my mouth. After chewing and swallowing— I wasn't raised in a barn— I asked, "What did you find out about the *Old Ones* and the possibility of retribution?"

She settled onto the brown leather recliner that sat beside my couch. *Not much. From what I can tell, they still exist, but have removed to another plane of existence. There simply aren't enough believers anymore to keep them fed.*

"Wait a minute," I said, pulling my feet off the coffee table, planting them solidly on the floor, and sitting up straight. "What does 'to keep them fed' mean?"

Just what it sounds like. They're like... I don't know... energy vampires. *They feed off the emotions of communities that believe in and worship them.*

"Yuck! And here I was thinking they were the good guys."

Well, they are. Sort of. At least, in comparison to the dark forces. They don't harm humans. Evidently we don't even notice the energy they draw from our worship. But that's what the rituals and cere-monies are for... they intensify the emotions of the worshippers, and thereby increase the amount of energy available to the Old Ones.

"Okay," I said, leaning forward, elbows on knees, chin on fists. "But don't people live a lot longer now than they did when the *Old Ones* were being worshipped? Modern science attributes that change to better diet, hygiene, and medical care. What if it's because we aren't having our energy siphoned off anymore?"

Sarah shrugged. *I suppose that's a possibility, but there's no way to prove or disprove it. Besides, what's that got to do with David Howe's murder?"*

"Probably nothing. Unless..." I stood and carried my plate and empty beer can to the kitchen while I allowed the thought coalescing at the surface of my mind to gel. After tossing the can in the recycling bin and putting the plate in the dishwasher, I turned to face her. "Jason Morgan murdered you to co-opt your power, right?"

Sarah eyed me warily, but nodded.

"What if this perp murdered Howe in a ritual sacrifice, at a very specific time and place, in order to feed on his life source, his energy?"

But the Old Ones have moved on, Sarah objected. *They've left this plane of existence.*

"All of them?"

I... I don't know.

"Let's review what we know," I said, pacing from the kitchen to the picture window framing a darkened view of the Willamette River, over to the built-in bookshelves and television, past the bathroom door and entry hall, and back to the kitchen. Doesn't take long to make a complete circuit of my studio apartment.

"One, Tammy Wilcox, a witch with demonstrable power and a believer in the *Old Ones*, was employed at *First Fruits*. Two, Tammy not only believes in the old rites, she told her employer they should be observed. Three, Tammy was twitchy enough to feel the need to ward the doors and windows of the shop. Four, someone... or something... was able to pass through her wards and lure its sacrificial victim to the shop at the appropriate time."

So, you're suggesting that an Old One *killed Howe in order to feed? Why David Howe? Why not Tammy? She's already a believer. She'd be easy prey.*

I shook my head. "Whatever it is, it couldn't sacrifice Tammy. She's its ongoing meal ticket. She provides a constant source of belief, and if left alone, is likely to add others. If she hasn't already, she's likely to develop a coven, and the more people she influences, the more energy the being gains for food."

But Tammy was dating David. Wouldn't killing him take away a potential believer?

I warmed to my subject, excitement buzzing through my veins. I was right. I could feel it.

"Not if Howe was eroding Tammy's faith. What if instead of Tammy influencing David, he was pulling her back toward the mainstream of modern thought? Our *Old One* can't afford to lose Tammy. She's its lifeline."

Sarah floated over to me and stared directly into my eyes. *If you're right, and I think you are, how do we bring a demi-god to justice?*

"We read up on exorcism," I said, without blinking, "and then we convince Tammy to help us free her boss from a danger-ous, perhaps even demented, *Old One*."

Adamson, she said, nodding. *Of course, it explains why his responses felt so off and yet neither of us could detect anything unnatural about him. He's human, but possessed.*

"I'm betting the *Old One* can bury himself deep enough in Adamson's psyche that the wards Tammy cast didn't affect it."

Which is why the purely human part of Adamson wasn't aware of my presence. She clapped her hands, though the action produced no sound. *Let's get to work.*

6

$\mathcal{T}$wo days later we had everything we needed to attempt to free Gerald Adamson from his *Old One* possessor.

Sarah and I left Jack out of the loop. We were dealing with forces he didn't understand and wouldn't believe even if we explained. So he and I did our due diligence, searching for incriminating evidence against Adamson—the only suspect who made sense from a purely human perspective. The tox screen came back clear, which bugged the hell out of Jack, but made perfect sense to me. An *Old One* would have no need to drug its sacrifice into compliance; it would have supernatural powers that would come into play.

When I wasn't working with Jack, Sarah and I studied exorcism and, when we'd learned what we needed to know, had a long, hard talk with Tammy Wilcox.

We sat in Tammy's living room again. Tammy and her black cat, Prissy, sat in the chair with the floral slipcover, while Sarah and I perched on the drab brown couch with the sprung cushions.

"So you're saying this is all my fault," Tammy said, tears

shimmering in her eyes. "If I weren't a witch, David would still be alive."

No, Sarah said softly, relieved that Tammy could hear her. *You're not to blame, and neither are your beliefs.* She reached toward Tammy's hand, remembered she couldn't make contact, and smiled sadly. *I'm not sure I even blame the* Old One, *though its certainly responsible. From what I understand of them, they're usually benign, avoiding harm to their believers. Unfortunately, this one has been starving for so long... I'm not sure its sane at this point.*

I cleared my throat to gain their attention. "At any rate, we need your help. If we can exorcise the *Old One,* Sarah will guide it to a point where it can cross over and join its fellows."

Sarah nodded. *I've sent a message that I hope will be received. If it is, another* Old One *will meet us and assist this one in its journey.*

"What about Mr. Adamson?" Tammy asked. "What will happen to him?"

I shook my head. "I'm not sure. So far we haven't found any tangible evidence against him, so the case could simply go cold, but..." I paused and took a deep breath. "It also depends on how he comes out of this experience. We just don't know."

Tammy bit her lower lip, but nodded. "Okay. What's the plan?"

7

I called Gerald Adamson and asked him to meet me at *First Fruits* that night at 11:00 p.m. He thought the hour was strange, but when I explained we were trying to recreate the scene of the crime, he agreed readily enough.

The shop had been released as a crime scene and had undergone a thorough cleaning by a company familiar with removing blood and gore. I was grateful that Tammy wouldn't be faced with entering a room where the blood of someone dear to her stained the floor and display cabinets.

Tammy had shivered when she first arrived, but then had set to work renewing the wards, though she left the one on the back door incomplete. We expected Adamson to enter through that door since he habitually parked just outside it. Once all the players were inside, she'd close that final ward. She had also cleansed the main sales floor with rosemary and sage and had placed candles scented with lavender around floor at the compass points.

We lit the candles, reciting an ancient prayer of thanksgiving to the four winds and invoking the protection of the four elements. When all was in readiness, we waited for Adamson to arrive.

At the stroke of eleven, a key turned in the back door's lock and Adamson stepped over the threshold.

"Detective," he said, nodding to me. "Tammy! I didn't expect you to be here." He appeared to be unaware of Sarah.

"Detective Collier asked me to come," Tammy said, stepping behind him to complete the ward on the door. "I'm happy to do anything I can to solve this horrible crime."

Adamson nodded, though he frowned as he watched her movements at the door. "Of course. What can I do to help, Detective?"

I gestured him onto the sales floor. "If you'll just kneel here," I said indicating the spot where David Howe had knelt on that fateful night. "I want to recreate the scene."

Adamson eyed the floor warily, but knelt facing the front door.

"No. I'm sorry," I said, "but if you'll just turn toward the display counter. I want to get the orientation right. Mr. Howe was facing east."

Adamson scootched around on his knees until Tammy nodded that his position was correct. I held up a hand and said, "Perfect. Now, if you'll just hold still."

Before the man had time to blink, Tammy, Sarah, and I began to chant the words to an ancient rite. Not in English, but in a long forgotten language that Sarah had coached us on. Tammy stood at the north compass point, Sarah at the west, and I held the south. As we chanted, we held our hands in front of us, palms up, and slowly raised them from waist to shoulder height, and then turning them outward, raised them above our heads.

At first, Adamson didn't move, but simply looked bemused by our actions. By the time our hands reached shoulder height, he'd begun to fidget, then he fell forward, writhing on the ritually cleansed floor. His body took on a bluish glow and something appeared to detach itself from the man.

A blue-green mist rose from the body, and Adamson lay deathly still. The mist continued to rise, and as it did so it coalesced into the form of a shimmering, ghostly man. He turned slowly, making eye contact with each of us as our hands reached the pinnacle of our ability to stretch. He stopped when his gaze reached Sarah.

You no longer live, he said in a cool, cultured voice. *Why have you agreed to challenge me?*

Sarah continued to chant without breaking her rhythm. We all knew that no matter what happened, we had to finish the incantation. The *Old One* undoubtedly knew it too.

He turned to Tammy. *You have worshipped me. Would you defy your god?*

Tammy didn't falter, though she did close her eyes. Tears trembled on her lashes.

Finally, he met my gaze. *You have no idea what you are unleashing on your world,* he said, his tone rising and becoming frenzied. *I will rip your limbs from your body. I will devour your soul.*

He turned back to Sarah with a sneer. *And you! You think death protects you? You have no concept of the immortal pain I will cause you to suffer! You think the Christian depiction of Hell is bad? Just wait until you taste the torments I will inflict on you for eternity.*

We were nearing the end of the incantation, and if anything, the *Old One* appeared stronger than he had at the start. A bead of sweat ran down the side of my face as I continued chanting. What if this didn't work? What if I'd led Tammy and Sarah not only to their deaths, but to everlasting torment? Could he really bring devastation to the world at large?

I closed my eyes and completed the incantation. We all

clapped a beat after the final syllable had been uttered. Even Sarah. I swear I heard Sarah's clap as well as Tammy's.

Absolute silence descended on the room.

An uncanny silence.

A silence so dense it felt like all sound had fled the universe.

I opened my eyes...

...and saw not one being, but two. So much for the efficacy of Tammy's wards!

The blue-green male had been joined by a golden radiance. A being inhabited the center of that molten gold glow, but I was incapable of assigning a gender to the being. All I knew was that it radiated peace... and acceptance... and a large measure of sorrow.

As I watched, the golden being engulfed the blue-green man, subsuming him into itself. The color of the newly joined pair mutated, ran through all the shades of the rainbow, and quite a few I had no words for, before stabilizing again at gold.

The newly joined being nodded to each of us and a bell-like voice rang through the room.

Well done. We will take our lost one home. Be at peace.

Light flared... and we were alone. Two conscious humans, one unconscious man, and one starry-eyed ghost.

I guess the Old Ones *got my message!* Sarah cried jubilantly.

I knelt beside Adamson. He was still breathing and his pulse felt steady, but I glanced at Tammy and said, "Call 9-1-1. Ask for an ambulance."

8

_____

Gerald Adamson suffered a stroke on the way to the hospital and died without regaining consciousness.

Jack and I closed David Howe's murder investigation without making an arrest. How could we? Our suspect was dead.

Tammy Wilcox stayed in Portland just long enough to help Adamson's heirs learn the ropes of the marijuana dispensary. Once the new owners had the shop up and running, Tammy relocated to the East Coast where she'd made contact with a coven of witches who were willing to mentor her in her craft.

And Sarah? She and I enjoyed a relaxing dinner at my place, complete with a great recording of her favorite jazz. Well, I enjoyed the dinner, but Sarah appreciated the music... and my company.

She's a great gal. Too bad we didn't meet until after she died.

Ah well. There's always the next homicide to look forward to...

PART II

DEATH OF AN ALCHEMIST

Uncollected Anthology

ALCHEMY

Issue 24 · UA · April 2021

DEATH OF AN ALCHEMIST

DEBBIE MUMFORD

PROLOGUE

*M*y name is Gus Collier and I'm a homicide detective for the Portland Police Department. Portland, Oregon, that is. My city. My beat.

My partner, Jack Barnes, is a solid detective, though you might not guess it to look at him. His graying hair is thinning, his cheeks are constantly stubbled and a little on the flabby side, and he's got a definite spare tire around his middle, but if you look closely into his gray-blue eyes, you'll see a keen intellect staring back... and taking your measure.

Jack is my official partner. The one Commander Abrams assigned to work with me. If you see me working a case, Jack will be by my side, but we won't be alone. Jack will never acknowledge her (because he has no idea she exists), but Sarah, my other partner, my *ghostly* partner, will be on the case too.

Sarah has been with me for a few months now— ever since I investigated her death at the summer solstice. When her case was solved and her murderer locked away for the rest of his natural life, I expected Sarah to leave. To move on. To *go into the light*. But she didn't. We'd developed a kind of working relationship, a bond of sorts, and she chose to stay on this plane to help me solve other murders.

So how is it that I can see and communicate with Sarah when no one else can?

Well, that's where it gets interesting.

You see, our desire to solve murders isn't our only bond. Sarah and I are both seventh-sevenths. I'm the seventh son of a seventh son, and while I always thought the legends were a bunch of hooey, I discovered I was wrong. Dead wrong, as it turns out. My abilities awoke on the summer solstice as I knelt over Sarah's dead body. That's when the impossible happened. Sarah opened her eyes, grabbed my wrist, and ordered me to find her killer.

To top it all off, it was my twenty-eighth birthday. Seven quadrupled.

I've got to say, I've had better presents than a corpse ordering me around.

So that explains me: seventh son of a seventh son. But what about Sarah? I mean, she's female, right?

Turns out, gender has nothing to do with it, but we're a patriarchal society and have been for thousands of years, so sons are the expected heroes. But the patriarchy is wrong. The definition should be: seventh offspring of a seventh offspring.

Whatever.

I'm not out to change the world's understanding of the supernatural. I'm just here to solve crimes... specifically, murders.

1

Portland's not exactly a hotbed of crime, but it's not always peaceful either. Sometimes the murders assigned to me and Jack are all too familiar patterns of life in a sizable city: drive-by shootings; bar fights gone wrong; domestic violence taken to the extreme. But today was going to be one of the unusual ones.

Not even zero-eight hundred and we'd already been notified that a prominent businessman had been gunned down in his own home. The maid found the body when she arrived for work and let herself in to his upscale home in the West Hills.

Jack parked our department issued dark blue sedan across the street from the crime scene, a beautiful specimen of a Tudor home, complete with steeply pitched gable roof and decorative half-timbering. I said as much to Jack as we studied the property, noting the lush gardens and sweeping views of the city and nearby hills.

He quirked an eyebrow at me. "You been studying architecture in your spare time?"

"Hey! I went to college," I said, stung. "And unlike you, I even remember a few things."

He grunted and headed for the nearest uniformed officer.

Sarah snickered softly. *I'm impressed.*

I managed not to jump when her voice whispered through my mind.

Barely.

I'd expected her to join us, but when she pops up out of thin air like that... well it still gives me an adrenaline rush that makes my heart hammer like a drummer in a rock band.

The uniforms had already cordoned off the area around the home with yellow crime scene tape, but even though the work day had begun and the neighbors could be expected to be at their offices in the city, they weren't. Curious onlookers craned their necks from driveways and porches all up and down the street. Experience told me that law-abiding citizens got a vicarious thrill out of being near the scene of a crime. Especially when one of their neighbors had been murdered in his own home. They might profess horror that someone they knew, or at least recognized as living in the area, had been killed, but deep down the experience excited them... a momentary shiver of fear, a brief brush with the seamier side of life.

Jack figured it was a result of too many cop shows on television. Everyone thought they understood police procedure... and knew how to do our jobs better than we did.

I thought their fascination with death was part of human nature. That it had existed long before the advent of TV crime shows, which were probably a symptom of the disease rather than its cause.

Whatever.

The neighbors were there, and we ignored them as we crossed the driveway and ducked under the crime scene tape. Occasionally the perpetrator would join the looky loos, curious about how his work was perceived, but not often. A quick glance confirmed that one of the uniforms was scanning the curious neighbors with a cell phone camera. Just in case.

Jack took the lead, and we flashed our badges as we approached the uniform we'd been told was first on the scene. The man stood about six feet away from the home's entrance, blocking the path to the front door.

"I'm Detective Jack Barnes and this is my partner, Detective Gus Collier," Jack said, pulling a small spiral-bound notebook from his pocket and clicking his pen open. Glancing at the man's name badge, he continued, "What can you tell us, Officer Abernathy?"

The uniform nodded. He stood at ease, relaxed but ready, feet solidly planted, thumbs hooked in his belt. "Dispatch called with the nine-one-one report at zero-seven-fifteen. My partner and I responded, arriving at zero-seven-twenty-two." He nodded toward the house. "The housekeeper was waiting on the front steps. Said she didn't want to be alone with the body. My partner and I cleared the house while she waited outside. Back-up arrived while we were taking her statement."

I nodded, glancing past him to the empty steps. "Where is she now?"

Abernathy hooked a thumb at the front door. "She's in the kitchen with my partner. The vic is in what looks like a home office. Want me to walk you through?"

Jack signaled one of the other uniforms to join us. A petite, dark-haired woman strode to Jack's side. He glanced at her name badge and said, "Officer Herrera, Abernathy here is going to walk us through the scene. Take over his station for him."

She nodded. "Of course, Detective."

Abernathy turned and led us through the open front door and into the house. He paused in the wide, wood floored foyer and pointed to another open door. He didn't have to tell us the vic was in there, the smell nearly knocked us off our feet. And that was with the front door open to the fresh late September air.

I turned toward the open front door, took a deep breath of the less tainted air, and noticed Sarah floating serenely behind me. I grimaced. She could afford to be serene. She could no longer smell the stench of death, the metallic tang of blood mixed with the foul odor of excrement and a lingering dollop of fear.

Not that I envied her being dead, of course. I had no desire to cross over to her side of eternity. Not for many long years to come.

She smiled sadly and nodded toward Jack, who was also working to maintain his professional demeanor in the face of the smell. Violent death in a small space was always harder to deal with than a body discovered out of doors.

It never gets easier, does it? she asked. Sarah had experienced her share of blood and gore. She'd been in her final year of residency as a doctor when a man she'd trusted had ended her earthly life. Since she'd just come off a double shift at the hospital when she died, Sarah was (and always would be) dressed in blue scrubs and white soft-soled shoes. Her long blonde hair was pulled back in a high pony tail. Even in hospital scrubs, Sarah was a beauty.

I sighed, wishing for the thousandth time my friend wasn't dead. If we'd met in life... well, a guy could dream, and I often did.

The opening to the room where the vic's life had ended was secured by French doors which opened into the foyer. Both sides boasted full, frosted glass panels, and each was etched with a large and detailed caduceus.

I raised an eyebrow and glanced at Abernathy. "Was the vic a doctor? What's his name?"

Abernathy pulled out a notebook and checked his notes.

"According to the housekeeper, our vic is Dimitri Xanthro-polous. A quick scan of that name pulled up this address, so I've no reason to doubt her statement. Not sure of his profession."

Jack nodded and stepped into the room with the body. "Did you take his prints?"

"No, sir. Procedure is to secure the scene and wait for the detectives and the medical examiner."

Abernathy remained in the foyer, but I followed Jack into what turned out to be Xanthropolous' office. The body was slumped against the front of a large walnut executive desk. Blood and excrement stained what had been an expensive Turkish carpet, its red, black, and gray pattern now blurred and indistinct in the area around the corpse. Glancing around, I noted a set of wide diamond pane windows looking out onto one of the front gardens, this one featuring rose bushes. Despite the lateness of the season, a few flowers remained, red, pink, and golden hued. Bookshelves lined the other walls, and a walnut credenza sat beneath the windows.

A younger-looking version of the vic sat in the black leather swivel chair behind the desk.

I was about to ask Abernathy what he was thinking to let a civilian into the crime scene, when Sarah gasped and floated around the desk to join the intruder. That was when my brain caught up with my sight and I realized the guy was almost trans-parent and he shimmered slightly.

Great. Another ghost.

I knew from my experience with Sarah that Xanthropolous wouldn't be able to tell us who killed him. For some reason beyond my understanding, the universe had decreed that while a ghost might be able to remember all the details of their death, they were unable to articulate them to the living.

However, Sarah wasn't living, and this wasn't *her* death, so it was possible I might get some, shall we say, *inside* information on the crime.

I left the ghost to Sarah and joined Jack in examining the body.

When I knelt across the corpse from him, Jack pointed his pen at the neat hole in the man's forehead. "Looks like a single shot to the head. Guy was dead before he hit the ground."

I nodded and glanced at his hands, which were open and relaxed. "Doesn't look like he struggled. The room's neat as a pin except for the body. No signs of a fight."

"Abernathy!" Jack yelled, and the uniform's face appeared beside the open door. "Did you see any sign of a fight in the other rooms? Anything look disturbed?"

The officer shook his head. "No, sir. The whole house is neat. Even the beds are made in the rooms upstairs." He moved back out of the doorway, and then reappeared a moment later. "Oh! And we found a safe room at the back of the garage. You know, one of those super secure rooms a guy can lock himself into if he feels threatened."

"Huh," Jack grunted. "Thanks, Abernathy. We'll take a look in a minute." He turned to me and cocked his head. "Sounds like Mr. Xanthropolous might've known his killer. No fight, and he sure wasn't shot while running for his safe room."

I nodded. "Why don't I poke around his office here while you check out the rest of the house." I was anxious to get Jack out of the room so I could check in with Sarah. One of the down sides of having a ghost for a partner was that I couldn't talk to her when anyone else was around.

Jack shook his head. "Nah. We can do that in a while. Right now we need to interview the housekeeper. I'm sure the poor woman would like to get as far away from this place as possible... as soon as possible."

"Right," I agreed, since I couldn't tell him I had a ghost to

2

The housekeeper, Angela Preston, wasn't much help. But then I hadn't expected her to be. Other than calling in the murder and telling us the dead man's name, she didn't know anything that would advance our search for the killer.

Abernathy's partner, a woman in her mid-thirties by the name of Langston, escorted Ms. Preston out the back door and to her older Subaru sedan, making sure the woman had our contact information just in case she remembered anything. She wouldn't. How could she? She hadn't witnessed anything.

Sarah and Xanthropolous' ghost floated into the breakfast room while Jack and I were finishing up our notes on Ms. Preston's interview. I caught Sarah's eyes and nodded. We needed to talk.

After sending Abernathy and Langston to canvas the neighborhood and take statements from anyone who might have seen anything, I turned to Jack. "Why don't you head upstairs and look around," I suggested. "I'll check out the rest of the downstairs, then we can meet back in Xanthropolous' office and see if we turn up anything interesting in there."

"Sure," he said, "make your aging partner climb the stairs."

I lifted an eyebrow. "You planning to ask the commander for a desk job?"

He scowled and, before stomping off, grumbled, "Not bloody likely."

Once my living partner was out of sight, I gestured to the ghosts. "Join me, please."

Sarah shepherded Xanthropolous over to the breakfast table, a beautifully polished white oak piece surrounded by four matching oak chairs. Diamond pane windows caught the morning sun and scattered refracted rainbow fragments across the table, chairs, and gold-toned slate floor. The ghostly victim looked totally bewildered as he floated beside the table he'd so recently owned.

I studied the man who was now a corpse on his office floor. He'd been a good looking guy. Late forties or early fifties, with a fit but not body-builder overblown physique. His hair had been dark, with silver wings at the temples, and his skin had a Mediterranean tone consistent with his surname. Dark eyes, chiseled cheekbones and chin, and a long, straight nose completed the picture of an adult male in his prime.

Gus, this is Dimitri Xanthropolous, and he has a very interesting story to share. Sarah turned to the vic's ghost. *It's okay, Dimitri. You can talk to Gus. He's not just a police detective, he's also the seventh son of a seventh son, so he has special, uhm, abilities. He can see you and hear you.*

Xanthropolous eyed me skeptically, but shrugged his shimmery shoulders, and said, *I am pleased to meet you, Gus. Though I wish I were still living. After my long centuries of existence, this... transformation... is something of a shock.*

My breath caught and I straightened in my chair. "Hold it," I said, my voice sounding less steady than I liked. I cleared my throat and continued, "Did you say *centuries*?"

The ghost nodded. *I was born in a small village in Greece in 326 B.C. by your reckoning. The name of the village is immaterial as it ceased to exist over a thousand years ago.*

I glanced from Xanthropolous to Sarah and back again. "How is that possible?"

I am, he glanced down at his semi-transparent hands, and amended, *or at least I was, an alchemist. Long ago I was known as Xanthos the Merciful. I was, have always been, a healer. I discovered an alchemical elixir that could cure any human ailment. I could even raise the dead, so long as the body had not sustained irreparable damage.*

He glanced mournfully in the direction of his office. *Alas, even were I to give you access to my panacea, my physical form is beyond repair.*

"So, let me get this straight," I said, making an honest effort not to sound like I thought this guy was a loony, which I did. "You're an immortal who, if you hadn't been shot in the head by an unknown perp, would've been able to heal anyone from anything? Including yourself?"

Xanthropolous nodded. *But the perp, as you call him, is not unknown. It was...*

But no further words came out, only a kind of strangled, gurgling sound. He closed his mouth, cleared his throat, and tried again. With the same result.

Sarah gave him a sad smile and shook her head.

"Don't worry about it," I told him. "It seems to be a rule, though who makes these crazy rules, I have no idea. Sarah couldn't tell me who killed her either. She had to show me."

He reached for my arm, but I threw my hands in the air and scooted my chair away from the table.

"Nope," I said, tempted to yell, but I didn't want Jack to come barreling down the stairs to my rescue. "I'm not doing that again. Besides, this time we have Sarah to intervene. You won't be able to tell her anything where I can hear it, but I'm betting you'll be able to give her all the details once the two of you are alone."

Xanthropolous nodded. *Very well, but you should know, there is another.*

"Another what?" I asked, hoping we weren't talking ghosts.

Alchemist. Another alchemist. My wife is also a practitioner and knows the secret of my elixir, though she has never been able to reproduce it. He shrugged and examined the fingernails of his right hand. *It seems a certain... talent... is required to produce an efficacious elixir.*

"Wait a minute. If your wife lives here with you, why didn't Ms. Preston mention her?"

His eyebrows flew toward his hairline. *Did I say she lived here? I think not! I merely said she was my wife and in possession of my alchemical formula.*

I frowned. "If she's your wife, why doesn't she live here?"

He shook his head. *You are very young, Gus. Though Korina and I remain fond of each other, living together amicably for over two thousand years is not as easy as the romantics of the world might think.*

"Right. So where do I find this Korina, and if she's not involved, why would you think I should bother?"

She lives across the river in Vancouver, Washington —we like to stay close to each other— and you should bother, as you say, because she will need protection. You see...

The ghost's speech was interrupted by another bout of strangled gargling. He scowled and tried again, *You see 'the perp' is aware that Korina also holds the formula.*

3

---

*T*urns out I was wrong about Xanthropolous' ability to communicate the name of his killer to Sarah. He choked with her just like he'd done with me, and since she had no physical body for him to grab hold of, he had no way to force his memories into her head.

Bummer.

Didn't change my decision not to allow him to touch me. I'd lived through Sarah's death, and it hadn't been fun. No way was I going through that again.

That left a trip to Vancouver, which we would've had to make anyway.

"Tell me again why we're driving to Vancouver?" Jack asked as he guided our dark blue sedan across the Glenn Jackson Bridge, over the mighty Columbia River.

"I found the vic's ex-wife listed in his contacts," I said without even a hint of a blush at the lie. "We need to notify her of Xanthropolous' death and find out what she knows... she could be involved."

Since I'd come into my power and Sarah had joined our team, I'd gotten used to misdirecting Jack. I consoled myself with the knowledge that we couldn't use any information I received from a supernatural source anyway, so the misdirections weren't really lies... they were alternate routes to information I already had. Routes that Jack would understand and the courts would accept.

It worked.

Most of the time.

A few minutes later we pulled into the drive of a sprawling riverfront mansion. I studied the graceful beige stone façade, appreciating the fluted pillars supporting the curved portico entrance. Eternal life evidently paid well. Both Dimitri and Korina Xanthropolous had lived well.

We strode to the door, and Jack rang the bell. A few moments later, a young woman wearing a gray dress covered by a starched white apron opened the door.

"May I help you?" she asked, eying us cautiously.

Jack flashed his badge and gave our names. "We'd like to speak to..." he glanced at his notes, "Korina Xanthropolous."

Sarah floated past the young woman and down the hall, disappearing into the home.

"Ms. Xanthropolous is meeting with another visitor at the moment," the maid replied. "Perhaps you could leave your card and I'll ask her to call you later?"

I was about to answer when Sarah reappeared behind the maid. *Come now,* her voice rang in my mind. *Korina is being threatened.*

Before I could say or do anything, a woman's scream sounded. "Sophie! Call the police!"

The maid startled and turned, but Jack and I pushed past her, racing toward the all too familiar sound of bodies in conflict.

We emerged into a spacious, light-filled room and saw a well-dressed man struggling to restrain a golden-haired woman.

She screamed again, bit the hand that was trying to silence her, and wrenched herself free.

Jack and I both unholstered our weapons, and Jack yelled, "Stop!" while I circled around to get between the woman and her attacker.

"We're police officers," I said, leveling my gun to aim directly at his heart. I neglected to add that we were from Portland and had no jurisdiction in Vancouver. "We're responding to a call for help."

Jack cuffed the man and, following the maid, escorted him into another room. Jack would stay with the man until the Vancouver police arrived to take custody. Leaving me free to interview Korina Xanthropolous.

Sarah floated beside Korina who had composed herself and now sat regally in a modern overstuffed chair upholstered in a soft blue fabric. Maybe velour? I settled on the matching sofa and glanced around the room. The light I'd noticed earlier came from floor-to-ceiling windows overlooking a wide stretch of lawn leading down to the majestic Columbia River. Lush flower gardens lined both sides of the lawn; available for the owner's enjoyment, but not detracting from the view of the river.

The room itself was spacious, with a river rock fireplace at one end and a cathedral ceiling of light wood. The floors were flagged in beige stone and covered with neutral toned area rugs. The furniture was simple and tasteful in a manner that practically screamed wealth.

"You are a detective?" Korina asked. Her voice was low and melodic. If I hadn't witnessed the altercation, I'd never have guessed that the calm woman sitting across from me had just endured a harrowing experience. She wore a light gray silk shirt, neatly tucked into charcoal gray slacks, and her honey-gold hair was pulled back in a high ponytail, not a lock out of place. Her skin glowed with health, and her dark blue, almond shaped eyes studied me with curiosity.

"Yes," I said, showing her my badge and introducing myself.

Glancing at it, she said, "You arrived awfully quickly."

I nodded. "We're not from Vancouver. Portland Police Department. We'd come across the river to talk to you."

She sighed deeply before replying. "Well, whatever the reason, I'm grateful for your timely arrival."

She won't be when she hears your news, Sarah said quietly.

Korina glanced at her sharply.

I jumped, the hairs on my neck prickling. "Excuse me. This may sound odd, but are you aware of another... presence?"

Korina turned back to me and cocked her head, studying me. "Of course. She was speaking to you?"

I nodded. "This is my unofficial partner, Sarah Allen."

Korina stared at me another moment and then turned to Sarah. "It is not often that I'm visited by a spectre," she said, "and even less often that we're introduced." She turned back to me. "What is it that you have come to tell me, Detective Collier?"

I took a steadying breath and said, "I'm deeply sorry to inform you that your husband, your ex-husband, was found murdered in his home a few hours ago."

The color drained from her face, her eyes widened, and she covered her mouth with her hand.

"Dimitri?"

I nodded.

"No! That's not possible. You don't understand, Dimitri can't be dead."

"I'm afraid he is," I said gently.

And we do understand, Sarah said. *He told us everything.*

"He... he told you?" she asked in a shocked whisper. Her spine straightened, and she said, "Then why isn't he here? Why did you come without him?"

I motioned to Sarah. This was her area of expertise, not mine.

The newly dead are bound to their bodies. Soon he will have a choice: remain in this realm or move on into the light. As you can see, I chose to remain. I doubt that your husband will.

Korina smiled fondly. "No. He will not. Dimitri has seen enough of this world. He will choose to move into the next." She closed her eyes and relaxed into her chair. Suddenly she sat straight again. "That man! The one who attacked me. Did he kill Dimitri?"

"We won't know for sure until we hear his story, but I suspect so. Tell me, who is he and why was he here?"

She reached out to the low table between us, picked up a business card, and handed it to me. "He said he was a pharmaceutical rep and was interested in a chemical formula of mine." She smiled sadly. "I suppose Dimitri told you about it?"

I glanced at the card before nodding. "He did. His house appeared undisturbed, so I assume his killer didn't search for it."

Korina shook her head. "If this man was the killer and he bothered to speak to Dimitri, he would've known that would be useless. Dimitri had mixed his elixir so often over the ages that he had no need for instructions. I possess the only written copy."

Dimitri told us you'd been unable to make an effective version of the elixir.

Korina shrugged. "It seems more than the formula is required. A certain... magical... talent is also necessary." She studied Sarah. "I suspect you might have been able to make it work. You were a healer, were you not?"

Sarah nodded.

"And not just a physician, in the modern sense of the word," Korina continued. "You also had a supernatural ability, I think."

I would have, Sarah said quietly, *if I'd been allowed to live.*

"Ah. A true tragedy. I would gladly give it into your keeping if you were corporeal."

"So," I said, interrupting, "you're saying this formula would be of no value to a pharmaceutical company?"

Korina turned those lovely almond eyes on me. "That is correct. But I doubt they wanted to produce the elixir. I imagine they would want to destroy the formula."

4

———

*J*ack made arrangements to exchange information with the Vancouver police since it looked like our cases were related. The Vancouver detectives were willing to give us an opportunity to interview the perp... once they'd had their shot at him.

Jack had tried to get him to talk while I was interviewing Korina, but the guy had clammed up and refused to speak. We wouldn't even know his name if Korina hadn't given me his business card. I snapped a cell phone pic of the card before handing it over to the Vancouver guys. After all, fair is fair, and this was their case.

As we headed back across the river to our territory, I filled Jack in on what Korina had told me. The whitewashed-for-normal-humans version.

"So our vic had some kind of snake oil remedy that a pharmaceutical guy was trying to buy." Jack glanced at me quickly before shifting his eyes back to the road.

"That's what it sounds like." I agreed.

"Sounds like a perfectly legit business transaction," Jack said, frowning in concentration. "So why'd he off him? And why go after the ex-wife? Makes no sense. Either they sell, or they don't. Can't see how killing either of them accomplishes anything."

That's because he doesn't have the whole story, Sarah said, leaning into the back seat so that her blue-scrub clad body disappeared into it. *He wanted to erase all evidence that a panacea had ever existed.*

I cleared my throat; our signal that I'd heard and understood her.

To Jack, I said, "It's a puzzle all right. We'll just have to see what he says once he realizes we have him on murder."

Jack slid a sideways glance my direction. "Do we?"

I shrugged. "We'll have his fingerprints as soon as VPD processes him and sends them over to us, and I'm betting they'll match whatever the crime scene team comes up with from our vic's home."

"Let's just hope he didn't think to wipe everything clean."

"Yeah, but I bet he didn't. That guy didn't strike me as an experienced killer, and amateurs make all kinds of mistakes." I paused as we crossed the imaginary line in the middle of the Columbia River that marked the border between Washington and our home state of Oregon. "Besides, how likely is it for a man and his ex-wife to both be attacked in their homes within a few hours of each other and it not be the same guy?"

Jack grimaced. "True. I just hope the evidence supports that theory. I'd hate for a killer to walk."

Once back in the office, Jack and I filled the time waiting for fingerprint analysis by researching both the vic and the perp. As expected, I found that Dimitri Xanthropolous was a well-respected practitioner of alternative medicine. His website was filled with glowing testimonials from patients he'd cured, as well as a number of references from traditional physicians, both medical doctors and osteopaths. I was frankly surprised to find the respectful comments from the MDs.

"Well," Jack said, blowing out a breath to break my concentration and gain my attention, "the perp is who he says he is. Nathan Johnstone. Found his picture on A2Z Chemical's website. It's a multinational pharmaceutical corporation and he's the director of their research and development department." He scrubbed his hands over his stubbly face. "Still makes no sense. If the vic had a promising formula, why kill him?"

I shrugged. "Maybe he wouldn't sell."

Jack glared at me. "Legitimate business men don't kill each other over formulas."

"If they didn't, we'd be out of business," I said. "Come on, Jack. The why isn't our job. We're just supposed to assemble the evidence and arrest the bad guy. We don't always get all the answers."

Jack shook his head and stared at the murder board across from our desks. "I know. But it galls me when the crime doesn't make sense."

I really wished I could explain it to him. But he'd never accept that the vic's ghost had told me he'd been an immortal (well... *almost* immortal) alchemist who could cure any human ailment and a pharmaceutical company had offed him to keep his cure from becoming public.

After all, pharmaceuticals was a huge business... that would no longer exist if a universal panacea existed.

Too bad the perp hadn't realized that only someone with a magic touch could produce the elixir.

After the lab contacted us with a positive match on the fingerprints, Jack contacted VPD to let them know that Portland PD would be charging the man in their custody with murder. No matter what Washington decided, Johnstone would be tried in Oregon.

EPILOGUE

*W*hen I finally got home that night, I went straight to the small safe built into the wall of the closet in my bedroom. Pulling an ancient but well preserved scroll from the inside pocket of my jacket, I locked it away carefully.

Nice of Korina to entrust that formula to you, Sarah said when I came out of the closet.

"I guess so," I said, sitting down on the edge of the bed and taking off my shoes, "but I've got to admit it makes me a bit nervous to have it in the apartment. After all, a man was killed for it today."

True, but he was a healer and was using it. You couldn't even if you wanted to.

I nodded. "I get that Korina is hoping I'll find another healer to pass it along to, but what are the odds? You're the only other seventh-seventh I've ever known."

And you didn't find me until I was a corpse, she said with a shrug. *Still, you were her best option.*

"I can't believe a woman who's been alive since before the birth of Christ will now die because of Johnstone. He should face two counts of murder."

Sarah didn't respond, and it occurred to me that I'd just been incredibly insensitive. Korina had lived for thousands of years. Sarah didn't even make it to her twenty-eighth birthday.

Perspective is an important tool, and I needed to use it more often.

"Well," I said into the silence. "At least she'll have plenty of time to put her affairs in order."

Later, while I enjoyed a slice of pepperoni pizza, Sarah popped back into view.

Who'd've ever thought we'd meet a real, live alchemist? she asked with a smile that told me my thoughtless remark was forgiven and we were back to normal.

"We didn't," I said around the gooey mouthful I was chewing.

She frowned and fisted her cute little hands on her blue clad hips.

I swallowed, took a swig of beer, and finished the thought. "The alchemist was dead before we met him." I decided it was the better part of valor to leave Korina out of our currently friendly banter.

Her eyebrows rose in surprise, and then she grinned. *So he was.*

I lifted my beer can in salute. "And we solved the death of an alchemist."

And allowed him to move on... into the light. She nodded and faded from view, but her parting words lingered in my mind, *We make a good team, Gus.*

I took another bite and nodded. "That we do, Sarah. That we do."

PART III

MISS BAINBRIDGE'S SUMMER ADVENTURE

DEBBIE MUMFORD

BESTSELLING AUTHOR OF *SORCHA'S HEART*

Miss Bainbridge's
Summer
Adventure

SPUN YARNS
A Story of the Erie Canal

1

_____

*M*iss Clarissa Bainbridge clutched her parasol and surveyed the packet boat that would carry her along the newly constructed Erie Canal from her home in Albany, New York to Buffalo, on the shores of Lake Erie. To think that she would view the glory of Niagara Falls in less than a week! The very thought caused her heart to race and her face to heat. To calm herself, she drew a deep breath and concentrated on the details of the boat before her.

The packet tied to the dock was long and narrow. The hull was painted bright red, and a long white cabin with a row of windows took up most of its deck. Red Venetian blinds covered the windows, adding to its gay appearance. The top of the boat was also a deck, very slightly rounded to allow rain to shed, and surrounded by a low iron railing. Already the packet's crew was stacking passengers' baggage in neat rows on that upper deck. At the bow and stern of the main deck were much smaller spaces, only a few feet above the muddy water of the Erie Canal. The captain and the helmsman would command the small deck at the stern as they manned the tiller. The forward deck, as well as the upper, would allow passengers a place to sit and breathe the fresh mountain air while enjoying the scenic delights.

Though the August day was warm and the packet's cabin would likely be close, Clarissa could hardly wait to board. She was tired of standing on the dock waiting for her adventure to begin. Not to mention anxious to be away from the odors of the near-by stables which housed the horses and mules that would plod along the towpath beside the canal, pulling the packet boats and liners to their destinations.

Adjusting her wide-brimmed straw hat and straightening the jacket of her olive green traveling dress, she noted that the crew had reached her bags and were loading them onto the upper deck. Surely the passengers would be allowed to board soon.

A moment later the steward called for the passengers to make their way to the gangplank.

"Have your tickets ready, please," the man called in a booming voice. "You'll need to show your ticket before you step on the gangplank."

Clarissa hurried to take her place in line, a little miffed that the gentlemen passengers did not immediately make way for her. Well, that was her own fault for insisting on traveling alone. Not having an escort to open the way for her was a bother, but the freedom to do as she saw fit more than made up for the momentary aggravation.

At first her mother had flatly refused to allow Clarissa to travel unaccompanied, but Clarissa had prevailed in the end. After all, only the wealthiest patrons could afford a place on the packet boats of the Erie Canal. The riff-raff had to be content with the slower, more crowded conveyance of the liners, squeezed in amongst the freight those vessels hauled. Clarissa would be surrounded by gentry, with her own sleeping berth— in a separate section for ladies only, of course—and meals prepared and served by the packet's crew. Her journey to the wilds of Niagara Falls would be a genteel and refined excursion to view the juxtaposition of nature's beauty and man's industry with her own eyes. For Clarissa Bainbridge couldn't imagine a higher form of technological achievement than the engineering marvel that was the 363 mile long Erie Canal.

When Clarissa reached the steward, she handed him her ticket without comment. He glanced at it, nodded, and handed it back.

"Very well then, miss. Would you like assistance boarding the packet?" he asked, glancing from Clarissa to the gangplank that was little more than a four foot wide board linking the dock with the packet's deck.

She almost accepted, but then remembered her desire to be free from male supervision for this journey and declined. "Thank you," she said, "but no. I can manage on my own." Holding tightly to her ticket with one hand and her parasol with the other, she stepped onto the gangplank and boarded her packet boat to adventure.

2

hree days later, Clarissa was ready for the voyage to end. She had seen lovely landscapes, to be sure, but she had also endured monotonous sections that lulled the senses and caused the hours to drag.

And she was heartily tired of the interior cabin. The novelty of watching the crew transform the sitting room into a dining room and later in the evening into sleeping quarters—separated into men's and ladies' sections by a thick curtain—had quite worn off. At least she was a lady and was not subjected to the extreme crowding that her male companions endured at night.

For while there were only six women to share the ladies' sleeping quarters, there were no fewer than sixty gentlemen. Since there were so few of them, the ladies each had lower berths, with no one sleeping above them. Not so the men. She'd seen their accommodations before the curtain was dropped. The gentlemen's berths were stacked three high with what had to be barely enough space between them to allow a man to crawl into his bed.

She shuddered to think of the close proximity... not to mention the smell since it was impossible to bathe on this boat.

Opening her fan, she waved it in front of her heated face. Two more days. They would dock in Buffalo in two more days. Then she would be free of this cramped, noisy, and too often dirty little packet boat.

"Very low bridge," the helmsman called, and Clarissa who was seated on the lower deck at the bow, glanced up to see a low stone bridge spanning the width of the canal. Above and behind her, she heard the men who were sitting on the upper deck scramble from their seats to lay flat on the deck. She'd experienced that scramble herself a time or two when she'd been unable to procure a seat on the lower deck, but had been unwilling to remain cooped up inside the cabin.

Smiling and fanning herself, she tilted her head back in time to see a young man climb onto the low stone wall of the bridge and prepare to jump.

Good lord! She hoped he wouldn't land on anyone. The passengers above would be unable to scramble out of the way, crouched as they were on the deck to avoid being scraped off into the canal's murky water. She passed into the shade under the bridge and immediately thereafter heard a thump and a yell as the newcomer landed on someone and both flattened themselves to avoid being hit by the stone solidity of the bridge.

Once the boat had cleared the obstacle, Clarissa jumped from her chair and climbed the stairs to see what was happening on the deck above.

A nice looking young man rose to his feet, dusted himself off, and offered his hand to a middle-aged man wearing a brown paisley waistcoat and a white shirt with the sleeves rolled to his elbows.

"Sorry about that," the young man said. "Hard to judge the landing when everyone is laid out to avoid the bridge."

The older fellow accepted the offered assistance and stood with some difficulty. "What were you doing jumping aboard in the first place?" If he sounded a bit testy, Clarissa couldn't blame him. She wouldn't have appreciated being jumped upon either.

The young man shrugged. "No docks nearby. This was as close as I could get to a packet boat."

"Well, you'll have to pay your fare, dock or no dock," said another deep voice. The captain had climbed the stairs at the other end of deck and now stood with his fists on his hips. "Come with me and I'll calculate your fee." The captain looked him up and down. "Our berths are full. You'll have to make do with a pallet on the floor."

"I expected as much," the new passenger said with a smile. He held out his hand. "Jeremy Pine."

The captain glanced at the man's hand, but didn't take it. Instead, he sniffed, jerked his chin toward the stairs, and said, "This way."

As the captain and the man retreated to the stern deck, Clarissa stepped down and resumed her seat.

"Well," she said quietly to herself. "That was unexpected."

3

———

*S*he couldn't have said why, but Clarissa found the newcomer unnerving. It wasn't his appearance; he was nice looking, to be sure, but she knew many young men with stronger chins, kinder eyes, and better grooming. It wasn't his manner; he was jovial and pleasant and went out of his way to be courteous to everyone, especially her. It wasn't even his speech, though his choice of words did strike her as a bit uncouth. But whatever it was, it jangled her nerves and kept her on guard whenever he was near.

She didn't trust him.

But other than his unorthodox method of boarding the packet, she had no reason to distrust him. Of course, the opposite was also true. But then, she had no reason to trust any of the other five ladies or sixty gentlemen who shared this cramped little boat with her. But none of them, nor any of the crew, concerned her. The newcomer did.

So she watched him.

She tried to be circumspect about her observations, but she watched him at meals, on the deck, she even tried to note where he placed his pallet every night, though that was not always possible, for once the curtain fell, it was not to be disturbed.

She carefully recorded all of her observations in her diary. Every. Single. One.

Her mother had given her the diary and made her promise that she'd keep a faithful record of her adventure and all that she observed on the way to and from Niagara Falls. But Clarissa doubted her mother had expected her to record the movements, expressions, and utterances of Jeremy Pine. A young man Clarissa would have never met had he not jumped from a bridge onto her packet boat.

At the very least, Mr. Pine relieved Clarissa's boredom with the plodding trip along the Erie Canal.

As they neared Buffalo, Clarissa's notes on Mr. Pine diminished. She didn't lose interest or cease to observe him, but he became quieter. Almost as though he desired to fade from other's notice. He drew into himself and his eyes narrowed. He watched everyone, and he noticed Clarissa watching him.

Clarissa stood at the rail of the forward deck, watching as the packet approached the dock in Buffalo. A shadow fell across her and she glanced around to find Jeremy Pine standing just behind her. Her heart pounded, but she remained still.

"You've been watching me," he said, moving to stand beside her. Too close beside her. "See something you like?"

She kept her gaze resolutely forward. "Not really."

He tapped a fist to his chest. "I'm wounded!"

"I doubt it," she answered, allowing herself a single sideways glance.

"Everyone else seems to find me amusing. Why not you?"

"Does it matter?"

He cocked his head and then turned to stare straight ahead. "I don't suppose it does. Still, our paths will part soon. I'd like to think you'll remember me fondly."

Clarissa turned to meet his gaze. "I doubt I'll remember you at all. Good day, Mr. Pine."

She turned and walked into the cabin, intending to gather her belongings, but stopped just inside the door, out of Jeremy Pine's sight. Listening intently, she heard him slip away down the narrow passage along the outside of the cabin toward the deck where the helmsman kept a steady hand on the tiller.

What could he be doing there? The passengers had been asked to steer clear of that small deck. Cautiously, she followed, but from inside the cabin. When she reached the back of the sitting room, she paused and eased open the door to the small galley where the captain's wife prepared their meals. Pressing her face close to the narrow opening she surveyed the room...

...and saw Jeremy Pine standing on tip-toe and reaching deep into an upper cabinet. When he pulled his arm out, he was grasping a small tin box which he quickly stuffed inside his shirt. Turning, he sauntered toward the door where Clarissa stood.

Without attempting to close the door, she turned and raced into the room, dropping into a chair and grabbing a book from a nearby shelf just as he pushed the door wide and stepped through.

Seeing her, he stopped short, then smiled and said, "Fancy meeting you here, Miss Bainbridge. I thought we'd said our farewells."

She glanced at him, hoping her cheeks weren't too pink. They certainly felt hot enough to give her away her exertions. "Indeed. I believe we've already said all that is necessary." She returned her gaze to the book... and noticed she was holding it upside down. Her breath caught, but she forced herself not to right it.

"Well," he said, "we'll be docking soon, so I'll leave you to your reading." He walked calmly down the length of the sitting room, onto the forward deck, and out of her sight.

Clarissa sat still for a moment, waiting for her heart to stop racing. Then she stood and walked through the galley and onto the stern deck. The helmsman stood at the tiller, carefully watching the horses as they plodded along the towpath, pulling the packet ever closer to its dock and the end of their journey.

How had Pine gotten past the helmsman unseen?

Or had he?

Clarissa bit her lip, suddenly unsure of what she should do. She'd expected to tell the helmsman of Pine's theft, but if he had allowed Pine to enter the galley without challenging him...

"Is there something you need, Miss? You shouldn't be back here."

She started, her heart racing again. "I know. I'm sorry to bother you, but I need to see the captain."

"And why would you need to see me this close to docking?" a gruff voice asked from behind her.

Clarissa whirled and found herself face-to-face with the packet's captain. She glanced over her shoulder at the helmsman before saying quietly, "If I could have a moment of your time, Captain, I'd like to speak with you... privately."

The captain raised his eyebrows, but gestured her into the galley and then through to the sitting room. "Now, how can I help you, Miss Bainbridge?"

She hesitated a moment, then blurted out. "Mr. Pine stole something from the galley. A small tin box." She gestured with her hands to indicate its size. "I saw him reaching into an upper cabinet and removing it."

The captain's eyes widened. "When?"

"Just a few moments ago."

The man turned and strode into the galley, going directly to the cabinet Pine had rifled. Reaching inside, he felt around, then withdrew an empty hand. His shoulders slumped.

"Well," he growled, "at least we haven't docked yet." Turning he spied Clarissa and smiled grimly. "Thank you, Miss Bainbridge. I'll take it from here."

Recognizing his dismissal, Clarissa hurried back through the sitting room and onto the forward deck. Relieved to find an unoccupied chair, she dropped into it, adjusted her straw hat to better shade her eyes, and watched the plodding horses while she listened to the commotion on the upper deck.

Voices shouted, but for once she didn't even try to understand what was being said. She had played her part. Now it was time for others to do the same.

4

─────────

*C*larissa sat in a padded rocking chair on the wrap-around porch of the Endicott Hotel in Buffalo, New York sipping a cup of tea flavored with lemon and honey. Beside her, Mrs. Hargrove, a fellow passenger from the packet boat, practically bounced in her rocker.

"I can't believe you foiled a robbery," the woman said, her eyes round and her voice awed. "You must have been terrified! I know I would have been."

"Really, Mrs. Hargrove, it was nothing. I merely observed Mr. Pine doing something he oughtn't and reported it to the captain."

"But you were so calm," Mrs. Hargrove exclaimed. "My Henry was there on the upper deck when the captain apprehended the scoundrel, and he said that Mr. Pine said that he'd spoken to you only moments before and that he was sure he didn't know *what* you were on about." The woman paused to draw breath before continuing. "But the captain wouldn't hear anything against you and insisted on searching the man."

Clarissa took another sip of tea, resisting the temptation to speak in the opening Mrs. Hargrove had provided.

After taking a sip of her own tea, the woman continued. "And you know," she said, lowering her voice to a conspiratorial whisper, "when the search was done, Pine didn't have anything he oughtn't to. Well, my Henry thought it was all over, that you'd been mistaken and that Mr. Pine was innocent, but the Captain bellowed for the steward to take the tiller and the helmsman to come up."

"And?" asked Clarissa, curious now despite herself. She hadn't implicated the helmsman when she'd spoken to the captain.

"Well, my Henry says that's when everything went to... uhm... heck," Mrs. Hargrove said, her cheeks pinkening at the near slip of her tongue. "Evidently the helmsman jumped right into the canal, which is terribly muddy, and tried to make his way to shore. But the horseman left his team and waded in after him and the captain's son, who was helping the horseman, joined in and they caught him and dragged him back to the towpath."

Clarissa nodded. "Trying to get away simply confirmed his guilt."

"Yes," said Mrs. Hargrove. "He confessed and said it was all Mr. Pine's idea." She sat back, satisfied with the outcome. "My Henry says they're both locked up in the Buffalo jail right this minute." She paused before continuing dramatically. "And it's all thanks to you, Miss Bainbridge."

"Well," Clarissa said after another sip of tea. "I can't really take any credit. After all, I simply made an observation and reported it to the proper person."

"Perhaps," Mrs. Hargrove said, "but the captain says you can take passage on his packet boat anytime you like. That tin held all the money from all of our fares. The captain and his family would've been hard put to keep their boat if they'd lost it."

Clarissa sighed contentedly and took another sip of tea.

She'd saved a good man and his family... and had quite the adventure. And she hadn't even seen Niagara Falls yet!

Mother was never going to believe the story Clarissa's diary would tell.

PART IV

THE WHITE DRAGON AND THE RED

DEBBIE MUMFORD

BESTSELLING AUTHOR OF *SORCHA'S HEART*

The
White
Dragon
and the
Red

1

The floor of Edith's chamber was strewn with fresh, sweet-smelling rushes and a warm fire crackled on the hearth adding the scent of pine and a whiff of smoke to the air. Harold, her hand-fast husband of more than twenty years, sat before the fire wrapped in a soft woolen robe of royal purple. Edith had washed the battle grime from his limbs with her own hands, and now, as he leaned back in the sturdy wooden chair, she combed his long auburn hair.

Once his hair had shone like burnished copper, alive with golden lights, but now those lights had dimmed to pewter and the copper had faded and lost its sheen. Placing the carved wooden comb on a low side table, Edith dipped her fingers in a small silver bowl of mint-infused oil and began rubbing it into Harold's temples. She knew from long experience that the pressure and motion of her fingers combined with the soothing odor of the mint would ease a headache and help her lord find restful sleep.

How many times had she performed such ministrations for this man? After how many battles had she eased his pain and helped calm his mind? Too many to count, and yet, she treasured the memories, and the knowledge that she had been a good wife to this powerful man.

She had been so young when her father had given her in hand-fast marriage to the newly named Earl of East Anglia. Harold had been in his mid-twenties, tall and handsome and battle-tested. A warrior of renown. She hadn't been loath to marry, but neither had she known the man.

Fortunately, she had found joy in their union.

And now, twenty years and six healthy, well-grown children later, she still loved her husband... and knew that he cherished her as well.

But Harold was no longer simply an earl. He was now King of All England, and beset by many foes. He had need of all the support he could find, especially from the powerful church whose archbishop had placed the crown upon his head. The same church that refused to recognize Edith as his lawful wife, had instead named her harlot.

Harold had been forced by the Dead God's church to take another wife, the widow of the King of Wales. Edith knew that this new marriage was one of political convenience, but that knowledge did nothing to bank the fires of outrage that burned in her soul.

Twenty years.

Six fine children, including three sons.

But instead of being Harold's queen, she was known as his mistress. His whore.

Still, after his defeat of the Norwegian king, Harald Hardrada, at the Battle of Stamford Bridge, Harold had returned to her, his hand-fast wife, not his pretty little Welsh queen.

Edith would always be the one Harold turned to, no matter what the Dead God's church demanded.

2

E dith woke to find Harold already dressed in a belted chainmail top over a rust colored tunic, his leggings and boots wrapped securely in place with leather thongs. A warm woolen cloak, pointed metal helmet and a sturdy, round shield of leather-covered linden wood waited beside the door.

"My lord," she exclaimed, "where are you going? You've only just returned from battle. You should be resting still."

He turned to face her, his expression grim. "Aye. 'Twas what I expected as well, but though I've defeated one foreign claimant to my throne, another threatens our shores. William the Bastard's ships have been sighted off Pevensey Bay. I must march south."

Edith swallowed her fear and forced her voice to calm. "But my lord, what of your men? Your housecarls and thegns sustained heavy damage against the Norsemen. Can they fight again so soon?"

Harold strode to the bed, took her face in his hands, and kissed her gently on the lips.

"They must," he said. "We must drive William back to Normandy." And turning, he strode from the room.

Edith sat alone in the large bed as fear curled in her belly and an ominous *knowing* bloomed in her mind.

He would die.

Her husband, her lord, her king.

Harold would die.

Closing her eyes and steeling her will, she made her choice. He would *not* die. She would protect him, and she would align herself with his pretty little Welsh queen to ensure that he did not meet his death in the coming battle.

What would it matter which of them was acknowledged Queen of England if the Bastard killed their King?

Ealdgyth, daughter of Aelfgar, widow of Gruffydd ap Llywe-lyn, wife of King Harold II would join Edith in the battle for their husband's life... or Edith would know the reason why.

3

---

*E*dith dressed quickly in her favorite deep blue tunic and fastened a rose mantle about her shoulders. She left the hood down, but braided her long dark hair and fastened the curling tendrils that escaped away from her face with a slender silver circlet. Her hair might no longer shine as it did in her youth, but it was still thick and dark.

When she was ready, she wrapped herself in a warm, fleece lined cloak and left the bower she had shared with Harold in the castle set aside for his use in York. Moving quietly through the unfamiliar passageways, she found her way up a stone staircase to a chilly tower. Heaving open a heavy wooden door, she stepped out onto the encircling walkway and leaned against the cold stone parapet.

Closing her eyes and opening her mind, she called to the White Dragon, the protector of the Midlands where she had grown to young womanhood. Never before had she sought the dragon's intervention in her husband's battles, but never before had he been threatened by a foreign duke when his own forces were weakened and battle-weary.

Great Wyrm, Wyvern of the low hills and gentle valleys of my birth, hear me now.

Edith poured all the belief and supplication of her early training into her prayer. Her mother, Matilda, had been a wise woman and an initiate into the mysteries before she had been given in marriage to Edith's father. Matilda had taught her daughters well, and though Edith had never had cause to call upon the White Dragon before, she knew with a certainty beyond mere faith, that the Great Wyrm would hear her.

Sure enough, a voice pealed through her mind. A sending so powerful she was forced to her knees and had to press her hands against her ears. The sound was within, to be sure, but she needed the outside pressure to keep the balance within her skull and forestall the faint that edged her vision with darkness.

Edith, daughter of Matilda, I hear your call and recognize your right of birth to petition my aid. What would you ask?

Even when he stopped speaking, his voice echoed like an avalanche of stones against her tender mind. When she felt sufficiently recovered, she responded, though she feared their conversation might cause her death.

If she died in this supplication, so be it. Harold must live.

Inhaling deeply she framed her request and sent it winging to the great White Dragon.

Harold, King of All England and the father of my sons and daughters, is in grave danger. He rides south to Pevensey Bay to fight against William the Bastard, Duke of Normandy. I ask that you protect Harold, Great One, and the men he leads into battle.

A strange prickling invaded her mind. Not painful, but unexpected and foreign. She braced for the pain his next words would bring.

What are the battles of men to me, little one? I care not which humans crawl along the earth in my domain.

Edith breathed a sigh of relief. He had moderated his sending. This time his voice soothed and warmed the edges of her mind, healing the hurts of his earlier message.

Her relief fled when his meaning registered.

But Great One, the Normans will not know you! They will not honor you as your deserve.

A soft, chiding sigh blew through her thoughts like a gentle breeze. *When have you honored me, daughter of Matilda? Have you thought of me even once since leaving your mother's domain?*

Shame overwhelmed her. The wyrm had the truth of it. What right did she have to ask his aid when she'd given him no thought, no honor, in the twenty years of her marriage. Only in her extreme need did she think of him now, and then only to seek his aid.

Forgive me, Great One.

A puff of solace touched her thoughts, followed quickly by a surge of ire.

You have betrayed me, daughter of Matilda, the dragon growled. *I see the shadow of another dragon in your mind. A great red beast with four legs as well as wings. Not a proper wyvern such as I!*

Edith shrank back against the stone parapet, her heart hammering in reaction to the dragon's clear wrath. What was he talking about? She'd had no thoughts of…

But she had. She had thought to seek Ealdgyth's aid in contacting the Red Dragon of Wales.

When her pulse rate slowed and she felt in control of herself again, she answered the White Dragon of the Midlands.

Nay, Great One. I know no other dragons, nor have I ever thought to seek congress with any save yourself. The red dragon you see in my thoughts belongs to Wales.

And what have you to do with Wales, little one?

Nothing, Great One, but my husband has another wife—do not ask me to explain, the ways of men are convoluted, especially where the Dead God's servants are concerned. This other wife was once married to the King of Wales, before he was killed in battle.

And what has that to do with me?

Edith closed her eyes and inhaled a deep, calming breath. Since she and I are both bound to Harold, I hoped she might seek the aid of the Red Dragon of Wales. She paused a moment before hurrying on, Tell me, Great One, if she made this request, would you join Wales to protect England's king?

A deep, rumbling grumble sounded in her mind and she made herself as small as possible as she huddled on the battlement. She had gone too far, suggesting that the mighty White Dragon might require the help of the Red Dragon of Wales. He would blast her mind to nothingness. Her children would find her crouched here, a drooling, helpless lump of flesh that had once housed their mother.

A shadow fell across Edith, and she opened her eyes to see a white dragon hanging suspended in the sky just beyond the parapet.

Come, little one. If you are so desperate for your lord's life that you would seek the aid of the woman who has supplanted you, I can hardly fail to grant your petition. Climb onto my back. I will carry you to your sister-wife.

Relief surged through Edith's heart and hope blossomed. Ealdgyth could hardly deny her if she arrived on the wings of a dragon!

4

----

*E*dith sat astride the White Dragon of the Midlands, secure in her position between two pointed spines taller than her seated height. Her booted feet were tucked beneath the dragon's wing joints, and she was very glad of her fleece lined cloak. She hadn't thought to wear gloves when she'd left York a-dragonback, but Ealdgyth had gifted her a fine, fur-lined leather pair before the two women left the castle in London.

She glanced to the west across the early October sky to see her sister-wife firmly settled between the neck ridges of a great red dragon. Wales had not failed to answer Ealdgyth's call. If the White Dragon would fight for Harold and England, then the Red would not be left behind.

The two dragons and their riders circled the skies above Hastings, observing the battle that raged below. The dragons had promised Edith and Ealdgyth they would defend Harold and his men, but only in extreme need. If men could win the battle on their own, they should do so.

From high above, Edith watched as her husband commanded his men. His army had marched more than 240 miles to intercept William's forces on the Sussex coast. Nearly 7,000 Normans stood against the weary Englishmen, but Harold's men stood firm behind hastily erected earthworks and prepared to employ their well-practiced shield wall, unaware that supernatural aid circled in the sky above their heads.

The armies were well matched, despite the forced march Harold's troops had endured, and the battle raged from early morning until well into the evening. The White and Red dragons withheld their aid until William's forces feigned flight, causing Harold's shield wall to break formation. When the Norman's turned and loosed a hail of arrows against the English, the dragons joined the fray.

They swept the arrows from the sky before buffeting the combatants with the wind from their wings, leaving none on their feet, on either side of the battle. Landing between the armies with a great bellowing roar, the Red Dragon of Wales scorched a line of fire into the land before William's men, while the White Dragon of the Midlands hung in the sky above the red's head.

As agreed in advance, the White Dragon spoke, and his words echoed across the field causing all men to cower.

"Invaders from across the sea," he boomed, "leave this land. The throne of England is for those who have grown here and love this land. It is not for the likes of you. Be gone from our shores."

"Be gone!" echoed the Red Dragon with growling menace.

William's men dropped their weapons and scattered, too anxious to find their ships to worry about carrying swords or spears.

The White Dragon turned to Harold's army. "Fear not, the White Dragon of the Midlands and the Red Dragon of Wales have come to ensure King Harold's victory. Return to your homes and live in peace, knowing that should the need arise, we will fly to your aid once more."

"But only we are given proper honor," added the Red Dragon. "And only if called upon by those who hold the right by blood."

The two dragons cleared a space on the battlefield and deposited their riders gently on the blood-soaked ground. Before departing, they allowed each woman to place a hand on their heads and bestowed a benediction on the sister-wives.

When the dragons were mere specks in the sky, Harold stepped forward to stand before his wives. "How is this possible?" he asked as his men milled around gathering their belongings and slapping each other on their backs. "How came you to bring dragons to the battle?"

Ealdgyth smiled and, placing a hand on his cheek, kissed him gently. "Ask Edith, your first wife." Then she turned to Edith and curtsied. "The Dead God's priests do not rule me, sister-wife. I am honored to be second to you in Harold's household. If it pleases our lord, bring your children and join our household in London. I would learn from you, Edith the Fair."

Edith inclined her head and responded solemnly. "Thank you, Queen Ealdgyth. I will discuss our future and our lodging with our lord and king." Turning to Harold, she threw her arms about his neck and whispered, "You are safe!"

Harold kissed her soundly, then stepped back and said, "Come, Edith. Tell me the tale of how you and Ealdgyth brought the White Dragon and the Red to the Battle of Hastings."

"Gladly," she said, taking his hand, content to *know* that she and Ealdgyth and the Great Dragons had changed the course of English history.

PART V

THE CAT LADY OF YELLOWSTONE

DEBBIE MUMFORD

BESTSELLING AUTHOR OF *SORCHA'S HEART*

The Cat Lady of Yellowstone

SPUN YARNS
A *Supernatural Yellowstone* Story

1

The world as we knew it ended on a Friday afternoon in July, during the height of tourist season. But since we live off the grid in a secluded mountain valley in Yellowstone National Park, we weren't aware of the devastation until Sunday morning.

Our homestead consisted of two log cabins, built of native pine logs of varying sizes with chinking made from local clay, sand, and good old Yellowstone mud. Both homes rested on thick foundations of large river rocks. The roofs were shake-shingled and the chimneys were also fashioned from smooth, rounded river rocks. A wide porch fronted the original cabin, and boasted a matching pair of log chairs. A wrap-around porch graced the newer cabin, built when Jason and I married. We had a sturdy porch swing on the front and two willow rockers on the side facing the forest.

A paddock in the back abutted a sturdy shelter for our horses, and a weathered barn with long, low rooflines stood guard over the rest of our livestock: six goats, a dozen chickens, and a few ducks. We'd had cows and pigs at one point, but had lost them to predators and hadn't yet replaced them.

Our gardens were in full bloom. A herb garden outside the kitchen door of the original cabin lent gentle fragrances of rosemary, thyme, and oregano to the sweetness of the flower beds lining the walkways between the cabins. A large vegetable garden teemed with life. Squash, beans, and potatoes crowded up against tomatoes, carrots, lettuce, and celery, while asparagus and marigolds guarded the borders.

On that fateful Sunday, Jason and I saddled our favorite horses and made the two hour ride from our home near Mary Lake on Yellowstone's Central Plateau to the Visitor Center at Fishing Bridge on the north shore of Yellowstone Lake. We had made this ride every Sunday since our daughter, Ruth, left home to study veterinary medicine at Colorado State University. Now that she had taken a job at the Denver Zoo, the tradition continued.

Thanks to long years of friendship between my family and the park rangers, we were allowed to use the computer equipment at the Visitor Center for a video call with Ruth on Sunday mornings; our only form of communication with our daughter.

As I said, our homestead was off the grid. We had no modern conveniences: no phones, computers, television, or any other form of electrical appliances. But we had everything we needed. And thanks the generosity of Yellowstone National Park, we had weekly contact with Ruth.

Maybe I should tell you a little about how we came to live in Yellowstone, but not be employees of the park service.

My family, as well as a few others, have lived in what is now known as Yellowstone National Park since before recorded history. When men of European descent first came to this region, we simply melted into the forests. They were unaware of our existence.

The local tribes, the Crow, Blackfeet, Shoshone, and

Bannocks, knew of us... and feared us. They considered us demons and avoided our lands.

But when Yellowstone became the first National Park, our forefathers came out of the wilds and *persuaded* the authorities to grant us our homesteads, to *grandfather* us in, as it were. It is well that the authorities acceded to their wishes; the park would not exist otherwise.

You see, the tribes were correct when they named us demons. Those of my bloodline, and of the lines of the other families included in that arrangement, are not strictly human.

We are a supernatural community that calls the Yellowstone region home... and protects it ferociously. Our unusual abilities have been fed for generations by ley lines of magical power that coalesce and knot in and around Yellowstone's geothermal features. Just as the region is unique in geophysical terms, it is also unique magically.

The women in my family form lifelong psychic bonds with animals. My bond-mate is a cougar known as Faithful Huntress, or Faith. My mother formed a bond with grizzly bear named Zell. So far, Ruth had avoided forming a bond. She wanted to leave the valley and go to university. Someday she'll return, and when she does, she will form a permanent bond.

Other families have different abilities. The men of the Jacobs clan are shifters, *skin walkers* in the old vernacular. My dad's rival for Mom's affection, Kam Jacobs, shifted into a black wolf and played alpha to a pack of normal gray wolves. Kam's jealousy forced Mom to reveal our nature to Dad prematurely, but... well, I'm living proof that their tale ended well.

Anyway, on that Sunday morning when we reached the populated area of the park near Fishing Bridge, we discovered that something had gone dreadfully wrong. The normal hustle and bustle of weekend tourist traffic was missing. Oh, we saw cars and trucks and SUVs, but none of them moved. The paved roads, the bridge over the Yellowstone River, looked like long, narrow parking lots. Ones where the vehicles had simply been abandoned.

We rode cautiously between the stranded cars, noting the people wandering dazed and aimless between the rental cottages and the beach. We reined our horses in, glancing at each other.

"Should we turn around?" I asked.

Jason nodded, his gaze sweeping the area. "Probably, but I'd like to know what's happening." His gaze returned to mine. "This is anything but normal."

"Agreed." I scanned the people, noting their interest in us... and our horses. "Let's go back to the forest and settle the horses. I'll ask Faith to guard them for us."

"Good idea. I wouldn't want to lose them," Jason said, turning his bay gelding, Sorkie, and moving back toward the tall timber, "especially to city folk who wouldn't know how to care for them."

My roan mare, Jezzie, followed with almost no prodding from me. While we ambled back to cover, I contacted my cougar. Like all bond animals, Faith was larger and stronger than others of her species. She was also exceptionally long-lived. We had bonded when I was just fifteen, more than thirty years ago. The usual life span of a cougar topped out at fifteen years, but Faith remained healthy and strong.

What do you require, She Who Walks With Strength and Grace.

A wave of love swept through me, and I smiled. Faith delighted in using the full form of my name. Everyone else just called me Grace. In fact, most people thought Grace *was* my full name.

We're near Fishing Bridge, I told her, *something is wrong and we need to investigate, but we don't want to leave the horses unguarded. Will you protect them?*

Of course, she said, her thoughts as calm and unruffled as a lake on a windless day. *I am not far. The forests and meadows are unusually quiet today, and the humans I have seen seem nervous and on edge.*

Thank you for coming. We have seen the same. We'd like to try to find out what's happening.

A few moments later, Faith appeared beside Jezzie. The two animals touched noses in greeting before Faith moved on to Sorkie. Our horses had long since accepted my cougar as part of the family. While another predator would spook them, Faith's scent caused no distress.

Jason and I dismounted and walked toward the visitor center, secure in the knowledge that Faith wouldn't allow anyone to approach Jezzie and Sorkie. Before we reached the bridge—the visitor center lay on the far side—we found David Andresson, a long-time park ranger and a friend.

"David," Jason said, extending his hand.

"Jason," David replied, shaking my husband's hand. "Grace. I was wondering if you two would venture down today."

As he spoke, he led us into a sheltered spot near the bridge abutment.

"Why wouldn't we?" I asked, puzzled.

David studied my face before nodding. "That's right," he said. "You're place is off the grid. You wouldn't have any way of knowing what's happened."

Jason shook his head. "No idea," he agreed, "but it's obvious something is wrong. Nothing is moving and from the sound of things, nothing mechanical is working."

He was right. We could hear the river singing and gentle waves lapping the shore of the lake. A buzz of voices reached our ears, but the hum of refrigeration units, air conditioners, motors, all the normal sounds of a populated area were missing.

"Whatever it was," David said, taking off his hat and wiping his forehead on his shirt sleeve, "happened on Friday afternoon. The first we knew was when all the lights went out in the Visitor Center. Gradually we've discovered that everything electrical ceased to function at the same time." He leaned closer, as if to avoid being overheard, though no one was near us. "Management thinks we've suffered an EMP." He caught our uncomprehending expressions and clarified, "Electromagnetic pulse. Knocks out technology."

"Oh," I said, stupidly.

"And that made the cars quit?" Jason asked.

David nodded. "Everything with computer chips and electrical starting systems. There are a few old, purely mechanical pick-ups around the park, but most of those are in disrepair. Still, we're trying to get them running. We've got tourists stranded in bear country. We need to get as many as we can find into the bigger park enclaves: Mammoth, Canyon, Old Faithful, here at Lake. Even Madison and Roosevelt will be packed."

"How can we help?" Jason asked.

David replaced his hat, tapping it firmly in place. "Head on back to your place. If you find stragglers, bring them down to us. I don't have any idea how long this outage will last, but we've got a good supply of food, fresh water, and we can cram people tight into the lodge and rental cabins. We'll hold out until help arrives."

"We can do that," I said, while David and Jason shook hands. "Good luck."

As Jason and I trudged back to our horses, I said, "I wonder if the outage extends all the way to Denver?"

Jason put an arm around my shoulders as we stepped beneath the trees. "I don't know, but Ruth is a smart girl, surrounded by animals she loves. She'll be fine."

"I wish we'd been able to talk to her," I murmured, my heart suddenly feeling very heavy. "I wish she was here with us, where Faith could keep an eye on her."

"I know," he said, squeezing my shoulders. "We're lucky to live where we do, to be as prepared as we are. We'll be fine."

I hoped he was right.

2

---

*D*avid's optimism was misplaced. No help arrived. No trucks or busses came to ferry tourists out of the park. No planes flew overhead to air-drop supplies into the over-crowded enclaves. Those who were able made their way out of the back country and down to the visitor centers. A few hardy souls shouldered backpacks and trekked out of the park and back to civilization.

David and the other rangers wished them well... and prayed that when they made it out, civilization would still exist.

Jason and Faith and I did what we could. Jason guided stragglers off the plateau and down to the rangers. Faith and I hunted, supplying David with game as often as we could.

At first, people were content to wait for the lights to come back on, for their cars to start, for life to return to normal. But when it became obvious that wasn't going to happen, and that the National Guard wasn't going to swoop in and rescue them, things got dicey.

Gangs formed.

The rangers did their best to establish strongholds and protect the non-violent from those who devolved into human predators, but they weren't trained or prepared for such circumstances.

Why would they be?

They were naturalists who, though they might be excellent marksmen, had never aimed at human targets. They were good men and women who wanted to do the right thing, and expected everyone else to play by the rules as well.

But the rules had changed, and the park service personnel needed to change as well.

Some were able to make the transition. Some weren't.

Good people died, both rangers and tourists.

Too many ruthless people survived.

On his last trip to Fishing Bridge, Jason led a family of five to what he still thought was the safety of the Visitor Center. Unfortunately, David and his charges had been overwhelmed by a group of desperate men who had allowed their savage natures to get the upper hand.

My husband, Ruth's father, died defending the family he had shepherded out of the wilderness.

The world as men knew it may have ended on a Friday in July, but my world ended on the Tuesday in September when Faith's cougar kin reported the slaughter of my husband and the people he'd been trying to save.

_____

A month after David's murder, Faith pushed me out of bed. I landed in a heap of filthy linens on a wooden floor littered with discarded clothes, dirty dishes, and dust bunnies the size of baseballs.

Enough, Faith growled. *Jason is dead. You are not. Bestir yourself and act like a woman again.*

My eyes filled with tears at her callous mention of Jason's name. "You don't understand."

She sat on her haunches before me as I struggled upright, pushing strings of matted hair out of my eyes and behind my ears. Cocking her head, she gazed into my eyes.

I do not understand death? she asked. *I, who deal it out to prey with regularity? Who has fed you this last month? Who fed the people David protected for months before that?*

"Not the same thing," I said, shaking my head and pulling the dirty sheets closer around my shoulders. "Jason is dead. My mate. The only man I've ever loved. How would you feel if I died?"

I would follow you into the summer country, she purred, *for it is only my bond with you that holds me in this world.*

I stared at her. Faith had never spoken to me of her belief in what lies beyond this life.

You are my world, She Who Walks With Strength and Grace, but there is more to your world than just me. You must get up and live. For Ruth. For me. For the youngling my kin herded to this cabin. She needs your protection.

"A youngling," I cried. "What youngling?"

A child's face appeared at the edge of my bedroom door. "Are you talking to me?"

A little girl, no more than eight, stepped into view, eyeing Faith warily and glancing curiously at me. The child's hair was easily as dirty as mine. It might have been blonde, then again, it might have been a light brown. Her jeans were caked with mud and torn at the knees. Her tee shirt might have been pink once; now it was too stained with grass and dirt to be sure. The jeans jacket she wore was too lightweight for October in Yellowstone, and her sneakers were little better than nothing. She'd clearly been wearing that outfit for far too long.

I stood as quickly as I could, which wasn't very fast considered how tightly the sheets were wrapped around my legs.

"Who are you and where did you come from?" I asked, rather stupidly, clutching my sheet and stepping past Faith so that I stood between her and the child.

"I'm Lacey. Who are you?"

"I'm Grace. I live here."

She leaned sideways, trying to see around me to Faith.

"Why is that big cat in here?"

"She's a cougar and she lives here," I said. "Her name is Faith."

"You have a pet cougar?" she asked, her brown eyes widening. "That's weird."

"She's not a pet, she's my friend," I said, a bit too sharply. I closed my eyes, took a deep breath, exhaled completely, and tried again, making an effort to sound calm and friendly... like unknown children appeared in my filthy cabin every day. "You didn't tell me where you came from."

Her eyes clouded with tears and she bit her lower lip, sniffling.

"Never mind," I said, dropping my sheet and striding toward her. I held out my hand. "You can tell me later. Right now, let's get you something to eat."

After that, you should both take a bath, Faith murmured behind me. *You reek.*

I didn't turn around and stick out my tongue, but it was very tempting.

Between them, Faith and Lacey brought me back to life. Caring for the child gave me a purpose again.

By the time we'd eaten, bathed, picked up and washed all the dirty dishes, and generally made the cabin livable again, I was feeling almost normal.

"Come along, Lacey," I said. "You can't wear that old tee forever."

After her bath, I'd pulled one of Jason's tee shirts over her head. It hit her mid-calf and the neckline threatened to fall off her shoulders. Totally unacceptable for long-term use, but her clothes were unsalvageable rags. No point in even washing them. Fortunately, I had options.

"Where are we going?" she asked, grabbing my hand and holding it tightly. "There are bad men out there."

I glanced at her. She was shaking so hard my arm tingled. Poor little mite. She still hadn't told me her story, but that would come.

"Just to the other cabin," I said, reassuringly, "and Faith will protect us. She might purr for you and me, but she can be ferocious if she needs to."

Lacey nodded and followed me onto the porch. I hesitated,

then swung her up into my arms for the short walk to what had been my parents' cabin. The child was barefoot, and while we didn't have snow yet, the stone path would be freezing beneath her little feet.

"Ready? Here we go!" I raced across the porch, down the steps, over the path, and up onto the older cabin's porch.

Lacey giggled as I deposited her onto her own two feet again. "That was fun!" Her face shone, and I wondered how long it had been since she'd had reason to smile.

I pushed the door open and ushered her inside. The house was cold, having been unoccupied since my mother died two years ago. Jason and I had made a point of keeping it clean and pest free, but no fire had been lit in the hearth in the month since his death. He'd laid a fire the morning he'd taken the family to Fishing Bridge, but I'd never struck the match.

I did so now.

Lacey huddled on the hearth rug in her inadequate tee shirt, waiting for the flames to warm the room. Faith laid down behind her, providing a back rest and additional warmth. To my surprise, the little girl leaned back into the big cat, accepting the offering of friendship and security.

She likes you, I said to Faith alone.

Of course, my cougar purred in reply. *I am very likable... and trustworthy.* After a moment, she met my gaze. *She reminds of Ruth, when she was a kitten. It is good that my kin brought her here.*

I nodded. "Stay with Faith, Lacey. I'll just be in the other room, rummaging around in some old boxes."

The child nodded, then curled up on the rug beside the cougar and closed her eyes. The poor little thing was undoubtedly exhausted. I'd had a month of nothing but rest... if existing in a dazed stupor can be said to be restful... and the morning's activity had tired me out. No telling how long it had been since the little girl had been fed and warm and safe enough to sleep soundly.

Faith would protect her. Time to get on with my search. I strode down the hall to what had once been my bedroom. The double wedding ring quilt on the queen-size log bed was dusty, but the room was as neat as it had been since Jason and I had moved into the second cabin. Hurrying to the closet, I unstacked boxes of out-of-season and outgrown clothing. The boxes were neatly labeled in magic marker, so I had no trouble finding the clothes I'd set aside from Ruth's childhood. I also found a box of toys. Rag dolls my mother had made, little cars and trains Dad had carved from bits of deadwood, and some wooden puzzles and games that dated to Mom's childhood.

Returning to the living room with my treasures, I found Lacey still fast asleep, Faith purring beside her. I rummaged through the first box of clothes, found a pair of underwear, jeans and a long-sleeved red plaid flannel shirt that I judged would fit, then opened other boxes until I had socks, boots, and a down jacket as well.

Hefting a couple of boxes, I headed for the door. *I'm going to take all this stuff home,* I told Faith. *Call me if she wakes.*

I will do so.

After several trips between the cabins, I not only had everything transferred, I also had Ruth's bedroom set up for Lacey. The bedding had been aired, clothes tucked away in the chest of drawers Dad had built for my daughter, and toys lovingly stowed in the toy chest. One calico bear, a favorite of Ruth's, rested on the pillow, ready to be snuggled by a little girl who'd lived through too much, too young.

Pleased with my progress, and more at ease in my skin than I'd been since... well, best not to think about that just now... I returned to my parents' cabin to wake Lacey and help her dress.

4

—————

*O*ur homestead soon became an orphanage of sorts.

Faith informed me that her cougar kin and Zell's grizzly kin reported many children wandering lost and alone in the back country.

Many had lost their parents to marauding gangs looking to rape and steal, others were orphaned through accident or attacks from predators not part of Faith and Zell's network. For though Zell had died when my mother did, her kin remembered our family as part of their own and continued to watch over our homestead.

Through the efforts of the cougars and grizzlies who claimed us, children appeared at the border where our homestead met the forest. Some were old enough to expect death from the large predators who herded them, and arrived terrified. Others were too young to walk the distance and were carried by their clothing, as if they were cubs or kittens.

However they arrived, Faith and Lacey and I welcomed them.

That first winter was hard. I'd been in deep mourning when I should have been harvesting and storing vegetables from the garden. By the time Lacey arrived to bring me back to reality, the garden was suffering. We managed to salvage a good amount of the produce, but not as much as we should have harvested. Fortunately, my family had been putting food by for years. Our pantry and root cellar were well stocked... even with all the extra mouths to feed, we would make it through the winter.

We were far better off than most.

The deep snows of December put an end to new children arriving. The bears were in hibernation, and the cougars no longer found living children. Our population stabilized at twenty-four: one adult, twenty-two children, and one cougar.

Besides being traumatized by events since that fateful Friday, our little tribe had some communication issues. Yellowstone had been an international vacation destination. Tourists came from all over the world... and so did the children who appeared at the homestead. Not all of them spoke English, but they all responded to food, warmth, and kindness.

Fortunately, a few of the kids were old enough to be of help. Lacey, though only nine, was serious beyond her years. Hiding under a bush while big, strong men beat your father to death and raped and murdered your mother will do that to a child.

Sam was our eldest at thirteen. He'd managed to save not only himself, but his ten-year-old brother, Jessie. Jamie and Ellen were twelve and a huge help with the younger children, as were Davey, Lynn, and Robbie, our eleven-year-olds.

The rest of our tribe ranged from nine to... well, I had no idea how old Caleb was. He was our baby, and I guessed he was around eighteen months. No name, of course. I'd dubbed him Caleb.

He was the last to arrive, just before Christmas. One of Faith's cougar-kin brought him in, a large male, who was unwilling to release the child.

Grace, Faith called, her mind-voice less calm than was usual. *Join us.*

I dropped the sheets I was folding and scanned the room for one of the older children. Spotting a dark-haired girl, I said, "Ellen, I have to go out for a minute. You're in charge."

The pretty little brunette glanced up, met my gaze, and nodded solemnly. All of these children were solemn. I wondered if they would ever be anything else?

Shrugging into my down jacket and pulling a knit cap over my ears, I stepped outside and looked around until I found my cougar. Faith sat at the edge of the forest on the far side of my parents' cabin. Another cougar, almost as large as Faith paced just beyond a dark bundle in the snow.

The bundle moved.

I ran to join them, slowing my pace before I arrived to avoid alarming the big cat.

My kin-brother has brought us another child, Faith said, as I stopped beside her, *but he wishes for assurances.*

I met the strange cougar's gaze, trying to ignore the child moving lethargically between us. *What is your request?*

This human is small and weak, he answered, *and I have kittens to feed. If the prey fails to live, I claim the meat.*

I inhaled sharply. I'd never liked thinking of humans as prey, but our world had changed, and the cougars had been incredibly helpful to all of us. I glanced at the child and my heart lurched. He was so tiny... at least I thought it was a boy. Too young to speak. Starving and dehydrated, the baby was too weak to even cry. I had to get him into the house and care for him.

I met the male cougar's gaze once more and nodded. *I accept your terms. If this small one dies, Faith will bring the carcass to your den.* I looked at Faith. *If she agrees.*

My cougar closed her beautiful tawny eyes, then opened

them slowly. *It is agreed. If this one lives, I will help you find other meat for your kittens.*

Very well. I leave this small one with you. And he melted into the snowy forest.

5

We survived the winter. All of us. Even Caleb.

When I first carried Caleb into the cabin, I'd despaired of saving him. His little belly was bloated and distended, his arms and legs little more than fragile sticks. He showed no interest in sucking the rag I'd dipped in warm water, and his eyes were crusted closed. Sam and Lacey milked one of the goats, while Ellen and I bathed him and swaddled him in soft flannel. Warm and dry and cuddled close, he suckled earnestly when I put the milk soaked rag to his lips. He'd turned the corner. The baby had decided to live.

After that, he improved rapidly. I kept him close, wearing him wrapped close to my heart while I tended to the other children and the myriad chores of keeping our homestead running. Before the winter was over, Caleb was toddling around the cabin with the other little ones.

Faith kept her promise to her cougar kin. She hunted for us weekly, but also made time to help her cousins keep their families fed.

I worried that we'd be vulnerable when the snows melted. While the winter had been hard, spring and summer would present a danger the snow had prevented: attack by roving gangs of desperate men.

The homestead was well supplied with rifles and ammunition, and I was an excellent shot. But I was only one woman, and I couldn't afford to waste ammunition teaching Sam or Ellen or Jamie to shoot.

Rather than worry the children, I shared my thoughts with Faith... and found her unconcerned.

You worry needlessly, she told me when I expressed my concern.

Needlessly? I was shocked by her seeming indifference. *Have you forgotten how Jason died? We have twenty-two children to protect!*

She stuck a back leg in the air and licked herself. I closed my eyes in exasperation.

I forget nothing, she purred. *You forget who and where you are. Excuse me!*

She sat up on her haunches, wrapped her tail around her feet, and gazed into my eyes. *You are bound to me. Your mother was bound to Zell, a grizzly bear. Her mother before her was bound to Arend, a golden eagle. You live on the land your ancestors have occupied since time began. All the clans who have ever been bonded to your family guard this homestead.*

She switched her tail in irritation.

Did you think we, who have benefitted from your people's protection for generations, would abandon you in your time of need?

Tears filled my eyes and I swiped them away. *Forgive me. I did not mean to insult you and your kin and all the others who have protected my family through the ages. I didn't think.*

She flopped onto her belly and rested her head in my lap. *Of course you didn't. Who could be expected to think with all these kittens underfoot? That is why I am here.*

Love and relief filled my heart... and I laughed. For the first time in many weeks.

Spring slid into summer bringing warm days filled with sunshine and cloudless skies. The children ran around the meadow jumping and chasing and playing games only they understood. I watched them with quiet pride. They were survivors, yes, but better still, they were remembering what it was to be children. And Faith and I, and the animals who had brought them here, had made that possible.

I wished Jason were here to see what we had accomplished. He would have loved seeing the homestead filled with life.

I wished Ruth were here, safe on the land of her ancestors. I prayed that wherever she was, she was safe... and as happy as my little charges.

I put away my longing for my lost loved ones. There was work to be done. Always.

Calling the children together, I laid out my plan. Now that warm weather had arrived we had no need to huddle together in one cabin. It was time to make use of both of our homes. Sam and Jamie would be in charge of my parents' cabin and the boys who would occupy it.

Privately, I shuddered at the thought of the damage a dozen little boys could do to the building, but we needed the space and there was only one of me. Besides, these weren't normal little boys. These were boys who had survived terrors and truly appreciated the warmth and security the homestead provided.

The nine girls and I would remain in the cabin Jason and Ruth and I had made our own. Caleb would also stay with me.

We divvied up the tasks and went to work cleaning the cabin that had stood unused through the winter, assigning personal space to each inhabitant in both cabins, and moving meager belongings into place.

Once everything was in place, we held a family council and

reviewed work assignments for the maintenance of our home. Sam took notes, and when everything was decided, he and Ellen made charts to hang in their respective cabins.

Our tribe was not only organized, we were, if not exactly happy, content.

I was working in the vegetable garden with Robbie, Lacey, Kamiko, and Sven, when Faith yowled a warning. I dropped my hoe and raced to the front of the cabin.

What? I cried to her. *What's wrong?*

Strangers! she yowled, her vocal cry melding with her mind voice. *A strange cat approaches. One whose kind I don't recognize. And a human comes with the cat!*

I stopped dead, scanning the trail leading to the cabins. At the edge of the forest, a single figure approached. A big cat accompanied the person. A very unhappy cat judging by its slink, the closeness of its belly to the ground.

Children crowded around me, alerted by Faith's yowl. I waved them back.

"Go inside," I said firmly. "Stay out of sight until I know what we're dealing with."

They melted away without argument, though I was aware of somber eyes watching from the cabins' windows.

Who is it? I asked my cougar. *Why did the guardians allow this person to pass?*

Faith didn't answer. She paced back and forth across the trail a few yards in front of me, tail switching, a low growl emanating from her throat. She was far more concerned with the unknown cat than with the human that accompanied it.

Suddenly, Faith froze. Nose in the air, ears pricked forward. She screamed and raced toward the strangers, her lean body low and sleek.

My mind overflowed with her joy!

She's home! She Who Loves with Purity and Truth is home!

I gasped, unable to catch my breath. My knees threatened to buckle, but I refused to allow it. I needed them to function. I needed to run!

My daughter was home! Against all odds, and who knew what hardships, Ruth had made it home from Denver.

Ruth, who my cougar had just announced using her full name.

She saw me coming and ran to meet me. We met in the middle of the trail with an impact that would've knocked us off our feet if we hadn't grabbed each other and hugged tightly.

I closed my eyes and wept, holding my precious daughter in my arms.

"You made it," I cried. "You're home."

"Oh, Mom," she whispered. "I never thought I'd see you and Dad again."

My throat closed, too choked by joy and grief to allow speech. Time enough to tell of Jason. Right now, I savored the fact that Ruth was safe in my arms.

At last, we broke our hold and gazed, grinning, into each other's tear-filled eyes. I looked past her to the strange cat. She looked beyond me to the children now lining the cabins' porches.

"Who..." we both said at the same time, then burst out laughing.

Faith purred and rubbed Ruth's leg. She reached down absently and scratched my cougar behind the ears.

The other cat growled.

"Hush, Snowball," Ruth said aloud, for my benefit. She turned to the big cat and said, "This is Faith. She's bonded to my mother and helped raise me. You will treat her with respect." Turning her gaze on Faith, she continued, "Faith, this is my bond-mate, Lady of Ice and Snow. You may call her Snowball.

She is still young and has had no cat to teach her. Will you guide her?"

Faith purred her assent and asked, *What manner of cat is my new sister?*

"You've formed a bond," I said quietly, pride filling my heart. Then, more loudly, "Faith wants to know Snowball's breed. Is she a snow leopard?"

Ruth nodded. "She was one of my charges at the zoo. When the EMP hit, everything was chaos. Her mother was killed. I managed to save her... and we formed a bond in the process." She stroked Snowball's sleek head, and the black and white cat closed her eyes and purred. "She's saved my life more times than I can count on our journey home."

The children were leaving the safety of the porches, sidling by twos and threes closer and closer to us. Ruth cocked her head and nodded in their direction.

"Looks like you've had adventures too."

I laughed. "That's an understatement. Let's go inside." I gestured for the children to join us. "Come on, everyone," I called. "I want you to meet my daughter, Ruth, and her friend Snowball."

They started forward, but stopped, all eyes on the snow leopard.

Ruth turned to me. "They're used to Faith, right?"

I nodded.

"It's all right," Ruth said encouragingly. "Snowball is like Faith. She won't hurt you, but please don't crowd her. She'll want to meet you one at a time."

And so, nearly a year after the end of the world, our tribe increased by two. We were now two adults, twenty-two children, a cougar, and a snow leopard. All protected by the wildlife of Yellowstone.

PART VI

THE WEDDING CAKE

UNCOLLECTED ANTHOLOGY

MAGICAL ARTS

ISSUE 26 — UA — DECEMBER 2021

THE WEDDING CAKE

DEBBIE MUMFORD

1

---

*S*ally Ann Grainger admired the spectacular cake she'd just finished decorating for her best friend's wedding. Sally had baked the three tier cake from scratch using only the freshest ingredients and imbuing the batter with her finest spells for health, happiness, and enduring love—though she'd been careful to limit the love spell to Amy and her soon-to-be husband Aaron. No need to include all the guests who would enjoy a slice of cake in that particular incantation!

And now the glorious confection was complete. Three tiers of rich, layered spice cake, iced smooth in almond buttercream frosting and decorated with sprays of fresh and fondant flowers cascading from the top tier. In deference to the fall season, Sally had tinted the frosting a pale peach and chosen fall blooms in vibrant reds, yellows, and oranges. Her fondant rosebuds were perfect and the marzipan leaves added an elegant finishing touch. Truly, Amy's wedding cake was a testament to Sally's skills, both as a baker and as a kitchen witch.

Sally Ann's magic was homey and comforting. She was a wizard in the kitchen. Her soufflés never fell. Her pies always had perfect, flaky crusts. Her bread rose consistently and the crust browned beautifully. And her soups and stews? Nourishing and healthful. Perfectly spiced and able to drive out the common cold with a single bowl.

Her pickles and preserves would have astounded judges at the county fair. If Sally Ann canned it, the jars sparkled and the contents glowed with color. Why, her pickled beets practically begged to be tasted! Not that Sally Ann would ever enter a cooking contest of any sort. It wouldn't be fair to the non-magical participants.

But Amy's wedding cake was another matter; it would be seen and appreciated by guests young and old. And all that was left for her to do was to deliver her masterpiece safely to the church, a mere six blocks away.

She was in the middle of casting a temporary protective spell over her creation, to ensure its safe transportation, when her doorbell rang. Momentarily distracted, she completed her incantation, wiped her hands on her apron and hurried to answer the door.

Pausing just a moment to catch her breath, Sally Ann swung the heavy, carved oak door wide and grinned at her visitors.

"I might have known," she said with a laugh, then hugged her mother and younger sister as they stepped across her threshold.

Ellen Grainger studied Sally Ann. "I had a feeling I should be here. Nothing is amiss, I hope?"

All of the women in the Grainger family were witches, but each had unique talents. While Sally Ann was a gifted kitchen witch, her sister Carol Lee's talent was gardening. To say she had a green thumb was a gross understatement. Carol Lee could grow *anything*. And their mother Ellen's specialty? Timeliness. Ellen Grainger always knew when she was needed and made sure she arrived to do what was required. She wasn't prescient, not precisely. Ellen never knew what was going to happen in advance, but she always knew when her assistance was needed... and she was never late.

"Not a thing," Sally Ann said, leading her mother and sister down the hall and into her kitchen. Stepping to the side, she gestured to Amy's wedding cake. "What do you think?"

Her sister's jaw dropped and her eyes widened. Then Carol Lee let out a whoop and clapped her hands. "Oh, Sal! You've outdone yourself this time. Amy's going to flip when she sees this."

"Well, let's hope she's still wearing jeans then and not her wedding dress," Sally Ann said drily, though she was thrilled with Carol Lee's reaction.

Ellen moved to her elder daughter's side and placed an arm around her shoulders. "It's truly a work of art, my dear. And now I know why we're here."

Sally Ann glanced at her mother and cocked an eyebrow.

"You're going to need help getting that beautiful cake to the church."

2

---

*A*n hour later the Grainger women had successfully transferred Amy's wedding cake from Sally Ann's kitchen to the reception hall at the church where the wedding would take place that evening. The frosted masterpiece now stood in pride of place on a table dressed in pristine white linen and dripping with fall flowers. Other smaller tables littered the reception hall, each with a white tablecloth and boasting a centerpiece of fragrant red and gold flowers.

Sally Ann had just stepped back to study her cake's final effect when she heard a quick indrawn breath and a sob. Turning, she saw Amy, the bride-to-be... and her best friend in all the world.

Amy stood frozen in the doorway to the reception hall, still dressed in worn blue jeans and a red and black plaid shirt. Her blonde hair was pulled back in a pony tail and her hands covered her mouth while her eyes glittered with tears. Sally Ann's heart plummeted; Amy was disappointed. The cake wasn't what she'd hoped for. And now it was too late to start again.

Moving quickly to her friend's side, Sally Ann gathered Amy

into a hug and whispered, "I'm so sorry, Amy," while her own tears thickened her voice.

Amy stiffened, pushed Sally Ann back, and stared at her. "Sorry? Whatever for?" A little frown creased her brow. "What do you know that I don't?"

Sally Ann cocked her head and studied her friend's confused expression. "Nothing," she said finally. "Except that you're disappointed in the cake and I don't have time to start over."

Amy's mouth fell open, but no sound came out. She glanced from Sally Ann to the cake and back again. "Disappointed?" she finally managed to say. "You think I'm disappointed by that amazing cake? Are you crazy? That cake is stunning! It's more than I could've possibly dreamed of."

"Then why are you crying?"

Amy managed to laugh and scowl at the same time, then hugged her friend tightly. "Because it's my wedding day," she said, her voice a bit wobbly, "and my emotions are off the charts." She pushed Sally Ann to arm's length and gripped her shoulders. "They're tears of joy, you goose. Now show me my wedding cake. I want to see every square inch of that amazing work of art!"

3

At seven-thirty that evening, Amy Elizabeth Jenkins and Aaron David Matthews were married in a candlelight service. Their vows were witnessed by two hundred of their closest friends and family and presided over by a pastor who had known each of them since birth. The bride was radiant in a full length white velvet gown with a fingertip length veil atop a riot of golden curls. The groom appeared both dazzled and proud in his white tuxedo jacket with black trim and matching black pants.

Sally Ann observed from the back of the sanctuary. Amy had asked her to be maid of honor, but the two had decided that adding those duties to that of creating the wedding cake was a bit too much responsibility for one woman and both knew that Sally Ann was the *only* person who could create the cake of Amy's dreams. So Sally Ann, dressed in a gown of autumn gold velvet, waited at the rear of the church to escort the bridal couple to the reception hall where she could be the first to give her best friend a congratulatory hug... and then help arrange the newly married couple and their parents into a receiving line.

While Amy and Aaron greeted their guests, Sally Ann

checked in with the caterer. Amy and Aaron had opted not to host a full sit-down dinner, but instead to serve hors d'oeuvres and other finger foods along with punch and, of course, cake. Satisfied that the caterer had the food service under control, Sally Ann moved quietly among the guests enjoying their comments regarding her cake.

"I've never seen anything like it," one woman exclaimed. "Not in the real world. In bridal magazines or online, of course, but in person? It's absolutely enchanting."

"I heard that Grainger girl made it," another observed. "What's her name? Oh yes. Sally, I think it is. Sally Grainger."

Close enough, Sally Ann thought with a smile.

"Why the decorating alone must have taken forever," yet another matron added. "I wonder what flavor they decided on?"

"We'll find out soon enough," said a distinguished-looking gentleman. "It looks like the receiving line is about to finish. They'll be cutting the cake soon."

Taking that last comment as her cue, Sally Ann glided past the wedding cake one last time, making sure the cake knife and server were in place along with dessert plates, forks, and plenty of napkins. Once Amy and Aaron had enjoyed their first taste—and the photographer had memorialized the moment, the caterer would step in and make quick work of slicing the tiered layers into servings for the guests.

As Amy and Aaron took their places beside the magnificent cake, Ellen Grainger stepped to Sally Ann's side. "Is there a problem?" she asked quietly.

Sally Ann gave her mother a quizzical look. "Not that I know of. Why?"

Ellen shrugged. "No idea. I just know I need to stay close to you... and close to that cake."

"Huh." Before Sally Ann could think of anything else to say, Amy picked up the cake knife, and with Aaron's fingers resting lightly on hers, attempted to make the first cut on the lowest tier of the cake.

A little frown appeared on Amy's face while Aaron's expression turned puzzled. The cake knife hung a fraction of an inch from the pale peach frosting. Sally Ann watched in confusion as the bridal couple exerted downward pressure, but the knife refused to budge.

Ellen grasped her daughter's hand. "Did you put a protective spell on the cake before we moved it?"

Sally Ann gasped. Of course! She'd intended the spell to be temporary, but the doorbell had interrupted the flow of her thoughts. She must have missed the final phrase that would ensure the spell's disintegration!

What to do? She could remove the spell in an instant, but not with Amy and Aaron exerting that much downward force... they were likely to topple the whole table. She needed them to relax, to try again once the spell had been removed.

"Mother," she whispered to Ellen, "I need you to distract the guests while I have a quick word with Amy and Aaron... and the cake."

Ellen nodded, stepped in front of the cake table, and clapping her hands turned to the assembled guests. "It looks like our beautiful young bride is having trouble deciding to cut into the masterpiece my daughter created for her wedding. Let's give the girls a moment more to admire the cake while we all have another cup of punch. I'm sure Sally Ann will call us back when she and Amy have had a last moment to be girls together."

While the guests moved away, laughing and chattering, Sally Ann stepped to Amy and Aaron.

"What's wrong, Sally Ann?" Amy asked, her eyes filling with frustrated tears. "Why can't we cut the cake?"

"I'm not a superstitious man, Sal," Aaron said, a frown furrowing his brow, "but this feels like a bad omen. Isn't sharing the wedding cake supposed to symbolize our future happiness? Does this mean our union is doomed?"

"Aaron," Amy cried, "how could you say such a thing?"

"Easy now," Sally Ann said, taking the cake knife from their hands. "Relax. Both of you. This is just a minor bobble in what will be a long and happy life together. Blame it on me! Just think of me as your lovable local witch who forgot a minor bit of magic in a thoroughly magical day."

That earned a smile from both of them. "You're such a goose, Sally Ann! Imagine calling yourself a witch on my wedding day. How silly."

"Right. What's a friend for if not to be silly when there's a minor crisis? Now, you two take a second to compose yourselves while I check this one little item."

When the happy couple stepped back to gaze into each other's eyes and sigh, Sally Ann recited a few words under her breath, traced a sigil over the cake, and then touched the tip of the cake knife to the frosting. It sliced through a fondant rosebud like, well, like a knife was supposed to do.

Turning back to Amy and Aaron, she handed them the cake knife. "Everything will be fine now." Catching her mother's gaze, she nodded and smiled, and Ellen clapped her hands and regathered the guests.

When the photographer nodded, Amy and Aaron sliced into the almond buttercream frosting, straight through the luscious layers of the lowest tier of spice cake and served each other a delicious sliver of Sally Ann's enchanting wedding cake!

4
***

When the happy couple had changed into traveling clothes and driven off in a car decorated with paper flowers and trailing streamers of white satin ribbon and rattling tin cans, Sally Ann sank into a chair at one of the guest tables. The remainder of the reception had gone off without a hitch, and most of the guests were now gathering their wraps and moving toward their cars.

"What a lovely wedding," Ellen said as she settled into a chair beside her daughter. "And that cake! Not only was it a work of art, but delicious as well."

Stifling a yawn, Sally Ann smiled. "And your timing was perfect as always. No one would've had a clue what the cake tasted like if you hadn't been here to help distract people while I removed that protective spell."

A small frown wrinkled Ellen's brow. "On the other hand, if our earlier arrival hadn't interrupted your concentration, the spell would've disintegrated as you'd intended." She tapped a finger to her chin thoughtfully. "Maybe I need a tune-up. It seems I was a bit *too* timely this morning."

Sally Ann laughed. "Whatever. Everything worked out." She

patted her mother's hand and smirked. "I even told Amy and Aaron I was a witch." At her mother's shocked expression she hurried to add, "Of course, I phrased it in such a way that they thought I was joking."

"Thank the Goddess!"

"Nothing to worry about," she continued with a wave of her hand. "Amy even called me a *silly goose* afterward."

No. There was nothing to be concerned about. Amy and Aaron were safely married, the wedding cake had been a success, and the top tier had been removed, packaged, and sent home with Amy's mother to be frozen. The happy couple would receive another dose of Sally Ann's best spells for health, happiness, and enduring love when they enjoyed the last of her cake on their first anniversary.

With a contented sigh, Sally Ann Grainger stood, and bending down, kissed her mother's cheek. "Thanks again for all of your help," she said, "but it's time to call it a day. I've had enough excitement to last for quite a while."

EPILOGUE

*I*n the bridal suite of a luxury hotel many miles from the church where they'd been married, Amy nestled into her husband's embrace and drifted to the edge of sleep. Suddenly, unexpectedly, her eyes popped open and she tapped Aaron's chest.

"Are you still awake?"

"Barely," he murmured drowsily.

"What did Sally Ann do to that cake? How did she fix it? We couldn't cut it, and then she said something, and we could! What did she do?"

Aaron cracked an eyelid and peered at his very warm, very lovely wife. "I don't know. Does it matter?"

She thought a moment, then shrugged and curled more closely into his arms. "I suppose not." But she didn't sleep. At least, not right away. Her mind was busy remembering her best friend's words... *Just think of me as your lovable local witch who forgot a minor bit of magic in a thoroughly magical day.*

Amy and Sally Ann were going to have a very frank, very heart-felt conversation when Amy and Aaron returned from their honeymoon. Witch indeed. What had Sally Ann been thinking to say such a thing?

Silly goose, Amy thought as she drifted into a deep and peaceful sleep.

PART VII

TREASURES

DEBBIE MUMFORD

BESTSELLING AUTHOR OF *SORCHA'S HEART*

Treasures

SPUN YARNS
A CONTEMPORAY SHORT STORY

1

---

 *M*amma has always had a love for other people's possessions. I've known this my whole life, so I hovered over her like a hawk eyeing a prairie dog.

"Oh, Mother Lange," I exclaimed. "What a wonderful piece of Lladro." I deftly removed my mother-in-law's prized porcelain statuette from Mamma's greedy fingers, and placed the little figurine back on the mantle. Taking a firm grasp of Mamma's elbow, I guided her to the center of Mother Lange's sofa. The most appropriate seat I could find for a kleptomaniac: nothing in arm's reach save a throw pillow.

"I'm so glad you like it, dear," said Roger's mother. I smiled up into her elegant face without relaxing my grip on my own mother's arm.

Roger, my husband of six months, had no idea how lucky he was to have been raised by this genteel and guileless woman. Mamma suffered by comparison. Of course, Mamma suffered by comparison to a baboon... whose females make remarkably good mothers.

"And you, Mrs. Wilson," said Mother Lange, "do you enjoy art?"

"Oh, aye," said Mamma, her gaze straying back to the little figurine. "I do love a well-made knick-knack."

Mother Lange looked startled. Doubtless she'd never heard a piece of her expensive collection referred to as a 'knick-knack' before. She recovered quickly, and leaned forward to begin the process of pouring tea.

"I'm so glad you could come today. I've regretted that we didn't meet before the children wed."

"Well," said Mamma, "I'm sure you remember how urgent young love can seem."

In truth, there'd been nothing urgent about Roger's and my courtship. Our mothers hadn't met for the simple reason that mine had been locked up in Attica until a month ago. They wouldn't have met today if I'd been able to think of any way around it. Though I had to admit, Mamma had cleaned up nicely for the occasion.

My mother, Senga Wilson, might have been a beautiful woman once, but her face showed signs of hard wear. Too much sun and wind in the prison exercise yard resulted in deep wrinkles around the eyes and mouth, and her once auburn hair had lost its luster to gray. Still, she'd made the effort to find a dark blue business suit that gave her the austere look of one of the prison matrons rather than an inmate. She'd even managed a bit of powder and lip gloss.

I released my grip on her arm, gave her a pat, and relaxed against the sofa's blue chintz cushions. Roger and I were happily married. Mamma couldn't hurt me, not this time.

"Elizabeth tells me you've been away for your health," said Mother Lange. "I do hope you're feeling better."

I felt Mamma's gaze bore into the side of my head, but refused to blush. Instead, I accepted a cup of tea from Mother Lange with a quiet, "Thank you."

"I've had cause to be away, aye," Mamma said. "In fact, I missed most of Lizzie's growing years."

"Lizzie?" Mother Lange set her own cup on the table and clapped her hands. "Is that what your family calls you, dear? But how charming! I don't remember ever hearing you referred to as anything but Elizabeth."

My face heated to scarlet as I wiped away the tea I'd just dribbled down my chin.

"Oh, she'll no want you to call her that," Mamma said hastily. "She's always put on airs, has my Lizzie. She'll want to be called 'Elizabeth,' to be sure."

Stung, I glared at her, before turning my attention to Roger's mother. "I'm not putting on airs, as Mamma so quaintly puts it," I told her, "but I do prefer Elizabeth."

In the tense silence that followed, Mamma rose and moved across the plush cream carpet to stand before a small oil painting, gilt-framed with its own recessed spotlight.

Mother Lange turned in her wingback chair to see what had captured Mamma's interest.

"That's my husband's pride and joy," she said, her voice conveying her own unmistakable pride, "the crown of his collection: an original Monet."

"Oh," said Mamma, examining the painting closely, "it's a bonnie wee picture, aye, but no an original. Whoever told you that should be tied to a post and whipped."

The effect of these words was utter chaos. Mother Lange jumped from her chair like she'd been shot from a cannon, while I managed to drop my cup on the mahogany table where it shattered, spilling the staining liquid into the carpet's deep pile.

"Whatever makes you say such a thing?" Mother Lange demanded, reaching Mamma's side.

"Mamma," I cried, "don't. Whatever you're scheming, just don't!"

Both women turned to stare at me, and I knew I looked a fright. My heart pounded, assuring my cheeks a hot flush, and I shook all over. My eyes had to be flashing, because anger boiled in my system.

"You can't ruin this for me," I yelled, holding up my ring finger for both to see. "We're already married; you can't hurt me this time!"

Color drained from Mamma's face and she stepped back as if I'd struck her. "Is that what you think, Lizzie? That I'm trying to harm you and yours?"

Mother Lange reeled away from Mamma, and perched unsteadily on a nearby chair, the painting forgotten.

"When haven't you hurt me, Mamma?" I dashed tears from my cheeks with stiff-fingered stabs.

"When were you ever there for me? When I started my menses, and thought I was dying? No. Daddy explained about the wonders of the female body. You were in prison for stealing Mrs. Davidson's emerald brooch. What about when I wanted to go to camp? I couldn't. We needed every penny to pay for your appeal."

Mamma stepped back with each accusation, until she pushed against the wall, as if willing it to absorb her. But that didn't stop me. I still had more to say.

Glaring at her, I continued. "What about when Daddy died of cancer? Were you there to ease him from this world and into the next? Or to comfort me in my grief? No. You've never been there for me."

I paused, took a deep breath, and finished my exorcism. "Other people's possessions have always been more important to you than me or Daddy."

Grabbing a linen napkin from the table, I blew my nose with such force that my ears rang.

"Well, I have my own family now, and it doesn't include you. Roger loves me, and I hope Mother Lange will still accept me after meeting you, but even if she doesn't, well, Roger loves me!"

I ran from the room without a backward glance, stopping only when I reached the safety of Roger's childhood room. I slammed the door, locked it, and collapsed on his bed amid ample evidence of his normal and well-loved childhood.

When I woke, having cried myself to sleep, I found Roger sitting beside me, stroking my back.

"How did you get in here?" I asked, sure I'd locked the door in my desire to lick my wounds in private.

He dangled a key before my eyes. "Used to be my room, remember? I know all its secrets." He leaned close and kissed my swollen eyelids. "Come downstairs, love. Our mothers have something to tell you."

I groaned and tried to bury my head in the pillow. "Just take me home," I whimpered. "I can't face them. Not today. Maybe not ever."

He picked up my hand and lifted it to his lips. "Yes you can. You're the strongest person I've ever known." He stood, pulling me up with him. "You were right, you know."

"About what?"

"I do love you, and we are a family, no matter what."

I took refuge in his arms and he held me tightly while I struggled to breathe. When I calmed, I lifted my head and gazed into his dark brown eyes.

"Do we really have to go downstairs?"

"We do." He kissed me tenderly and led me to the door.

Mother Lange met us at the living room threshold and squeezed my hand before walking us to the sofa.

"Senga and I have had a long talk," she said with a glance at Mamma. "I want you to know, Elizabeth that nothing that happened here today has caused me to think less of either you or your mother. In fact, I'm more honored than you can know to have you in my family, and your mother has done us a great service."

I must have looked skeptical, because she hurried to explain.

"It's true. Your mother explained her reasons for believing the painting to be a fraud, and I must bow to her expertise. I phoned Howard, and he agrees. We're having the painting examined and its provenance authenticated."

She stood and reached for Roger's hand. "Now, we're going to leave you and Senga alone for a few minutes." She caressed my cheek with her free hand and, cupping my chin, raised my eyes to meet her own. "You might want to rethink your decision to ban Senga from your family."

I sat in miserable silence until Mamma came to kneel in front of me.

"I'm that sorry, Lizzie," she said quietly. "I can't change what's been, and you're right about me never being there, but I hope you'll let me try to make a wee spot for myself in your future." She rose to sit carefully on the edge of the wingback chair opposite me.

I raised my eyes then, and gazed at her worn face. Thief she might be, but she'd never lied to me, never claimed to be anything but what she was.

And she was my mother.

"I'm sorry, too, Mamma. Sorry for everything we've missed." I sighed and managed a weak smile.

"As to the painting," Mamma paused and clicked her tongue

reproachfully. "You should have known better, child. When have I ever stolen from family?"

I gazed at her with a calmness that astounded me.

"Really, Mamma? You've never stolen from family? What about Daddy's peace of mind?"

I rose and walked to the door, ready to join my husband; ready to leave the past in the past. I paused on the threshold and glanced at her over my shoulder.

"What about my childhood, Mamma?"

*T*hree years to the day later, Mamma and I once again joined Mother Lange in her comfortable living room. The changes in the room and its occupants were understated, but significant. The fake Monet had been replaced by a Renoir of impeccable provenance, thanks in large part to Mamma.

Who knew that a life of crime could have marketable value in the world of art?

Certainly not me, but my father-in-law's insurance company had been quick to offer Mamma a job. She had recently reached a milestone: two-and-a-half years of diligent service. A few more and she'd be bonded in her own right—able to work without a supervising partner.

More important to me than her gainful employment was her new outlook on life. Mamma could now play with other people's treasures with impunity. The life suited her. She looked younger and healthier than I'd ever seen her, and radiated a quiet calm when we were together, which was often these days.

The most significant change in our lives raced across the room and threw himself into Mamma's arms.

"Choo-choo?" my son asked.

Mamma pulled the sturdy two-year-old onto her knee before rummaging in her capacious purse. To his delight, she pulled a little train engine from its depths and presented it to him.

"Run along with ye now, and don't be marring yer granny's table."

He slid from her lap and moved to the stone-floored entryway to play with his prize.

"He's such a good boy," Mother Lange said. "So like his father at that age."

"Aye, he's a bonny lad," agreed Mamma, turning a proud gaze on me. "And verra lucky in the parents who brought him into this world."

I smiled at the compliment. Mamma and I would never regain the lost years, but I was content. My son had two loving grandmothers in his life, and true to her word, my mamma no longer stole from family.

knew without a doubt that we were more important than other people's possessions... and that knowledge was balm to my healing heart.

PART VIII

DELIA'S DECISION

Delia's Decision

A Short Delia Laubhan Mystery

DEBBIE MUMFORD

1

My name is Delia Laubhan. I'm a no-nonsense kind of person dedicated to the facts. Opinions are nice, but they're open to discussion. Facts are facts.

These are the facts about me. I'm female, twenty-nine years of age, single, and currently between jobs. I served my country as active duty military police for eight years overseas. The job was both tougher and easier than I imagined when I signed on the dotted line with my recruitment officer. I learned a lot in the military, not the least of which involved police procedure and investigative technique.

When my tour of active duty ended, I mustered out and headed home to Denver, Colorado a wiser and somewhat more jaded woman. I'd seen the worst of human behavior, but I'd also witnessed acts of self-sacrifice that could only be described as heroic.

Now that I was home in Colorado and retired from military life, I had options, but those options called for decisions, and after taking orders for eight years, I was unaccustomed to making my own choices. But life is all about change, and those who can't—or won't—change wither and die.

I had no intention of rolling over and playing dead, so I needed to pull myself together and make a decision: what did I want to do with my life?

With my background, I was probably best suited for police work. The boys and girls in blue would undoubtedly welcome me with open arms, but did I really want to join the force as a rookie after the years of investigative experience I'd accumulated?

I could go back to school. I had an undergrad degree thanks to the military, but I could use my G.I. educational benefits to get a law degree or train in one of the many branches of forensic science. But returning to the sedentary existence of classroom lectures and study groups after leading an active life as a military investigator didn't really appeal.

While I was pondering those weighty choices—and trying to convince myself that I was qualified to make such a decision—a challenge fell into my lap. One that would allow me to procrastinate on the decision making, while telling myself I was doing a good deed.

My mother's Honda Accord was stolen.

She reported the theft immediately, but the police held out little hope of finding the car. Honda Accords were the most frequently stolen vehicle on the Front Range. When I heard Mom's plight, I knew what I had to do: find her car.

Great! A legitimate excuse to set aside the uncertainties of my future and concentrate on a mission. One I was uniquely qualified to undertake.

"No worries, Mom. I'll have your car back in the carport in no time."

Famous last words.

2

*T*racking down a car thief in the civilian world was harder than I'd anticipated. I no longer had a badge, a gun, or investigative resources at my fingertips. Nor did I have the military chain of command to bolster my authority. I couldn't just order civilians into interrogation. I had to be friendly, chat up the neighbors, and hope they unwittingly dropped a clue I could follow up on.

What a waste of time and energy!

On the second day of my attempted investigation, I loitered in the downstairs hallway of Mom's apartment building, hoping to encounter a neighbor willing to talk. The front door opened and a middle-aged woman I'd known since childhood entered the building.

"Hey, Mrs. Malloy. How ya doin' today?" I asked brightly.

"Why, Delia! I had no idea you were back in Denver. Are you on leave?" The slightly frowsy little woman beamed up at me. Now, I'm not exactly an Amazon, but it doesn't take much to tower over Mrs. Malloy's five-feet-nothing.

"No, ma'am," I answered. "I finished my tour and mustered

out. I'm home for good, though I gotta say, being a civilian feels a bit strange."

"Oh, your mother must be so happy to have you home. Are you staying with her?"

"No, ma'am. I've got my own apartment. It's in another complex, but it's only a few miles away. Mom will get sick of seeing me, I'm sure."

Mrs. Malloy laughed. "I doubt that. She's spoken of you often during your deployment." She stepped past me down the hall to her first floor apartment, which faced the back of the building and the covered parking that was reserved for tenants. "Would you like to come in for a cup of coffee?" she asked. "Or are you on your way up to visit your mother?"

"Actually, I'd love some coffee and a chat."

"Wonderful. Come right in."

Gesturing for me to follow, she unlocked the door and stepped into her living room. Mrs. Malloy's apartment was laid out just like Mom's. The hall door opened into a decent sized living room with a sliding glass door opening onto a small concrete patio—Mom's, being on the fourth floor, opened onto a minuscule deck—across the way, a breakfast bar separated the living room from a compact kitchen. Next to the kitchen was a short hallway leading to a bathroom and two small bedrooms.

Mrs. Malloy's living room put me in mind of a tropical forest. She had plants everywhere. African violets and gloxinia covered the end tables on either side of a deep burgundy sofa. A huge rubber tree stood in the corner beside the patio door, and philodendron runners crept along shelves and bookcases. She'd even arranged some of the runners to drape across the ceiling between the living room and kitchen. And then there were the hanging pots! English ivy, spider plants, ferns, and some sort of succulent with little round leaves dripped from macrame hangers.

"Have a seat, dear," the woman called as she pulled off her jacket and stowed it and her purse in the closet near the front door. "It won't take but a minute to fix that coffee. I have one of those new-fangled machines that brews it by the cup. Do you take cream or sugar?"

"Black is fine, ma'am," I said. "The military cured me of the fancy stuff."

She trundled off to the kitchen, chuckling. "I'll just bet it did."

A few minutes later we were settled with good-sized mugs of coffee, Mrs. Malloy in a well-used wooden rocker and me on the sofa. The mug was warm in my hands and I inhaled the bitter-sweet aroma of the brew. Closing my eyes, I appreciated the fresh scent. I'd downed too many cups of stale coffee during my stint in the service. Finally, I lifted the mug to my lips and sipped. Delicious!

"So what are you doing with yourself, now that you're home?" Mrs. Malloy asked.

I opened my eyes and met her gaze. "I'm still getting my bearings," I said. "Haven't made any concrete decisions about the future yet." I took another sip, then found a place for my mug among the pots of flowers on the end table. "Right now, I'm helping Mom out with a problem."

"Oh?" she asked. "And what might that be?"

I grinned. "I'm glad you asked, 'cause I wanted to ask you a couple of questions."

She lifted a questioning brow, and I continued.

"Someone stole her car late Tuesday night or early Wednesday morning, and I was wondering if you might've seen or heard anything unusual that night?"

Her eyebrows drew together in a frown of concentration. "I'm sorry to hear that. Tuesday night, you say? I don't think so, but then I go to bed as soon as the news is over."

I sighed. "I was hoping... since your patio looks out over her parking spot, but..."

She clicked her tongue, and I glanced up again.

"It's not that unusual, but Greg Jennings and a group of his friends were hanging out in the parking area that night. Just talking and smoking, you understand, but they would've still been there after I went to bed. You might check with them."

"Thanks, Mrs. Malloy. I'll do that."

I picked up my mug and enjoyed another swallow of coffee while Mrs. Malloy caught me up on her son and his wife, and their three boys. I might not be living up to Mom's expectation in the progeny department, but it sounded like Stan Malloy was doing just fine.

3

---

*G*reg Jennings lived in the next building over from Mom's. I was aware of his family, but didn't know them well. They'd moved into the complex about a year before I left for college in Boulder. If I remembered right, Greg had been about nine at the time, which would make him in his late teens now.

The perfect age for the male of the species to start causing trouble. Not that they all did, of course, but enough did to raise my suspicions.

How to approach my quarry?

I could use the direct approach. Simply knock on his parents' front door and ask to speak to him, but that would put him on his guard. Better to arrange a *chance* encounter somewhere. I decided to stake out his apartment and follow him. Surely he'd end up in some public place where I could approach him casually.

As I hung around the Jennings' building, I had a moment of deja vu, realizing I was back to loitering in an apartment building. Fortunately, I'd spent enough time with Mrs. Malloy that even a teenage boy would be up and about on a warm summer's day like this one. I'd barely taken up a post standing at the top of the third floor staircase when the door to the Jennings apartment opened and Greg stepped out. Since I didn't want to call attention to myself, I started up the stairs to the fourth floor while Greg sauntered down the hallway and headed to the first floor. When he reached the landing, I turned and followed him down and out of the building.

Three blocks later, I ducked into a convenience store and pretended to study a revolving rack of sunglasses. The mirrors on the rack allowed me to keep an eye on Greg as he moved along the snack aisle. When he neared where I stood, I *accidentally* bumped into him.

"Hey! Watch it," he said in a slightly belligerent tone, scrambling to keep hold of the bags of chips and cookies he held.

"Sorry about that," I said. Turning to face him I feigned surprise, widening my eyes and raising my eyebrows. "Greg?" I asked. "Aren't you Greg Jennings? Wow. It's been, like, forever!"

A frown creased his forehead. I stuck out my hand and when he freed one of his and took it, shook his vigorously. "Delia Laubhan. My mom lives in the building next to yours. I've been overseas for several years." I looked him up and down. "You've really grown up."

"Uhm, yeah," he said. "Nice to meet you."

"What say I buy you a cola and then we can walk back together?"

He didn't exactly jump at the offer, but shrugged his shoulders and muttered, "Sure."

After a couple of blocks, I said, "So, I hear you were hanging out in the parking area of Mom's building Tuesday night. Did you see anything unusual?"

He gave me the side-eye and said, "Depends on what you call unusual." He took a sip of cola, then asked, "Why? What's it to you how I spend my time?"

I shrugged and winked. "Couldn't care less... unless of course you were in on the theft of my mom's car."

He stopped dead, and I turned to face him.

"That was your mom's Honda?"

I nodded. "What do you know about it?"

He bit his lip and a trickle of sweat ran down his temple as he studied me. After a moment's pause he seemed to make up his mind.

"Nothing really. The guys had just left and I was about to head home when this guy hopped out of a car and ran over to this silver Honda Accord. I was out past curfew, so I kind of hunkered down so he wouldn't notice me.

"The car drove away and I thought he was just picking up his own ride. But I did think it was kinda strange that he was dressed all in black... I mean black jeans and a black hoodie with the hood up even though it was a warm night. Then I realized he didn't have a key; he was jimmying the lock on the driver's door."

He shrugged, chugged his cola, and started walking again.

"Once he had the door open, he hot-wired it, slid into the seat, and took off."

"Did you recognize the guy?" I asked

Again with the side-eye. Another swig of cola and he lobbed the empty can into a trash bin. "Yeah. I saw his face when the door light came on."

"And..." I prompted.

"It was Mrs. Malloy's grandson, Mark. Mark Malloy."

My turn to stop dead. "Wait a minute. You're telling me Mark Malloy is old enough to boost a car?"

Greg shook his head sorrowfully and gave me a look that said I was too stupid for words. "He's the same age I am, and I've had my license for a year."

Not that you needed a license to steal a car.

I stood there feeling old and tired. Mrs. Malloy was going to be so disappointed to learn one of her beloved grandsons was a car thief. At least, I sure hoped it was only one... I didn't have a clue who'd dropped Mark off at the parking area.

"Shame," I said. "I really like Mrs. Malloy." I started walking again and Greg and I continued to his building. "You willing to tell the police what you saw?"

He grimaced, but nodded. "Sure. I guess since I told you I don't really have a choice."

"Appreciate it," I said. "It'll sure make it easier for Mom to get her car back. Come on, I'll drive you down to the precinct."

4

A week later, I watched the local news while I ate my version of dinner: a frozen chicken pot pie fresh out of the microwave. Mom wouldn't consider it a meal—she still believed the evening meal consisted of meat, vegetables, some form of potato, and a side salad... and if you ate all your veggies... dessert—but it worked for me.

The news show flashed mug shots of Mark Malloy and his cousin Devon Harris. I sighed as the reporter droned out the story of the teens' arrest for stealing cars. Evidently the pair had been at it for a while. When the police arrested them at the Harris's auto body shop, they discovered a dozen stolen vehicles.

I'd kept my promise to Mom. She had her car back, but she was not happy about the circumstances. Comforting sweet little Mrs. Malloy wasn't a pleasant task. Not when I'd been the cause of her grandson's downfall.

Never mind that the real reason for Mark's trouble were his own poor choices.

Decisions could be a bear at any age.

I hit the button on the remote, turning the television off, and leaned back in my chair. Past time to face some decisions of my own. Hopefully with a better outcome than Mark Malloy and Devon Harris had seen.

Apply to the police force and be a rookie again?

Go back to college and train for a new career with another degree?

Weren't there any other choices?

I pulled my laptop from the table beside my chair and looked up the qualifications for a Colorado private investigator's license. Studying through the website, I discovered I more than qualified. I could apply for a license and open my own business next week!

But what did I know about investigating in the civilian world or running a small business?

Not as much as I should if I wanted my business to succeed.

I did a search on private investigators in the Denver area and made a list of the ones that struck me as professional and having solid standards. Surely one of them would be willing to take on apprentice and teach her the ropes.

I closed my laptop and relaxed. Decision made. I was on the way to becoming *Delia Laubhan, P.I.*

And the choice felt good.

PART IX

FOOL'S PUZZLE

Fool's Puzzle

A Short Kristi Lundrigan Mystery

DEBBIE MUMFORD

1

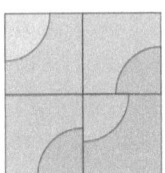

*K*risti Lundrigan sailed into Delectable Mountain Quilting, her ankle length patchwork skirt swirling around her legs. She grinned at Mattie Stebbings, her best and most experienced employee. Mattie nodded in acknowledgment as her hands were busy measuring a length of gorgeous deep purple batik print for a customer who stood with her hand resting possessively on a stack of at least six additional bolts of fabric.

Business was good. Barely past their 9:30 a.m. opening and Mattie was already preparing to cut a good-sized sale.

Kristi smiled and said. "Good morning, Mattie." She turned her attention to the customer. "Thanks for coming in, Eleanor. Did you find everything you need?"

Eleanor beamed at her, running her fingers lovingly over the stack of bolts. "Oh, Kristi, I just love these new batiks. I've got a Double Nine Patch planned and with these..." she paused, sighing happily, "it's just going to sparkle."

"How wonderful. Be sure to bring the top in when you get it pieced. We'd love to see it."

"Oh, don't wait that long," Mattie added with mock concern.

"Bring the blocks in as soon as you have enough to lay out the design!"

Kristi laughed, waved, and moved to the kitchen to put away her purse, acknowledging several other customers as she passed. What a great way to start her day! She was so lucky that Mattie had agreed to come to work for her.

The petite, dark-haired woman had owned the shop until last spring when she'd been forced to sell in order to cover her husband's gambling debts. Kristi had been fortunate enough to buy the whole package: building, land, and inventory. Of course, she hadn't known the reason for the sale at the time. That had come out later, when Mattie's husband, Gary, had been murdered just outside the shop's back door.

But all of that was behind them now. The grand opening of Kristi's new and updated Delectable Mountain Quilting had taken place nearly six months ago, and thanks to her marketing savvy and skillful redesign of the shop's floor plan, the business was doing better than anyone had dared to hope. After three months of employing only one sales clerk, Kristi had approached Mattie about coming back. The former owner had jumped at the chance. She was still mourning the loss of her husband—not to mention her mother's betrayal—and was glad to have a reason to get out of the house and interact with people who loved quilts and fabric as much as she did.

Back out on the sales floor, Kristi re-shelved bolts of quilting cottons as Mattie finished cutting, chatted with customers, and offered suggestions as to which fabrics might blend well in blocks.

She was straightening books in the notions room when Anna Marsten approached her. "Excuse me, Kristi."

Kristi turned to the heavy-set woman. Blonde and blue-eyed with a florid complexion, Anna had been a beauty in her youth. Now the rancher's wife and mother of six could best be described as warm-hearted and sturdy. "Anna, how nice to see you. How can I be of help?"

Anna clutched a bolt of white-on-white backing fabric to her ample bosom, licked her lips, and asked, "Have you ever done any appraisals? Quilt appraisals, I mean."

Kristi cocked her head to one side, considering the question. After a moment's hesitation, she said, "Well, yes. I'm certified by the American Quilter's Society, but it's been several years since I've done any. Do you need an appraisal for insurance purposes?"

Anna shook her head. "No, not me. I don't need anything." She bit her lip and glanced at the rack of books Kristi had been straightening, her demeanor tense and uncertain. Finally, she blurted, "It's Carl's mother. A man has contacted her about quite a few of the items in her estate. He's making all sorts of wild claims about the money she could have if she follows his advice. Carl is convinced it's a scam."

Kristi's brow furrowed. "That's awful, but I'm not sure how I can help."

"Well, part of his advice concerns her quilts. He's suggesting that they're worth thousands of dollars ... each. Now, you know that I love quilts, and I value them, but I'm pretty sure the market value is nothing like what he's quoting. Carl and I, we just don't know how to counter his hold on Momma Marsten. But I thought if we could bring in a quilt expert and disprove what he's saying about her quilts, maybe she'd be less likely to fall for his lies about all her other things."

"I see. Well, as I said, my market information is out of date, but I'd be happy to inspect her collection, document the designs, types of the fabrics, the stitching, the binding... the general condition of the quilts, and then do the market research to give her an accurate appraisal."

Anna's expression cleared and her grip on the bolt of fabric eased. "Oh, thank you, Kristi. What would you charge?"

"Let me give you my email address. If you can tell me approximately how many quilts you'd like appraised, I'll work up an estimate for you. Then you and Carl can decide whether or not you want to proceed." She paused for a moment, and added, "But I have to warn you, depending on the number and types of quilts, this may not be a quick project."

Anna nodded, relief evident around her eyes and the set of her jaw. "I understand. I'll get the information to you this evening, and thank you so much. Just to be able to tell Carl we might have this option means a lot to me."

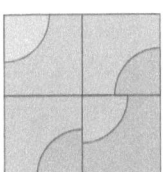

2

*L*ater that evening, Kristi sat across the table from her ex-husband, Jason Reynolds, at Rizzoli's Fine Italian Restaurant. Rizzoli's was also Garnet Gateway's *only* Italian restaurant, but since it was a favorite of Kristi's, the couple ate there often.

Recorded violin music wafted dreamily through air spiced with the aroma of roasted tomatoes, garlic, oregano, and beeswax from the candle flickering on their red and white checked tablecloth. Kristi gazed contentedly at Jason. He was focused on trapping the last bite of linguini between a bit of crusty bread and his fork and didn't notice her fond expression. After their divorce a year ago she'd never have believed that they could even be friends, and yet, here they were, dating again.

She'd had a brush with death during the investigation into Gary Stebbings' murder, and Jason, Garnet Gateway's sheriff, had reacted by declaring his continued love for her and asking for a second chance.

Kristi had been glad to grant his request, and now, six months later ... she was even more at ease with her decision.

The repairs to their relationship would take time, but Jason was worth the effort.

The object of her concentration, looked up, noticed her gaze, and the undoubtedly sappy little smile on her lips, and reached for her hand.

"You look happy," he said, his gray eyes twinkling in the candlelight. "Did you have a good day?"

"I did," she said, squeezing his fingers. "And I had an unexpected request. Actually, it was a bit odd."

"Oh? Tell me about it."

When she finished explaining the conversation with Anna Marsten, Jason frowned.

"I'd appreciate it if you'd keep me informed about this," he said, his tone more serious than she'd expected. "If someone is preying on our elderly citizens, I want to put a stop to it."

"Preying? That seems like an odd word choice."

He released her hand and leaned back against the cushioned booth. "It may be nothing, but the fact that Carl and Anna are concerned enough to ask for your help raises a red flag for me."

She nodded. "Yes, I agree their agitation is concerning. But I can't see what this man stands to gain. So far, he seems to be promising Carl's mother *more* than her things are worth."

Jason clenched his jaw, then relaxed. "Yes. That's part of the problem. It sounds like he's running a con on her, but I can't see what it is with the information we currently have."

"Maybe I'll discover more when I inspect the quilts." She shook her head and amended, "If I inspect her quilts. I haven't been hired yet."

She glanced at the time on her cell phone and sighed. "Speaking of which, I need to get home so I can work up that estimate." She smiled at Jason as she scooted to the edge of the booth and stood. "Thanks for dinner, Jason. Sorry I have to cut our evening short."

He stood as well, nodded to the waitress, and said, "I'll be right back, Jenny." Then to Kristi, "Let me walk you to the door." When they stood outside in the evening shadows, he pulled her into his arms. "I like having dinner with you, Ms. Lundrigan." He kissed her gently, sweetly, not invoking heat, but promising so much. "Maybe someday soon, we'll decide that we should have dinner together every night... for the rest of our lives."

She couldn't see his eye color in the soft light, but she imagined his gray eyes were edging toward the blue they wore when emotion was high. She kissed his cheek, a little scratchy this late in the day, and stepped out of his embrace. "Maybe someday," she agreed, and turned to unlock her bright red Subaru Outback.

As she settled into the driver's seat and fastened her seat belt, she heard the jingle of the restaurant door as Jason returned to settle their bill. It wouldn't do for the sheriff of Garnet Gateway, Montana to fail to pay for his meal.

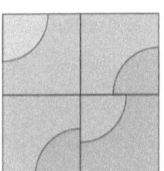

risti guided her bright red Subaru Outback over
the rutted dirt road that led from the paved
county road to the Broken M Ranch. The mid-September day
was fine, the weather not yet cold enough to require a full down
coat, but the high overcast of the sky spoke of snow in the near
future. She'd been on enough ranches to know this was a busy
time of year as the cattle were brought down from the high
meadows and preparations were made for the coming winter.

The fact that Carl and Anna were taking time to meet with
her about a quilt appraisal now spoke volumes about their level
of concern. Events like this were usually saved for dreary winter
days.

Pulling into the ranch's main compound, Kristi parked in
front of a two-story home that probably dated back to the mid-
1800s. White with black shutters and door, the front steps led to
a wide porch. Bare now, she imagined it furnished with wooden
rockers and small tables in the summer months. Across the way
stood a younger version of the home, this one painted yellow
with white shutters. Anna and Carl and their children lived
there, but this one, the original ranch house, was the domain of

Momma Marsten. This was where she and her late husband had raised Carl and his siblings.

Kristi had just stepped onto the front porch when someone called her name. She turned to see Anna crossing the yard to greet her.

"Welcome, Kristi," she said as she reached the steps to her mother-in-law's home. "Glad to see you found the place."

Kristi waited until Anna joined her on the porch to extend her hand. "Your directions were easy to follow. Thanks."

"Carl's out with the cattle," the rancher's wife said, "but he should be back by noon."

Kristi's eyes widened in surprise. "Whatever for? I mean, he's welcome of course, but we won't need his help to lay out and measure quilts."

Anna grimaced and glanced at the still closed front door. "I certainly hope not, but..." She stopped herself, drew a deep breath, and waved the thought away. "No sense borrowing trouble. Let's go in and get started."

She knocked on the door before pushing it open and calling, "Momma Marsten? It's Anna and I've brought the appraiser for the quilts."

Kristi followed Anna past a stairway leading to the upper floor and into a long hallway, its walls lined with framed photographs, many of them going sepia with age. There were pictures of this house in various stages of its existence: a lone building with an indistinct man and woman standing before it; the same house with a sturdy barn with a high-pitched roof in the background; other views as the out-buildings multiplied; and finally a color photo of the current ranch compound with its two homes and multiple out-building in sharp focus.

There were family photos as well. Many featuring long-dead ancestors, but there were also relatively current photos of Carl's family and the families of his siblings. Kristi smiled, appreciating the history of the place, the lives these walls had known and sheltered. Too many Montana ranches had been broken up for development; it was good to see this one alive and well and prepared to move forward into the future.

Doors opened off the hallway into several spacious rooms. Formal living room. Sitting room—Mrs. Marsten probably still thought of it as a parlor. A library that doubled as an office, and a dining room where the lady of the house waited.

"Momma Marsten," Anna said, stepping to where the older woman sat at the head of a beautifully polished walnut table with clawed feet, "this is Kristi Lundrigan. She bought Delectable Mountain Quilting last spring and she's an AQS quilt appraiser."

Mrs. Marsten nodded and held out a hand that Kristi hurried to shake. "Pleased to meet you, Kristi, though I'm not quite sure why Anna dragged you out here."

Kristi gave her a winning smile and released her hand. "Anna's told me about your quilt collection. I'm thrilled to be able to help you document the pieces. You know how important it is to record vintage quilts. They're part of our heritage, a history of Montana's women written in fabrics of their day and tiny stitches."

Mrs. Marsten smiled and nodded. "I hadn't thought of it that way, but you're right. They're so much more than just bed coverings."

Anna's expression expressed her gratitude for Kristi's quick explanation, but she only said, "Shall I bring down the first set, Momma Marsten?"

The older woman nodded her permission and rose to clear the table to provide a work surface. "Do we need to put a leaf in?" she asked.

Kristi eyed the table, which was easily six feet long without the leaf. "Let's start with this. We can add the leaf later if needed. If you'll excuse me, I'll go get my tools."

When she returned, Kristi found the table clear with all the chairs pulled back to the walls, and a stack of six or eight quilts folded neatly on the walnut sideboard.

Anna took the cardboard from Kristi and covered the table's gleaming surface—it wouldn't do to accidentally mar that polish with pin scrapes—while Kristi laid out three sets of white cotton gloves, her digital camera, measuring tape, magnifying glass, and the tablet she'd use to record the data. Anna had indicated Mrs. Marsten had at least two dozen quilts to be appraised. They had a full day's work ahead of them.

The women were working on the third quilt of the morning, a beautifully executed crazy quilt, when a knock sounded at the front door.

"Shall I get that, Momma Marsten?" Anna asked.

"Don't bother. I'll take care of it. You girls keep working."

When her footsteps had receded down the hall, Anna caught Kristi's eye. "I didn't have a chance to thank you," she said. "She was all set to send us packing, but your answer smoothed her feathers and made everything work." She studied Kristi's face and nodded. "You know a thing or two about people, don't you?"

Kristi cocked an eyebrow and said with a sly smile, "I can't imagine what you mean, Anna. I simply stated the truth."

Anna laughed. "The right truth at the right moment. You're good, Kristi, and you're a fine appraiser too."

Footsteps on hardwood and a murmur of voices announced Mrs. Marsten's return. A moment later she entered the dining room followed by a well-dressed man in his late forties. Clean shaven, with neatly groomed dark hair and light brown eyes, the man was not much taller than Kristi's five foot six.

"This is my son's wife, Anna," Mrs. Marsten told the man,

gesturing to her daughter-in-law, "and this is Kristi Lundrigan, a quilt appraiser who's helping me document my collection. Ladies, this is Mr. Benedict Peters."

Peters shook hands with each of them. "A pleasure to meet you, Anna. I've heard such wonderful things about you. Ms. Lundrigan, how nice of you to help Emma with this project."

A sidelong glance at Anna's face told Kristi that the man's use of Mrs. Marsten's Christian name had shocked her as well. Kristi hadn't even known what the older woman's given name was until she needed to enter the information into the appraisal form... and then Mrs. Marsten had seemed reluctant to give it.

"It's always a pleasure to be allowed to examine quilt collections," Kristi said.

He nodded, leaning over the table to study the embroidery stitches on the Crazy quilt. "The history of these quilts is important," he said, "but I hope you're not bothering to do an appraisal." He straightened and met her gaze. "I've already done that."

"I see," she said with an easy smile. "I didn't realize you were a quilt appraiser. We have something in common."

"Not officially," he said, stepping away from the table and waving airily. "I'm an antiques dealer... from New York." He added this detail as if it gave him all the credentials he needed. "I've worked with enough estates to know what's of value and what isn't."

"How fascinating," Kristi said, widening her eyes. "And what brought you all the way to Garnet Gateway, Montana?"

His gaze slid away from Kristi's and he moved to Mrs. Marsten's side. "A friend of a friend mentioned Emma's wonderful antiques to me," he said with a shrug. "Six degrees of separation. You know how it is."

Kristi was beginning to believe she knew exactly how it was. Jason was right. This man was running some kind of scam on

Mrs. Marsten and he didn't want a certified appraisal to be completed. The quilts were unlikely his main focus, but if she could prove he was lying about the quilts, she could cast doubt on the rest of his patter.

Benedict Peters was a con artist. She was sure of it, but what was his end goal? What did he hope to accomplish?

Peters tried, very suavely Kristi thought, to dismiss her when Carl came home and the work stopped for lunch, but by that time Emma Marsten was invested in documenting her fore-mothers' work for posterity.

Anna and Carl went to their home for lunch, but Kristi was invited to join Mrs. Marsten and Peters for a bowl of fresh vegetable soup and a ham sandwich. Their conversation was light, consisting mainly of observations about the quilts they'd worked with that morning.

Peters tried to draw Kristi out about her background, but desisted when she mentioned her relationship to Garnet Gateway's sheriff.

"You were married to Sheriff Reynolds?" Mrs. Marsten asked in impressed tones. "I absolutely adore that young man. He's been out here several times. Always so helpful, and so dedicated." She eyed Kristi thoughtfully. "I'd've thought he was a keeper."

Kristi felt her cheeks flame. "Well, we had some difficulties," she said quietly. "But we're trying to make amends. I have hope that this time..."

Mrs. Marsten patted her hand. "I'm sorry, dear. I didn't mean to pry."

When the last quilt had been documented, Kristi packed up her supplies while Anna and Mrs. Marsten put the room back in order.

They said their good-byes and Anna, who was heading home herself, walked Kristi to her car.

"You'll let me know what you turn up about the value?"

"You can be sure of it. I'll give you a complete report and a print out of the historical information that you can share with Mrs. Marsten. You can decide whether or not to share the results of the appraisal itself."

"Perfect," agreed Anna. "And again, thank you for everything, Kristi. I'm not sure we could've accomplished this without your deft handling of the situation."

"You're very welcome. I'll be in touch."

Kristi had a lot to think about during the drive back into Garnet Gateway. As she neared town, she called Jason. "Are you at the office?"

"I am," he responded. His deep voice soothed away the day's concerns.

"Great. I'll be there in just a few minutes."

"Okay," she heard the wariness creep into his tone. "Is there a problem I should be aware of?"

"Not exactly," she said, "but I want to discuss the situation at the Broken M with you."

"What did you find out?"

"I'll tell you when I get there."

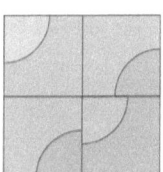

4

Fifteen minutes later she sat in one of the uncomfortable visitor's chairs across the scarred wooden desk from the man she loved, though she was still hesitant to admit that, even to herself.

Jason Reynolds wore his uniform well, looking every bit the capable law enforcement officer that he was. His gray eyes were clear and cool, his forehead high and his jaw firm. He radiated calm assurance; this wasn't a man to tolerate outsiders preying on those in his care.

"Have you ever heard of a man named Benedict Peters?" Kristi asked.

"No," he said, scribbling the name in a notebook, "but I'll run a background check. What does he do?"

"He claims to be a New York antiques dealer."

"Claims?"

She squirmed on the hard wooden seat. "I don't know. Something about him rubbed me wrong." She frowned, trying to pinpoint exactly what had made her suspicious. And then it hit her. "He called her *Emma*," she said quietly.

"Excuse me?"

She glanced up and met his confused gaze. "Sorry. I just realized that was what did it. He called Mrs. Marsten by her given name. It was too familiar... and she didn't object." She stood and paced across the room. "I don't know what he's up to, but he's got her mesmerized, and she's a strong-minded woman." She stopped and rested her hands on the back of the chair she'd just vacated. "I think he expected to be able to dismiss me, but we'd connected— Mrs. Marsten and I. We'd established a bond over the history of those quilts, so he wasn't able to get rid of me."

Jason nodded. "As you said, she's strong-minded, which makes it even more concerning that he's managed to worm his way into her confidence. What else?"

Kristi detailed the day's events, trying to remember every word Peters had spoken, his every gesture and tone of voice.

"Wait a minute," she exclaimed as Jason finished writing his notes. "I've got a picture of him. Just a second."

She dashed out of the station and returned a few minutes later with her digital camera and a USB cable. Jason fired up his computer while she found the picture she was looking for. Once it was downloaded onto the sheriff's computer, they studied the image.

"I knew he wasn't from around here even before the introductions. Look at that suit. I bet it's hand tailored. You won't find anything like that even in Billings. And his hands. You can't see them in the picture, but they were soft, his nails manicured. Definitely not a rancher's hands, and I bet even the lawyers and accountants around here have more calluses than he does."

Jason studied the picture, but glanced at her with admiration. "You do notice details, Kristi. And good job getting this picture. If Benedict Peters is an alias, this photo will go a long way in figuring out who he really is."

She blushed. "Thanks. If he's a legitimate business man, I'll eat my Fool's Puzzle quilt!"

He laughed. "I'm betting on your instincts; I think the Fool's Puzzle is safe, but I'm not so sure about the fool who calls himself Benedict Peters."

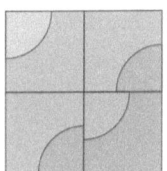

5

*J*ason called Kristi bright and early two days later. Glancing out the window as she answered her cell phone, she saw that the day was anything but bright. Gray clouds obscured her view of the majestic Absaroka Mountains; the snow wouldn't hold off much longer.

"Have you given that report to Anna and Carl yet?" Jason asked.

"Of course not," she answered, mildly irritated. "I'm barely awake and not even dressed yet."

"Great," he said. "I'm coming over."

"What?" But he'd already disconnected.

Kristi stared at the phone in her hand. What was he up to? She glanced around the mess that was her living room. She'd been up late last night researching quilt values and finishing her appraisal of the Marsten quilts. The coffee table was littered with books and print-outs, and her clothes were scattered across the floor. She'd been too tired to be neat. Plus, she lived alone...if she didn't count her two moggy cats, Stitches and Between, and when it came to messy rooms, who counted cats? They didn't care if the sink was piled high with dirty dishes.

But Jason? He was an entirely different matter.

Unless she got her butt in gear, got dressed, and met him outside.

Properly motivated, Kristen accomplished the feat. When Jason's Trail Blazer pull into the drive, she was out the front door, carefully locking it behind herself, and across the lawn before he had a chance to climb out.

He reached across the seat, opened the door for her, and leaned back while she settled into the passenger seat and fastened her seat belt.

"Where are we going?" she asked.

"I would've come in," he said.

"I know. I repeat, where are we going so early in the morning?"

He put the vehicle in gear and backed out of her driveway. "The Garnet Gateway Inn. I want to catch Peters before he has a chance to leave his room."

"Ah. I take it you found something."

He glanced sideways at her. "I found a lot, mainly thanks to that picture you took."

"Well?" she asked. "What's he up to? Tell me."

He shook his head. "You'll hear it all when we get there."

"Uh-huh. And why am I tagging along?"

"Oh, I just thought you'd enjoy watching me put the fear of God into a no-good hustler." He smiled. Kristi thought he looked like a shark. "And when we finish with him, we're heading out to the Broken M. I need to apprise Mrs. Marsten of the situation and you need to deliver your report."

"I can hardly wait," she said drily.

Jason parked in front of the Inn, and Kristi followed him inside. Definitely not a hardship; he had a fine butt and his determined stride showed off his physique nicely.

She jerked her thoughts back to their mission as he reached the front desk and spoke to the clerk on duty.

"Hey, Dave," he said, leaning on the counter. "I need the room number for Benedict Peters."

"Hey yourself, Jason," Dave responded. "You know I'm not allowed to give out that information."

"You are when the sheriff asks," Jason said, a hint of steel edging his voice. "This isn't a social call, Dave. Police business. Now, what room is he in?"

"He's up top," Dave answered, looking a little shaken. "The penthouse suite. What's he done?"

"Nothing that concerns you or the Inn, Dave."

Dave nodded, his expression somber.

The Garnet Gateway Inn was an historic building. Built at the turn of the last century, it was five stories high with a vintage elevator, all gilded ironwork and polished glass. The Inn's owners hadn't updated because the elevator was part of the Inn's charm, but it was inspected regularly and kept in peak working order. Everything else in the place was up to date, including in-room microwaves, refrigerators, and Wi-Fi connections.

"The penthouse," Kristi said as Jason pulled the elevator grill closed behind them. "He must have some excellent backing."

Jason grunted his agreement and they rode up in silence.

Kristi stood a little behind Jason when he knocked on the penthouse door. After all, he was law enforcement; she was just along for the ride.

The man she knew as Benedict Peters opened the door and frowned at Jason. He was casually dressed in khakis and a light blue polo, but he still appeared polished.

"I'm sorry. Do I know you?" he asked, frowning at Jason.

"I'm Sheriff Jason Reynolds. I believe you've met Ms. Lundrigan."

He peered past Jason and nodded at me. "Of course, Kristi isn't it? But that still doesn't explain why you're here."

"May we come in?" Jason asked, and his expression said that the answer should be "yes."

Peters opened the door completely and stepped out of the way. "Be my guest."

They moved into the sitting room of the penthouse, a spacious room tastefully decorated with fresh flowers, beautifully upholstered sofa and chairs, and plush carpeting in a deep plum. A certain tension in the air kept everyone standing.

"You are Benedict Peters," Jason stated. He pulled out a small notebook, flipped it open, and, after a glance, continued. "Also known as Reginald Lewis, Maximilian Davenport, and Xavier James?"

Kristi watched in fascinated silence as the color drained from Peters' face. Then his eyes flashed, color returned to his cheeks, and he straightened his shoulders.

"I don't know what you're talking about," he said, his tone waspish and full of disdain. "Certainly I'm Benedict Peters. I have no idea who those other men are."

"Uh-huh," said Jason, watching Peters with those cool cop's eyes of his. "Well, they're all aliases for Jimmie Fredricks, a smooth talking hustler out of Denver. Now I can add Benedict Peters to the list."

"I assure you, you can't. I have no idea where you got your information, but your little backwater connections are mistaken. I am a prestigious antiques dealer from New York." He glared at Jason and moved toward the door. "Now, if you'll kindly leave, I have business to attend to."

Jason sat down on the pretty little sofa with its muted lavender and green floral pattern. Kristi raised an eyebrow, and at his nod, followed suit.

"I'm sure you think you have business, Fredricks, but you

don't. Not in my jurisdiction. My *backwater* connections include the FBI database, and the photo Ms. Lundrigan took when you met the other day was a positive match for all the names I've stated."

Peters, or Fredricks, or whoever he was, folded into a chair. The man seemed to shrink in on himself.

"Now, before I give you your options, I need to know, do you have any documents signed by Mrs. Emma Marsten?"

Kristi's brow creased, but she sat still, certain that the con was about to be revealed.

Peters shook his head. "I'd intended to have her sign a contract the other day," he said, glaring at Kristi, "but events didn't unfold as planned." He shook himself and straightened in the chair. "But you have nothing to hold me on. The contract was simply an agency agreement giving me permission to arrange for the sale of her possessions after her death. I have better contacts and can get better prices than a local dealer."

"Yes," Jason said. "I'm sure that's what you told her, and that's what the document would've said when she read it."

Peters expression cleared and some of his bravado returned. "Of course. I can let you see the contract if you like."

Jason nodded. "I'd like a copy for my files." He smiled that shark smile again. "And I'm sure I'll find that the signature page is separate from the rest of the document... as it was in all the other contracts you've negotiated with wealthy ranchers in this state. Easily removed from one document and attached to another." Jason shrugged and leaned back into the sofa. "Not the best business practice for a legal document," he continued, "but what can you expect from these *backwater* lawyers?"

"Now see here, Sheriff," Peters blustered. "You can't just make accusations like that. You have no proof that I've done anything illegal."

Jason straightened. "You're right. I don't have any proof. If I did, you'd be in cuffs right now. And you haven't done anything illegal in my territory yet... and you're not going to. Because when I leave this room, you're going to pack and leave town. Immediately. No need to contact Mrs. Marsten. I'll be paying her a visit to explain things as soon as we finish our business here."

Jason stood, and Kristi jumped up as well. She followed him to the door, where he turned back to Peters and said, "I'd leave the state, if I were you, and I'd find new associates. I've sent out a statewide alert with your picture attached. I think several rural districts are interested in what you can tell them about ranches being unexpectedly left to development conglomerates instead of their expected beneficiaries. I've also sent a report to the state attorney general's office."

Jason opened the door and Kristi stepped through. "Get out of my town," he growled. "Now. Before I *discover* something to charge you with."

Kristi didn't say a word until they were out of the Inn and safely ensconced in the Trail Blazer. "That's really what he was doing?" she asked. "Trying to get Mrs. Marsten's signature on a legal document that he could then switch out?"

Jason turned to face her. "He's done it at least three times in other parts of the state. He's working with some shady developers, essentially stealing ranches. In a couple of the cases, there wasn't anyone close enough to the victim to protest; no one contested the false documents."

He turned back to the dashboard and started the car. "That's not the worst of it. In at least one case, the victim seemed to be living too long. It looks like these people may have gotten impatient and arranged for her to have a fatal accident. The sheriff I spoke to last night will be reopening that case and reexamining the evidence."

Kristi shivered as big fluffy snowflakes began to drift onto the car's windshield. "How awful. Emma Marsten has had a close call. She's lucky you're here to protect her."

He smiled grimly. "She's lucky Carl and Anna are careful... and that you had the good sense to snap a picture of Peters. And I'm going to make sure she appreciates what all three of you did for her."

Kristi settled back for the ride to the Broken M Ranch. The first snowfall of the season was always lovely. This early in the fall, when the weather was still fairly warm, the flakes were large and drifted lazily, making it easy to enjoy their beauty. Later when the temperatures dropped and the blizzards raged, the flakes would be tiny and driven... and they'd pile high, burying the countryside.

Quilts were a great comfort during a Montana winter.

"You know," Kristi said when they turned off the pavement onto the packed dirt road. "We make a hell of a good team."

Jason kept his eyes on the road, but reached for her hand and clasped it tightly. "We do, indeed," he said quietly. "And I hope we always will."

PART X

WILDFIRE!

Wildfire!

A Short Kristi Lundrigan Mystery

DEBBIE MUMFORD

1

*K*risti Lundrigan sat at her scrubbed oak breakfast table and stared out the window at what was usually a serene view of Montana's Absaroka Mountain range. But this morning, the scene was anything but calm; it was downright worrisome. A storm overnight had produced lightning, which had kindled a fire in Garnet Canyon, which led straight down Garnet Creek and into the Paradise Valley town of Garnet Gateway... and Kristi's home.

Situated as her home was on the eastern edge of town, Kristi had a clear view of the black clouds billowing up from the canyon. The only good news was that the smoke continued to hover above the rocky, tree-lined slopes. The wind had died down as the storm passed, so the smoke and flames weren't being pushed toward town. Yet.

Dragging her gaze away from the ominous scene, Kristi forced herself to finish her breakfast. Usually the creamy blend of rolled oats, honey yogurt, and apricot nectar delighted her, but this morning she ate her refrigerated overnight oats mechanically, concerned only with finishing as quickly as possible. She knew she'd need the fuel for what was likely to be an uncomfortable and harrowing day, but she begrudged the time.

Not being in the habit of watching early morning news shows, she'd been blissfully unaware of the fire as she showered and dressed for the day in her favorite long patchwork skirt and a white cotton shell, but Stitches and Between, her moggy cats, had been uneasy, pacing the bedroom and bumping up against her legs repeatedly as she dressed, applied her usual minimal make-up, and pulled her long blonde hair into a high ponytail.

She'd scolded them for their insistence, thinking they were simply anxious for breakfast, but the moment she stepped into the breakfast room and saw the cloud of smoke hanging over the canyon she'd known her cats were more attuned to Mother Nature than she was. Trouble was brewing... and it had chosen a dangerous form: wildfire!

Now, as she carried her bowl to the sink, she wondered if her house would still be standing at the end of the day. Glancing down at her cats, she noted they'd barely touched their own breakfast.

"Too worried to eat, huh, kids," she said as she rinsed out her bowl and placed it in the dishwasher. "Well, it won't matter. You're in for an adventure today. How'd you like to come to the shop with me? I'll set you up in the back with a basket, a blanket, and your food bowls. You'll be quilt shop cats for the day."

As she chatted to the cats in what she hoped was a normal voice, she found their cat carrier, packed a bag of their favorite toys and blankets, and grabbed bags of kibble and litter. Once their things were safely tucked into a box, she packed a small suitcase of her own. After stashing the luggage in her bright red Subaru Outback, Kristi sat down in the middle of the living room floor and opened the door to the cat carrier. To her amazement, Stitches, the older of the pair, took the lead and stepped regally into the carrier and curled into a gray tabby ball, hiding all four white paws beneath her tail and nose. Between (who'd been named because his claws reminded Kristi of the tiny, sharp needles used in hand quilting) followed without even a *meow* of comment. The little tuxedo male curled up beside his best friend and stared at Kristi as if to say, "Well? What are your waiting for? Close us in and get us out of here!"

Kristi did just that, hefting the carrier and settling it safely on the floor of the Subaru's backseat. "All right, kids, we're off to *Delectable Mountain Quilting.*" As she pulled out of the garage, she couldn't help glancing at her neat, one story home with its freshly mown front lawn and wondering if she'd ever see it again.

She really hoped so.

She'd been happy in this little house. Her first real home. Not her parents' where she'd lived as a child, or her husband's where she'd lived as a spouse, but her very own, purchased after the divorce that had nearly broken her heart. Her home, and her kitty-kids, had seen her through a tough couple of years, but things were better now. She now owned *Delectable Mountain Quilting,* and after more than a year of hard work, business was thriving, and best of all, her relationship with Jason was healing.

Her ex was not only the sheriff of Garnet County, Montana, he was also her personal hero. He'd saved her life when a murdering mad woman had decided Kristi had to die... and that close call with death had opened both their eyes. They might be divorced, but there was still a lot of love between them. They'd started dating again, but were taking things slow and easy as they worked to rebuild the trust his infidelity had destroyed.

She was just pulling into the parking area behind the shop when her cell phone rang. She finished parking, then pulled the cell from the pocket of her embroidered denim shoulder bag and glanced at the display. Jason. Of course.

She answered with a smile. "Hi, Jason. What's up?"

"Are you still at home?" he asked, his voice gruff and official sounding.

"No, the cats and I just parked behind the shop."

"Good, the cats are with you. Then you're aware of the fire."

She nodded, though he couldn't see her. "It was pretty obvious from my place. How bad is it?"

"Bad enough that we're going to be evacuating the homes on the east side of town, yours included. I'm glad to know you and the cats are already in town."

"Yep, and I packed a bag. I figured I wouldn't be going home again until things settle down."

He sighed and when he spoke again, his voice had mellowed and lost its official edge. "Good to know you're safe, Kristi. I'll stop by the shop later and check in with you, but for now, I have emergency crews to mobilize."

"Stay safe, Jason," she said quietly.

"Always," he responded, and disconnected the call.

2

———

*B*usiness at *Delectable Mountain Quilting* was beyond slow. It was non-existent. Kristi and her sales clerks, Ruby Andrews and Mattie Stebbings, busied themselves by checking the inventory of quilting cottons, moving new bolts to the sales floor to replace ones that had sold out, and cutting a new supply of fat quarters to replenish the shop's stash of the popular 18x22 inch rectangles. Ruby hadn't been scheduled to work that day, but she lived alone on the east side of Garnet Gateway and when the sheriff's department called with the evacuation order she'd decided she'd rather spend her day at the quilt shop than in one of the town's emergency shelters.

Each of the town's four churches had opened their fellowship halls for those who'd been displaced, and the community center on the town square was also taking in refugees. Knowing those sites were likely to be overloaded, Kristi had contacted her employees, including DeAnna Waters (the shop's bookkeeper), who worked from home, and told them they were welcome to shelter at *Delectable Mountain Quilting*. The accommodations wouldn't be luxurious, but they'd have a nice bathroom and a fully functional kitchen... and Jason had volunteered to supply them with cots and blankets if those items became necessary.

Kristi really hoped they wouldn't need to shelter overnight.

After all, the Incident Management Team for the Northern Rockies had arrived mid-morning and firefighters were pouring into Garnet Gateway from all across the state. The IM team had set up a helipad near where Garnet Creek emptied into the rolling Yellowstone River. Kristi and Ruby had taken a break and stepped outside to watch the helicopters dip their buckets into the river like so many giant dragonflies before zooming off to drop their loads on the flames raging out of the 'Sorkees.

Later in the afternoon, the IM team expected bombers to lend their efforts to dousing the wildfire, but Kristi had no idea where the massive planes would land or how they'd refill their tanks. However they accomplished the task, Garnet County would be grateful for their help.

Around 11:00 a.m., Ruby and Mattie left to take a shift at the community center, volunteering to distribute box lunches to the firefighters. They promised to bring lunch to Kristi when they finished their shift. Alone in the shop, Kristi was surprised to hear the front door open. Glancing up, she discovered a young woman wearing jeans and a T-shirt, with a baby wrapped against her chest and clutching a toddler's hand.

"Hello, I'm Kristi. How can I help you?"

The young woman licked her lips and glanced over her shoulder nervously. "W-would it be all right if we... uhm... if we took shelter here?" She pulled the toddler further into the store and glanced again at the front door, or maybe the street beyond. "I mean, I know this isn't a designated shelter, but..." The baby squirmed in its wrap and the young woman patted its back and shifted her weight from side to side, murmuring soothing sounds.

"Of course," Kristi said quickly, moving around the cutting

table to the young woman's side. Odd that she'd chosen the quilt shop. Kristi didn't recognize her as a customer, nor as a relative of one of her students. "You're welcome to wait here, but are you sure you wouldn't be more comfortable at one of the churches? They have nurseries and toys for your little ones."

The young mother shook her head, and now that she was closer, Kristi noticed a bruise on her left temple. She looked a bit unkempt, as did the toddler, neither of them looking as if their dark hair had been combed recently. They must have left home in a hurry. Of course, nearly everyone who'd been forced to evacuate had done so hurriedly, and getting two little ones ready to leave couldn't have eased this woman's process. Still, she seemed unusually nervous, glancing over her shoulder repeatedly.

Almost as if she were hiding from someone.

Kneeling down, Kristi spoke to the toddler. If she had to guess, she'd say the child was a boy, though at this age and with that wildly curly head of dark hair, it was impossible to tell for sure. "Hi there. I'm Kristi. What's your name?"

The little one's eyes widened, and he stepped behind his mother, hiding his face against her jeans. She released his hand and stroked his hair.

"His name is Jesse. He's a little shy."

Straightening to standing, Kristi smiled at the mother. "He's a fine boy, and you're welcome to stay."

The woman glanced at the door again, and Kristi decided they might be more comfortable deeper in the store. "Why don't you come with me," she said, leading the way to the back. "The restroom is over there, and this is our kitchen / breakroom. I don't have any kind of playpen, but I can get you a box and one of my quilts for the baby, if you want to unwrap her and put her down? Is she a girl, or another little boy?"

The moment the door closed behind them and they could

no longer be seen from the front door or display windows, the young woman's shoulders relaxed and her hand went to her forehead. She looked exhausted. Kristi gestured toward a chair, and the mother sank into it.

"Girl," she said. "Jill. I call her my little Jelly Bean." When his mother sat down, Jesse scrambled under the table and leaned against her legs.

"And you are?" Kristi asked.

"Charlene Jenkins," the woman replied. "But everyone calls me Char."

"Well, Char, you and Jesse and Jill are safe here. Shall I set up that makeshift cradle for you?"

"Yes, please." Char said with a weary smile. "It'd be a relief to put her down."

Kristi scoured the storage room for a box, the end of a roll of batting, and two of her early quilts that she sometimes used in classes as examples of how *not* to piece. Once Jill was nestled safely in her makeshift bed, and Kristi had folded the other quilt into a pallet on the floor for Jesse, she checked the kitchen cabinets.

"Ah-ha! I thought I still had some granola bars in here." She pulled a box off the shelf and offered it to Char. "You and Jesse are welcome to share these, and there's bottled water in the refrigerator."

"You're very kind," Char murmured and unwrapped a bar, broke off a piece and offered it to Jesse. The little boy didn't hesitate, but grabbed it and stuffed it in his mouth.

"I'm sorry I don't have any toys, Jesse," Kristi said with a smile, "but my cats are visiting the shop today. Maybe Stitches and Between will come out of hiding now that we're all settled in."

Jesse's eyes widened and he looked around the kitchen while he chewed.

"If you sit very still, they might come out for a visit. Stitches is gray with four white feet, and Between is black with white markings. Do you like cats?"

The little boy nodded, still searching the room with his gaze.

Kristi beckoned to Char, and the two women stepped to the door to the sales floor.

"Are you in trouble, Char?" Kristi asked quietly. "You seem frightened."

Char glanced at her son, but Stitches had decided to put in an appearance, and the little boy was absorbed in watching her. His mother glanced at Kristi before lowering her gaze and nodding. "It's my husband. He's abusive. He's always knocked me around, but the other day, he hit Jesse." Glancing again at her son, she continued, "I've put up with it for myself, but I won't let him hurt my kids. So, when the order came to evacuate, I decided..."

She paused, took a deep breath, and continued quietly. "I decided to take a chance. I've never been in this shop before, so he shouldn't think to look for me here. I know he'll check the community center and the churches, but..."

She stopped, licked her lips, and met Kristi's gaze. "I don't know what to do now. Even if he doesn't find us here, what do I do next? I don't have a car... or money... or family to call for help." She bit her lip and her eyes filled with tears. "This was a mistake. I shouldn't have bothered you with this. There's no way out for us."

Kristi placed a gentle hand on the woman's arm. "Yes. There is. You may have picked my shop at random, but it was a good choice. I know Sheriff Reynolds. He's a good man and he'll see that you get to a shelter in Billings. You and Jesse and your little Jelly Bean are going to be fine."

Char's eyes widened and she drew in a sharp breath. "Really? You'll help us?"

"Of course I will." Kristi smiled and nodded to where Jesse sat on his pallet with Stitches stretched out beside him and Between curled in his lap. "And so will they."

3

*K*risti left Char and her little ones in the kitchen and returned to the sales floor. She'd just pulled her cell phone from the pocket of her long patchwork skirt when the door opened and a man strode in, an unusual occurrence on any day for *Delectable Mountain Quilting*, but ominous after Char's confidences. A large, overblown man with a full head of unruly dark hair and a belly barely contained by his chambray shirt and blue jeans, he stopped just inside the door and surveyed the sales floor.

"You alone in here?" he asked, his voice deep, his manner brusque.

Kristi moved away from him, behind the cutting table. "I don't see that that's any of your business," she said, though she tried to keep her voice pleasant. "Did you want to buy some quilting cottons?"

He glared at her and drew himself up to his full, and substantial, height. "No. I'm looking for my wife and kids. Are they here?"

Kristi feigned innocence and glanced around the shop. "Do you see any children here?"

He turned, as though to leave, but two things happened to prevent that. The front door opened and Ruby and Mattie came in carrying four box lunches, and...

...a baby cried.

Char's little Jelly Bean had chosen the wrong moment to wake up in a strange place.

"They *are* here," the man bellowed, and charged toward the door to the kitchen.

Kristi threw herself into his path, yelling to her friends, "Get help!"

Mattie dropped the box lunches on a counter and ran to help Kristi as she struggled to keep the big man away from the kitchen door. Not that the petite sales clerk carried much weight to throw around!

Ruby screamed, "Stop!"

And amazingly, the man turned to stare at her.

She glared at him. "I don't know what's going on here, but the sheriff is joining us for lunch, so I suggest you leave." Stepping away from the door, Ruby pointed at the man, then at the door. "Go. Now!"

He glared at Ruby, then turned to Kristi and growled, "You won't get away with this. You can't keep a man from his kids."

The front door opened again, and Sheriff Jason Reynolds stepped into the quilt shop. He took a quick look around, his gaze resting on Kristi's flushed face for a moment, before nodding to the man and saying, "Jenkins. Didn't know you were a quilter."

"I'm not," Jenkins answered. "This bitch is hiding my wife and kids and I want them back. Right now."

"I see," Jason said, walking into the shop and stepping between Jenkins and Kristi. "Well, you should know that this *bitch* is *my* wife and I don't appreciate you bullying her." He glanced at Ruby and Mattie, then returned his gaze to Jenkins. "I suggest you leave now. I'll look into your claims and let you know what I find."

Jenkins straightened his back and stared into Jason's eyes. "You'll find my whore of a wife and her brats," he said in a surly tone, "and you'll bring them back to me."

"That's enough, Jenkins," Jason said, his voice soft, but with a deadly edge. "Leave. Now. Or face arrest for menacing."

"Fine," Jenkins snarled. "I'm leaving." He stepped to the side so that he could make eye contact with Kristi. "But I'll be back."

4

*W*hen the front door slammed behind him, everyone turned to Kristi.

"What was that all about?" Jason asked.

"Come with me." Kristi turned and led them all to the kitchen where they found Char huddled on the floor beside the exterior door, cradling Jesse and Jill.

Kristi moved to crouch before the frightened woman. "Char, this is Sheriff Reynolds, the man I was telling you about."

Then she pivoted to face Jason and her clerks. "This is Char Jenkins and she's trying to escape an abusive marriage."

Jason took off his official Stetson, laid it on the kitchen table, and turned to Mattie and Ruby. "I think we're going to need a couple more box lunches."

The women took the hint and left the kitchen.

"Mrs. Jenkins," Jason said, "why don't you join me at the table and tell me your story. Kristi and the others will watch your little ones, won't you, sweetheart?"

Kristi smiled and held out her hands to take Jelly Bean. "I'd be delighted. Come on, Jesse, let's go find Stitches and Between."

She could relax now. The Incident Management Team

5

A week later, Kristi and Jason sat at their favorite table near the window of *Rizzoli's Fine Italian Restaurant* enjoying steaming plates of flavorful lasagna and generous tossed salads. Kristi felt truly relaxed and at ease for the first time in days, and Jason's presence had everything to do with her state of mind. Of course, the perfectly spiced beef, rich tomato sauce, and generous layers of gooey cheese in her lasagna didn't hurt. Neither did the bottle of Chianti wine Jason had ordered for them. The red wine's tart cherry flavor, along with its alcohol content, made Kristi want to purr with satisfaction.

Jason smiled at her across his wine glass. "It's been a week, hasn't it?"

"It sure has," she nodded. "And not one I'm anxious to repeat."

The Incident Management Team had declared the wildfire under control and had packed up and left three days ago. Since then, Jason and the Garnet County fire chief had been busy mopping up the aftermath, while keeping a watch on the canyon to make sure no hot spots erupted into flames.

Everyone had returned to their homes, which were all still

standing, and cattle herds that had been moved from the ranches in peril to the safety of those on the west side of the Yellowstone were in the process of being returned to their home ranges.

"I'm sure glad Garnet Gateway escaped without loss," he said, placing his glass on the table and reaching for his fork.

"So am I," Kristi agreed. "Stitches and Between were really glad to get home again. Cats aren't fond of upheaval."

Jason smiled and his eyes softened. "Neither are people." He reached for her hand. "You were great with Char Jenkins and her kids, by the way. Protecting her from her thug of a husband took courage."

She squeezed his hand. "Well, I didn't do it alone. Mattie and Ruby were there to back me up, and we were all relieved when you arrived."

"Good thing I'd planned to have lunch with my favorite quilters."

Kristi took a bite of lasagna and closed her eyes, savoring the blend of flavors. When she opened her eyes again, she met Jason's gaze and asked, "So what happened with Char and her little ones? Were you able to get them to safety?"

He swallowed, wiped his lips with his red checked napkin, and said, "Yes. They're safely settled in a shelter in Billings. I introduced Char to the district attorney, and between the two of us, we convinced her to press charges. The DA's also going to help her find a divorce attorney." He took another sip of wine. "And he had a doctor examine Char and the children, and the DA thinks between the doctor's testimony and mine he'll be able to get a conviction." He ate another forkful of lasagna and swallowed before continuing. "At the very least Char will be able to get a restraining order against the man."

"But they're safe right now?" Kristi asked.

"They are. The shelter doesn't give out names of its residents and it has a great security system. Plus, no one in Garnet Gateway knows where I took them." He paused, his eyes taking on that expression Kristi so often thought of as his *cop's eyes*. "Not even you."

She nodded, satisfied. They finished their dinner in companionable silence.

It had been a long week, but ultimately a good one. The wildfire was in the past, Char and her little ones were safe, and Kristi and her kitty-kids were back in their snug little home.

Plus, her relationship with Jason was becoming more solid and trusting by the day.

She smiled and reached for her wine glass. All was right in Kristi's world.